SALT WATER GRAVES

BOOKS BY B.R. SPANGLER

Where Lost Girls Go

The Innocent Girls

SALT WATER GRAVES

B.R. SPANGLER

bookouture

Published by Bookouture in 2020

An imprint of Storyfire Ltd.
Carmelite House
50 Victoria Embankment
London EC4Y 0DZ

www.bookouture.com

ISBN: 978-1-83888-260-0
eBook ISBN: 978-1-83888-259-4

To my friends and family for their love, support, and patience.

PROLOGUE

The clouds of a summer storm rolled over the Outer Banks. The tree-covered jogging trail became dark as night. The footpath lights flicked on, and their orange glow reached Ann Choplin's feet. She slowed her jog, a large raindrop blooming on her arm, another running down her cheek, the dusty path becoming flecked by rainfall. As the rains grew heavy, light flashed in the sky above and a thunderous boom shook her insides. Thick trees lining the trail began to sway, their ballooning foliage spitting leaves across the path, the weather turning fast.

Ann sucked in a deep breath, welcoming the front, inviting the breeze, thinking any change in weather could provide a respite from the unusual heat. The storm filled her nose and touched her tongue with the smell and taste of rain as she jogged in place with short dance steps, trying to keep to the beat of the music in her ears. Her watch at quarter past six in the evening showed the outside temperature was still in the nineties. She didn't need an app on her watch to tell her the air was hot and sticky, making a poor combination when trying to finish a three-mile goal. She'd only jogged her first, and thought to go home, to give in to the change in weather.

Change begins with you, her trainer had said. She'd heard the same from her therapist too.

"Fine," she mouthed, deciding to finish the miles. Maybe a jog in the rain would do her some good. Who was she to argue with professionals? The year since the bankruptcy and her separation had proved challenging. Like the weather steeped in heat, her life had been an onslaught of marital woes and financial tragedies. Any change had to be good. It wasn't just recommended, it was needed.

First, though, a drink. In the thick humidity, her water bottle was coated in sweat and slipped through her fingers, the bottom of it striking the footpath and bouncing with a thud, toppling end over end until it disappeared into a bushy thicket.

"Let me." A voice came from behind. Ann spun around, yanking out the cords to her earbuds. A man jumped into action, chasing her water bottle and disappearing behind the thicket. Branches broke and the bushes shook. There was quiet then, a moment growing long and leaving her to wonder where he'd gone.

"Are you okay in there?"

No answer. The shrubbery trembled with the man's laughter, his hand appearing in the open, the water bottle in his clutched fingers. "I found it!"

"That was very nice of you," she said as he reappeared and then dropped to one knee, tightening the cap and cleaning the sides, the sweat having collected dirt from its tumble.

"Here ya go," he said, handing it to her, his head lowered, his hat and sunglasses hiding his face.

"Thank you," she said, annoyed that she'd been clumsy, appreciating the gentlemanly gesture. A lightning strike turned the sky white, a sharp crack making her jump. "Whoa! That was a real close one."

He twirled a finger up at the sky, "You might want to take cover from this." He tipped his hat and removed his glasses to show his face briefly, his blue-green eyes and dimpled chin snagging a memory.

"Hey," she said, flipping her hair. The earlier unease disappeared. "I didn't know it was you."

"It's nice to see you, Ann," he replied, staring at her, sparking another memory. A silent flash of light, and they crouched as a boom sounded and rolled over them. He hung his thumb over his shoulder. "I'm parked in the nearest lot if you want to wait this out, maybe catch up?"

"That's very sweet of you, but I'm braving the rain today." She gripped the bottle, trying to remove the cap, cursing as she realized the threads were crossed. "Stuck."

"Here, let me," he offered, and took hold, his arms muscled and toned, his shoulders chiseled, his face handsome. He'd clearly had an ugly-duckling transformation since she'd last seen him at school.

"You look really different," she said, surprising herself with her boldness. Her face warming bashfully, she added, "I mean that in a good way."

"Thank you," he answered, the corner of his mouth turned with a smile. He handed her the bottle again, and made a tipping motion, encouraging her to drink. She did, gulping deeply, her body sweating. He mimed a weightlifter's stance, saying, "I've been taking care of myself."

Ann pegged her toe into the pavement, looking him up and down, and offered a flirty smile. *Change is good,* she heard in her head, liking what she saw, and surprising herself with her next question. "Maybe we could run together sometime?"

"Sure thing," he answered, his sunglasses back in place, his hat tipped down. "I'm sure I have your number."

"Don't be a stranger," she said, capping her water bottle, her skin turning cold, her workout interrupted. "I better get moving; don't want to lose the momentum and risk a muscle cramp."

He offered a comical thumbs-up. "That's good advice."

It was in the last half of the third mile when it hit her, her feet slapping clumsily against the pavement, the music in her ears turning garbled, and her skin aflame with a ferocious heat. She was sick but had no idea what it was. She stopped on the jogging trail, wispy steam rising from the blacktop, the storm heading east into the ocean, her car parked a hundred yards away. It was hard to breathe, her lungs dying, too weak to draw in air and exhale it.

"You drank the water," she heard, and realized he was standing next to her, his hands on his hips, hat and glasses still on as he glanced around to see if they were alone.

"Mouth is so dry," she managed to say, opening her bottle, her tongue swollen and as arid as the desert. "Can't get enough."

"Yeah, that's one of the side effects."

"Wha—" she began, fear striking in slow motion as she fell on her side, paralysis taking over, her arms and legs turning rigid.

"And there she goes," he said with confidence as he knelt and looked around cautiously. When he was sure they were alone, he hoisted her in the air, carrying her into the woods, branches swiping her arms and face, wet leaves brushing against her skin, rainwater dripping from her face and acting as surrogate tears for the ones she wanted to shed but couldn't.

"Wh—" she tried again, a groan escaping her lips.

"This is for someone else," he answered, stopping when they reached a car. The back of the wagon was open, a white sheet spread out, a bundle of rope with three sections cut and a roll of tape already prepared. The real tears came then, as she thought back, remembering him jumping into the shrubs and chasing her bottle. He'd drugged her.

When he finished tying her wrists, ankles and knees, he showed her an empty syringe. "That break in the weather made this easy for me," he said.

She groaned again as he layered tape over her mouth, his blue-green eyes sharp in the sunlight breaking through the clouds. What had happened to him that would make him do this? Why her?

His hands gloved, he brushed his fingers across her cheek. "I always thought you were beautiful. It'll be over soon."

She moaned as the car door slammed shut, trying to muster a scream that wouldn't come, her eyelids growing heavy. As the car started, she tried with all her might to stay awake, watching the storm overhead, a gale wind pushing the tops of the trees, listening as the road beneath changed from gravel to pavement. But it was when the sound of the ocean waves came that the drug finished its bidding, putting her to sleep, leaving her to wonder if it would hide how death would come. Distantly, in her trailing consciousness, she thought maybe that wouldn't be so bad.

A splash. The water was cold. She sank like a stone, a wave crashing over her head. She reared and kicked and thrust her hips, trying to swim, but the currents were already on her, swirling and squeezing her body like an inescapable blanket. The sky was dark. In a boat nearby, the shadowy figure of her killer stood at the bow. Her shoes, her phone and her earbuds dangled lifelessly from between his fingers.

"It was good to see you again," he shouted. The boat idled in the middle of nowhere, twin motors puffing smoke. His voice had changed, becoming low and menacing. "You can live. That is, if you can swim."

And she could swim. Or at one time she'd been able to, on the swim team at school. But could she swim with her arms and legs bound? The current spun her around as the ropes cut and bit her wrists and ankles, her skin opening with vicious stings. Her head dipped beneath the surface, ears filling until clogged, her muscles weak from the drug.

With the little motion she had, she swam upward, finding a place on her back, floating a moment, breath rasping, the moon emerging between the clouds, a beam of moonlight falling on the boat, on him. The motors let out a choppy low growl as he steered the boat closer to her, his face empty.

Then the motors really came alive, roaring and spitting water, showering her with a pummeling force that drove her under. It was too strong, her mouth and lungs sucking in the sea, her momentary reprieve becoming her last. She kicked like a dying fish, but it only made her descent more violent, delaying the inevitable. With her lungs filling, the ocean became eerily calm, the pressure on her ears pushing until she thought they'd burst. Above, the boat sped away.

ONE

Late summer in the Outer Banks brought crowds to our beaches. It brought red-shouldered and freckled masses to our boardwalks. And it brought droves of traffic funneling onto the island with every seat filled, bodies pinched and squeezed, voices tangled with songs on the radio, luggage strapped to the rooftops, pillows and beach towels shoved against the side windows, bundled folding chairs heaped in the rear atop coolers stuffed with food and drink swimming in melted ice. From the windswept beach grasses in Carova to the spiraling lighthouse steps in Ocracoke, every inch of the islands would be visited before the end of the season.

But the only destination I had in mind was home. Never had I wanted to be back in my apartment as much as today. I dropped my things on the kitchen counter and secured my gun in its safety locker, officially relieving myself of the day and the responsibilities and the tools that came with being a cop. We were always cops, always on duty—twenty-four hours and three hundred and sixty-five days a year. But there were also moments of being who we'd been before, and who we were without a badge. This was one of those moments.

I was home early today because I was late. A cold sweat returned, carrying fright and nerves this time, the number forty on my lips. I swore that the count couldn't be right. *I was late.* It had been almost six weeks. To be sure, I checked the calendar on my phone, confirming just how late I actually was.

Peeing on a stick is easier said than done. I considered a gallon of water, or a cold glass of juice, but didn't know if that would cause a misread. On my way home, I'd stopped at a drug store pharmacy and stood in front of a wall of pregnancy tests. There were too many choices. Never had I seen such a wall dedicated to selling one thing. There were more than a hundred boxes, all with similar claims, all saying the same thing but wording it differently. There were even digital tests, and one offering an app I could download onto my phone. I snuffed a laugh, a tear pinching my eye. I'd share it with Jericho later, knowing he'd get a laugh about there being an app for pregnancy tests.

Concentrate, I thought, clenching, my leg shaking, the sole of my shoe tapping the bathroom's tiled floor. My mind raced like bees buzzing about a hive, thoughts zinging haphazardly. I was restless, and yet I was also strangely excited by the idea. A baby. Mine and Jericho's. I cupped my mouth, swiping at an errant tear, and willed the pee to come.

Hoping the cold would help, I stripped off my shoes and socks, putting my bare feet on the bathroom floor, a chill rising into my legs, followed by a shiver that helped me to wet the stick. And now I had to wait.

I was alone in my apartment, the single bathroom bright in the indirect light that shone through the rear patio doors. Sunlight entered on a sharp angle, the sun rising above the roofline, nearing its trip overhead before it landed on the other side for the afternoon. I checked the time, seeing it was nearing noon. Jericho's schedule showed he was working a rally for his mayoral campaign. His every hour, every minute, every breath was occupied by meetings and interviews and speeches. *Vote Flynn to Win* stickers, buttons and banners were all over his house. How would he take the news? Would he quit the campaign? Would there *be* any news? My phone's timer showed I had two more minutes before reading results that might change our lives.

With so many questions, my nerves were getting the better of me. Had I been this nervous with Hannah, my firstborn? This scared? I thought back to my old place in Philly, the apartment on Broad Street, Hannah's father and me sitting in the bathroom doorway, the two of us half naked and sweating out a mid-August heatwave that had turned the city into a humid oven. Back then, we didn't have air conditioning. I remember the happy excitement; we were young and wanted more than anything for me to be pregnant. We'd both moved up in our careers and had recently plunked every dime of what we had into a down payment on our first house, with a move date already set. The timing was right.

But that was then. What about now? What about our age? I wondered, aimlessly picking one of a thousand frightening concerns. We weren't young newlyweds. Heck, we weren't newlyweds at all. Would Jericho want to get married? Did he still believe in marriage? Did I?

We're young enough! I decided with a flit of optimism, emotion returning. The optimism waned as my thoughts returned to Hannah. I'd only just gotten her back in my life.

After she was kidnapped as a child, I spent nearly fifteen years with a broken heart, obsessively searching for her. My evenings were filled with nightmares, the memory of Hannah being taken from our front yard, snatched almost right out of my hands. My life and career changed soon after—my marriage ending and my cases shifting to concentrate on kidnappings, some ending in murder, the victims around Hannah's age. A gut-level fear of one day identifying her remains was ever-present. Sometimes, when I close my eyes, I can still smell the morgue back in Philadelphia, the cold touch on my skin and the unbearable relief of not seeing Hannah's face when the sheet was pulled back.

I'd arrived at the eastern barrier islands for a respite during the latter part of the previous summer, but I had also come to continue my search for Hannah. I'd been following up on an old lead, the case having a possible connection to her kidnapping. And although I was the detective, it was Hannah who'd found me. It was the sweetest possible relief after years of searching. Now the two of us were navigating what it was to be mother and daughter again, chasing time to make up for the loss of it.

One more minute, according to the timer. My pants were crumpled around my bare feet, and I realized I was still sitting on the toilet for no reason at all. I got up, the empty tub across from me turning on its side, a heady lightness making me shut my eyes and brace against the sink and wall. I had felt like this before, the memory a strong one from the first time I'd been pregnant.

I turned off the timer and put my phone back in my pocket. My hands shook, palms sweaty, a hot stew in my gut urging me to look at the pregnancy test.

"Casey?" I heard Jericho calling. He appeared in the doorway. "What's wrong?"

"I didn't hear you come in," I said, glancing at the test perched on the sink and drying my hands nervously against my legs. "What are you doing here?"

He was clean-shaven and dressed in one of his best suits, a *Vote Flynn to Win* button neatly pinned to his lapel, his wavy brown hair combed back. A television interview was scheduled for early afternoon. His eyes narrowed, showing more green than blue in my apartment's light, a deep concern cutting ridges between his eyebrows as he said, "I got a call that you'd left work sick."

When it came to working at the largest police station in the Outer Banks, there were no secrets. Especially when your boyfriend had been the sheriff for as many years as Jericho had, and was running for office. He knew everyone and everyone knew me.

"Someone called you?" I asked. In the years since I'd become the lead detective, I'd never been ill, had never called in sick or even had a cold. I'd had a feeling that my abruptly leaving in the middle of a team meeting would raise a question or two. "Dr. Swales?"

Jericho gave a nod, catching the annoyance in my voice. Dr. Terri Swales was the town's medical examiner. She was also one of Jericho's closest friends. "She was concerned."

"That's sweet, but what about your interview?"

He checked his phone, a screen showing a list of messages. "Rescheduled," he answered, though I could tell he was lying. A part of me was glad he'd lied, that he was here with me, the pregnancy test sitting on the sink waiting to be read.

His eyes flashed with the bathroom light as he spotted the plastic stick. I didn't try to hide it and picked it up, covering it in my palm so I couldn't see the results. "I'm late," I told him, my voice shaking.

With those two words, Jericho's expression changed instantly with a recognition I was certain had been shared by every man who had ever heard the same phrase.

"How late?" he asked, brow raised, an odd smile showing.

"Almost two weeks," I answered with a stir of excitement as I rechecked the math in my head.

"Well?" he asked, a smile inching from ear to ear. I almost burst into tears, his reaction answering one of my biggest concerns. "Aren't you going to look?"

"I can't," I said, hands trembling.

"Together?" Jericho said, emotion breaking in his voice. My knees were weak and my head felt light again. I dropped to sit, and he joined me, no care for wrinkling his suit. Shifting closer to me as I held the test in front of us, he cupped my hand, and said, "On three?"

"Okay," I answered, barely able to get the word out.

"One," he began, his voice changing as the excitement grew. "Two."

"Three," I blurted, opening my palm flat, the test results revealed.

I held my breath. I had to hear his reaction before I said another word. Jericho studied the results, all emotion gone from his face. Then tears stood in his eyes, and his smile returned. "Question now is, do we have a little girl, or a little boy?"

TWO

We'd decided to share the news after breakfast the next day. We were both nervous, having no idea how Jericho's son Ryan and my daughter Hannah would react. Jericho side-eyed me, biting his lip, ready to reveal the news to all. I gave him a warning glance, the fun of it almost unbearable. Hannah definitely caught on to the shenanigans, but said nothing. No matter what she was thinking, she was definitely going to be surprised, and I hoped it was in a good way.

"This French toast is terrific," Jericho said. My stomach was surprisingly settled as the smell of our late breakfast filled the kitchen. He stabbed another piece, holding it in the air, looking at Ryan. "When did you learn to make this?"

"Wasn't me," Ryan said, giving Hannah a nod. "I only assisted."

"You did this?" I asked, happily surprised. "I didn't know you could cook."

"I've got a few tricks," she said. "You should see what I can do with a can of Spam."

"Spam?" Ryan asked, and grimaced jokingly, clutching at his throat as though sick. He shook his head, saying, "Hard pass!"

"Hey, I like the stuff," I warned. "It's not as Philly as scrapple, but it's in the top ten."

"No, not scrapple!" Jericho mocked with a shout, dropping his fork and mirroring Ryan with his hands around his throat.

"I love scrapple," Hannah said, delight in her eyes. "I should have added that."

We laughed a long minute, before quieting to finish breakfast. I couldn't stop smiling, though, the news pressing to come out. I glanced at Jericho to see that he was feeling the same, the two of us like children the night before Christmas.

Hannah took to her phone between bites of food. Her hair was pulled back in a ponytail, her piercings gone, and her neck tattoo covered slightly with makeup. She'd been changing subtly since entering my life again, working a lot of hours while going back to school. I touched my own neck, asking, "Why did you cover it up? It's so beautiful."

"Really?" she asked, dimples showing with a faint red warming her cheeks, glancing at Jericho and Ryan to gauge their reactions. She cocked her head bashfully. "I wasn't sure it fit in."

"Who cares what fits with what. Just be you," Ryan said, his mouth full as he flashed her a smile. "Who knows, maybe I'll get one too."

"What? What's that?" Jericho spoke abruptly, then laughed it off, adding, "Let me know when; I might join you."

"You guys are full of jokes," Hannah said, sounding more comfortable.

"Seriously, Dad?" Ryan asked. "Can I get one?"

"We'll talk about it," Jericho told his son.

Ryan was a mirror image of his parents. I could see resemblances to both Jericho and Jessie from any angle. Approaching nineteen, a freshman in college, he had Jericho's wavy hair but without the salt-and-pepper grays, and with light brown highlights like his mother's. He also shared Jericho's eye color, a rich blue-green, but they were Jessie's eyes too, the shape of them matching what I'd seen in the framed photographs Jericho kept in the house. He was home for the summer, working long shifts as a lifeguard. While we only saw him a few times a week, I could always tell it made Jericho happy to have him near.

"Ryan's right, you only need to be you," I told Hannah.

"Thanks, guys," she answered, her eyes fixed on Ryan. It was great to see them getting along. They'd hit it off almost instantly, the two of them sharing the same interests, talking movies and music. Ryan had even offered to help Hannah with school, where she was studying to take a high-school equivalency exam. With a diploma, she'd mentioned taking some classes at the local community college in the fall.

I eased back into my chair, a sudden burst of emotion warming my insides with a giddiness that pushed upward like a park fountain and forced a smile across my lips. I covered my mouth with a napkin, not wanting anyone to see. For the first time since my daughter's kidnapping, I had a family again.

The touch of Jericho's hand on my shoulder came with a soft sting in the corner of my eye. I put my hand on my belly, imagining a high chair between the two of us, an eruption of baby sounds, a tray covered with bits of French toast and sticky with syrup, a stub of crust in the baby's fist, half chewed. Was that what this scene would be like a year from now? I pinched my eyelids shut, wishing it with all of my being, with every fiber of me.

"Babe?" Jericho asked.

"I'm good," I answered, my hand on his, a smirk forming on his face, knowing I was about to break the news.

"Okay, what's going on?" Ryan asked, dropping his fork onto his plate. He folded his arms, casting a glare at each of us. "There's news? Don't tell me you're moving?"

"Well, yes and no," I said. His brow rose as Jericho speared another stack of French toast. "My apartment's lease is up at the end of the month."

"We've been talking," Jericho began with some hesitation. "We decided to move in together."

Hannah stopped mid chew, the news of a move coming as a surprise. She had only just settled in with me, and I could see she was afraid. Her life had been filled with lies, and after a tumultuous year living in a corrupt detention center, she ended up on the streets. "All of us!" I said, reaching across the table, taking hold of her fingers.

"Yes," Jericho said. He dared a touch of affection, his hand on her arm briefly. "I thought you would like the guest bedroom. It has a full bath, all yours, private."

"Really?" she answered as Ryan's interest in the conversation waned and he seized another slice of toast, shoving it into his mouth. She searched his face, looking for a response. "You're okay with it?"

Ryan shrugged. "The more the merrier." Though he barely showed it, I could see he was considering the change. Jericho could too. This was his mother's home—a house she'd rebuilt, restoring it over the years. And it was the only home Ryan knew. His knee bobbed, his shoe tapping the floor, a look of concern appearing. "Do you think that maybe we could keep some of Mom's things around, though?" he asked.

"Ryan, of course we can," his father answered, his voice breaking.

Ryan gave a nod, focus shifting from me to Hannah and then to his father. "It'll be good to fill this big house," he said, offering a reserved grin. "I think Mom would want it that way."

There was a sense of relief in the room, clearing the air enough for me to risk what I had to tell them next. Jericho's eyes were locked on mine, waiting for me. "Thank you," I began, my nerves shaky. "We've still got a few weeks, giving us time to pack and get things sorted. And then the three of us will be here. Me and Hannah, and your new baby sister or brother."

Ryan gave a nod, slow, his head moving and then stopping as the words registered. "No way!" he laughed. "A baby! That's awesome."

"Really?" Hannah asked, the shock on her face priceless. "You guys are having a baby?"

Ryan raised his hand. "I can babysit, but I'm not so sure about changing any stinky diapers."

I took a moment, looking at Jericho and Ryan and then Hannah. I had a family, and we were adding one more to our happy home.

The moment was stolen as my phone buzzed. As I read the message, the warm family gathering feeling drained out of me like water through a sieve. I cleared my throat and wiped my lips, Jericho's hand on my arm, understanding on his face. A body had been discovered, and it was my job to determine if it was murder.

THREE

"Female, mid forties," I said, taking a knee next to the body. The woman's skin was pale and creased by deep grooves, the morning light reflecting in her dead eyes, the side of her head partially buried and her arms and hands covered entirely with sand.

"Detective White." Tracy Fields greeted me as she took a photograph. Daybreak colors glowed on her face and her sandy hair, lightened by the sun. She smiled with a show of dimples that reminded me how much she looked like my daughter, and how close they were in age.

"Tracy," I said, motioning to the victim's exposed neck and shoulder. Without missing a beat, the camera's strobe struck with a blinding flash, its charge cycling, followed by two more. "Good, get coverage of her torso and legs too."

Without questioning, Tracy followed my lead. She was the youngest crime-scene technician I'd ever worked with, and also one of the brightest, having received multiple certificates and college degrees at a very young age. I'd gotten close to her, mentoring her and helping with school and career decisions. She worked full-time on my team while she continued her path to becoming a crime-scene investigator, which I was sure was just one of many successful career's she'd have in her lifetime. "Anyone else joining us?" she asked.

I checked the time and the running surf, then shook my head. "For now, I think we're alone on this one." I tapped my watch. "Time-sensitive."

Tracy followed my gaze into the ocean and refocused her camera, a ring flash mounted on the nose of the lens. "The surf buried some of the victim's body. Should we roll her?"

"Not quite yet," I answered, adjusting my position carefully. Air bubbles erupted through the sand, threatening to steal my foot. "Female, early to mid forties," I repeated, making an adjustment while flicking a ghost crab from the victim's neck. There was substantial evidence of the critters having consumed portions of the body, the fattier pockets of flesh gnawed. "Get a picture of this," I said, motioning to the damage, believing it might assist us in constructing a feasible timeline.

As Tracy framed the pictures, she said, "That's not something I'll ever get used to seeing."

"You shouldn't have to," I said. "But they'll help tell a story."

"Like the flies we see further inland," she commented, referring to fly larvae and other insects infesting a body, their presence used to determine time of death.

"Correct."

Although the side of the victim's face was covered by sand, I saw enough to make out her appearance. Short salt-and-pepper hair framed a narrow face with high cheekbones. She wore a pale blue jogging outfit, the kind meant for working out. Her legs below the knees were buried in the sand too, one heel showing, the color bright and easily mistaken for a seashell. Her running shoes were missing, her feet bare. "No blunt trauma immediately evident," I continued.

"She drowned?" Tracy asked, bright speculation on her face. "Drinking and a late-night swim?"

"I don't think so," I said, eyeing the woman's hands, her slender fingers interlaced and poking through the packed sand like colorless flower stems. "It's the clothes. Exercising, yes. But a swim when fully dressed?"

A car engine rumbled over the breaking waves, the medical examiner's van pulling up to the scene and parking along the packed sand, which glistened wet and reflected the blue and red flashing lights of the pair of beach patrol vehicles bordering the scene. I gave the island's chief medical examiner a nod as she exited the vehicle and followed a rutted footpath toward us. Dr. Swales ducked beneath twisted yellow and black crime-scene tape slung from the beach patrol vehicles, the corners anchored.

"Be right there," she said, stopping at the patrol car, holding her finger in the air. "Gloves and boots." Her rigor for protocol was a constant, regardless of where we were. She stuck her familiar dark-green Crocs in a bootie box, the elastic of the shoe covers snapping around her ankles. Latex gloves went on next, the wind batting the empty fingers like a balloon until she sleeved them thoroughly.

"Morning," I said.

"Detective," she answered. A rush of seawater ran toward her feet. She peered over a thick pair of fogged glasses, nudging her chin toward the receding wave, a frown forming. "Looks like we'll have to make this quick.

I checked my phone, opening an app Jericho had suggested: a chart showing the times when low and high tides would occur. Urgency ticked, a clock setting in motion like a countdown. "We only have forty minutes before all of this is under water."

"We'll be racing the tide," Dr. Swales said, cupping her hands around her mouth. "Derek!" she yelled over the surf and wind. "We're falling short on time. Get the van ready to receive the body."

When she rejoined us, her glasses slipping to the end of her nose, I said, "I didn't expect to see you here."

"I heard the call over the radio," she answered, her frizzy hair blown briefly across her face. She pointed toward the ocean's lip curving unevenly, the hazy surf a blur of white and blue along an endless coastline. “This is almost in my backyard.”

“It’s good to have you,” I said, my confidence firmed knowing what she’d lend to this investigation. “We better make the most of the time we have.”

“Where are we?” she asked.

“Discussing the possibility of a drowning,” Tracy answered.

“And?”

“I’m questioning it,” I said, motioning to the woman’s outfit, the jogging pants and top. “Especially with the exercise clothes.”

“Drowning is still a possibility,” Dr. Swales replied. “I’ve seen it before.”

“I suppose. But odd that her shoes are missing,” I commented.

Tracy took another picture, adding, “She could have taken off her sneakers before going in the water?”

“Maybe. Here, help me with this,” I said, carefully freeing the woman’s arms. Wet clumps of sand tumbled to reveal a binding around the wrists, a white rope with a pattern of green interspersed across the threads. I leaned back, clearing the body, saying, “That changes everything.” The three of us stared, frozen by the sight. “Tracy, photograph.”

Tracy repositioned and focused on the binding. “It’s a type of polypropylene rope, used for boat anchors and mooring.”

I’d recognized the rope, having seen it used in marinas, but didn’t know the details. “How do you know about it?” I asked, Swales tilting her head.

Tracy lowered her camera when she saw us staring. “Uncle Daniel,” she answered. “He taught me about all the ropes and knots used on a sailboat.” To Tracy, Daniel Ashtole had been her favorite uncle, one of her closest family members. To the rest of us, he had been a well-respected and well-liked district attorney. He had also been a lifelong friend of Jericho's, someone I'd come to admire and whose company I very much missed. His recent murder on a case we'd all been close to had been devastating, and hearing his name came with an aching sadness. I could only imagine how terribly Tracy missed him.

"Do you recognize the knot?" I asked, my voice unsteady, feeling Tracy's heartbreak.

She refocused her lens as I carefully brushed wet sand from the woman's bare feet, the skin on them deeply wrinkled, the toenails lifting from their nail beds. She photographed the rope binding the ankles, then nodded, saying, "I think I do."

"Research it, find out what kind it is," I said. Beneath the rope, the victim's skin was raw, peeling from a nylon burn, signs of her fighting the restraints, but there were no obvious signs of other injuries. "I believe this victim was put in the ocean while alive."

"Someone dumped her in the ocean with her hands and feet tied?" Tracy asked, a look of horror on her face. She was still young, and over time, this job, and seeing the worst in people, would erode her innocence like heat melting ice.

Dr. Swales leaned closer to the victim's face, shining a light in the eyes, assessing them. "Drowning is a possibility," she said. "Of course, I'll have to confirm it at autopsy."

"Given what we can see, that is our leading cause," I said.

"I know this woman," she said, surprising me, hard concern on her face, a splash of seawater dotting her glasses. "She's a local. I think her name is Ann. She has a daughter named Christina."

As I made a note of the names, Tracy's camera flash caught something beneath the woman. "I think we have something here," I said. "On the lapel of the victim's jacket."

She knelt next to me, her camera close to her chest, an arm guarding it from the seawater. "It looks like something is pinned to it," she said. "I think it's a button."

"Help me roll her," I said, motioning to show her where to place her hands on the victim.

The woman's body came loose from the dense sand, the suction gurgling. On her jogging top was a campaign button I knew intimately. I'd been surrounded by them for weeks. The words *Vote Flynn to Win* were picked out in colorful letters against a background showing Jericho's hometown of Kitty Hawk.

"It's definitely Ann Choplin," Dr. Swales said, her voice pitched high. "She owns a public relations firm on the mainland."

"Choplin," I said, the name registering with a memory, a cold twinge in the pit of my gut. The victim was a friend of Jericho's. The three of us even had a dinner date planned for the end of this week. I'd never met her in person, and now I never would. "She's working with Jericho on his campaign."

"Like a campaign manager?" Tracy asked.

"Exactly like that," I answered, dread stealing my thoughts.

Dr. Swales stood and searched the beach, looking north, then pivoting and searching south.

"What is it?" I asked.

"I don't like this," she said, fingers picking at her lip as she scanned the sand, back and forth, a shake coming to her face, jowls jiggling.

"What?" I asked, the look of her and the tone of her voice putting me on edge.

"Jericho's wife. She… this feels like that. She was found washed up on the shoreline not far from here."

Beach sounds erupted over our silence, gulls calling, surf crashing, the murmur of onlookers questioning and speculating. A hard lump set in my throat. The ghost of Jericho's wife, her murder two years ago, struck a chill in me and raised bumps up and down my arms.

"Could just be a coincidence. But of course we'll look into any link," I said, water rushing around my shoes as I tried to cover my emotion with steely professionalism. "I think we better hurry."

I spurred us on with the tasks of collecting evidence, taking pictures and securing the victim's body for transport to the morgue. Ann Choplin had been somewhere out there in the ocean, her hands and ankles tied. Who would want her dead? And was there anything to what Dr. Swales had said about the similarity to Jessie Flynn's murder?

FOUR

As a cop, I'd been trained for the gruesomeness of death, the vileness of murder. And at times, I'd seen as bad as Choplin's murder, even worse a few times. The training could only do so much, though. I'd learned early in my career to put away what I saw and what I felt, reserving a place deep in my heart and my mind where I could plant the images and emotions like seeds to root and to grow and to branch, fostering ideas to help with the investigation. Securing what I saw this way was also how I was able to cope, and it let me recognize when to be grateful for what I had, which was a hard-learned lesson for me.

This early afternoon came with one of those rarest of moments, the scene of the morning locked away in my mental vault and everything being right. After a frantic morning directing my team, now the sea air filled my lungs. The taste of the ocean on my tongue and the touch of salt on my skin; the moment was like breathing joy.

"You okay?" Jericho asked, a breeze playfully teasing a tangle of his brown hair, a gleam shining in his blue-green eyes. I stopped walking, wanting to share whatever it was that had taken hold of me.

"I'm good," I said, tightening my grip on his hand, weaving my fingers with his. The moment welled inside like a warm gush ready to explode. "In fact, I'm very good."

"You better get used to it," he said, leaning in for a kiss, his pepper-colored scruff scratchy on my cheek.

"That's just it, I'm not used to it," I confessed. He cocked his head, questioning. In my life, I'd become used to seeing happiness being reserved for the lucky, the ones who knew what it was and how to hold onto it. That hadn't been me. Not until now, anyway. I clutched Jericho's hand, pulling him close and saying, "This. I love this."

"I love this too," he whispered, his eyes tender, his palm gentle on my belly. "And I love you."

We continued forward, reaching the top of the boardwalk as the planks of wood sounded a foot parade. The restaurants and shops were filling with the bodies that spilled over from the bordering sands and the ocean play. Jericho drew me into his arms without a care in the world who was watching. We stood in the middle of the boardwalk, surrounded by a beautiful Outer Banks afternoon, hair windswept, and I let out a giddy laugh.

"Casey, it's called happiness, and you deserve *all* of it," he said with emphasis. There was emotion in his voice as he continued, "What you've been through… what you and Hannah have been through, that's not normal. This is—"

"This is normal," I said, finishing for him. Maybe he was right. As a cop, a detective, I'd only glimpsed what normal was, seeing the worst in people, living and breathing it. "You deserve it too."

Jericho broke our embrace, eyeing the boardwalk and the beaches. "If I win this election, I might see a whole other side of this place I never knew existed."

"And it might see a whole other you it never expected," I exclaimed. He pondered my words as I scanned the beaches, the lifeguard stands, tanned bodies at attention. Beneath them, the sands were strewn with pitched umbrellas and laid towels. There were children in the surf, running, yelling, some kicking up water while others glided along on stout wakeboards. Their parents were near, lazing in beach chairs, feet buried to their ankles, skin slick with sunblock, magazines or books on their laps as they kept a cautious watch while aimlessly leafing through the pages.

But just as I relished my happiness, I knew it was short-lived. I heard Dr. Swales' voice in my head, telling me about the beach where Jericho's wife had been discovered, the location of her body eerily close to Ann Choplin's.

"Can I ask you something?" I said with hesitation, afraid of how he'd react.

He raised his brow, hearing the caution in my voice. With a slight frown, he answered, "I suppose."

"You haven't said anything about Ann Choplin's death." We walked to the beach-facing side of the boardwalk, bench seats empty and inviting, and sat with our backs to the ocean, the wind blowing my hair around my face. "Will her firm continue with your campaign?"

He shook his head. "Ann Choplin *was* the firm. If anything, I think the company will probably dissolve, or end up with her husband Joseph."

"You knew him too?"

Jericho rolled his eyes. "*Knew* isn't quite the word. It wasn't by choice."

"I don't follow?" I said.

"Ann and Joseph were my high-school friends, along with Jessie and Daniel."

This was news. While I'd known Jericho had met his wife in high school, I didn't know they'd been friends with Ann Choplin. "How close?"

He crossed his fingers, "Tight. We did everything together, even dated a few times."

"You and Ann Choplin?" I asked, surprised. I'd always believed he and Jessie had been the classic couple who got together young and stayed together.

Jericho smirked. "Everyone dated everyone. And it was almost always brief. Trust me. She had eyes for Joseph and I already had eyes for Jessie."

Dr. Swales' words returned. "You know, you've never told me about that day."

"Which one?" Jericho asked, his attention stolen as a campaign supporter flashed a massive *Vote Flynn to Win* button and signaled a thumbs-up.

"Jessie's murder," I answered.

Jericho's expression went blank, his gaze falling to the boardwalk. "What's there to tell? You know what happened."

"Look at me," I insisted, knowing how personal, how sensitive and intimate this was for him. He granted me a look, letting me see into his eyes. I cupped his hand in mine. "But you never told me what it was like for you. Jericho, I have shared everything with you, every moment, every heartache. I'm only asking you to do the same."

Jericho froze. He didn't speak. He didn't show emotion or even look at me. I began to feel uncomfortable, as though I'd crossed some invisible line and intruded on a guarded area. I realized then that he had his own place too, a place in his heart and mind where he locked away the hurt and the ugliness. The seconds ticked into a minute, maybe more, the unease growing and becoming unbearable. "It's okay…" I told him.

"It was awful," he began, meeting my eyes briefly, his voice gruff. The pain of the memories must have been too much for him, his gaze returning to the boards. But even with the struggle, he continued to tell me of that day, that terrible day that changed his life forever. As he spoke, he took me back to the moment his wife's body was discovered. The boardwalk and the parade of tourists slowly faded to some distant place, disappearing from around us as the bench we sat in became his squad car.

Jericho had been dressed in full uniform. He was the sheriff back then. Slacks and shirt pressed, sunlight glinting on his gold badge. His face was years younger, skin smooth around his eyes, all evidence of mourning and worry yet to come. The squad car's radio had squelched, a tinny voice on the speaker, dispatch calling about a body discovered on the beach. Jericho picked up the radio's receiver. "Pamela, Jericho here. I'm closest to the location."

"Thank you, Sheriff," Pamela answered.

The patrol car's motor revved, the front heaving as Jericho stomped the accelerator. He wove through Outer Banks traffic, humming along to the nineties tune "Everybody Hurts", the song a peculiar memory he'd later marry forever with tragedy. The song hit its peak as Jericho parked along the beach in the early-morning sun.

This feels like that, Swales had said, the beach the same as where Ann Choplin's body was found.

When Jericho arrived, the normally tranquil sands had been littered with patrol cars, blue lights blinking sharply, a small gathering behind crime-scene tape being questioned and peeking for a gruesome look.

"Officer Wilson," Jericho said, greeting Emanuel, a patrol officer at the time. Their heels dug into the sand, and Emanuel took Jericho's arm when the depth stole his balance. "What have we got?"

Emanuel swiped the sweat from his brow, his full uniform warm for the morning, and produced a small pad and pencil, flipping over the cover to read his notes. "White female, possibly mid thirties, discovered at daybreak by two joggers. The body appears to have washed up onto the shore, possibly deceased for more than a day. There were no immediate signs of trauma—"

"Anyone touch the body?" Jericho asked, interrupting.

"Nobody yet, but we have a call to Dr. Swales."

"That's good," he answered, his hands on his hips, the first sight of the body showing nothing more than a lump in the wet sand covered by seaweed. "You said there are no signs of foul play?"

"None as yet. We'll have to turn her over," Emanuel answered. "She's fully dressed, though."

Jericho paused. "Clothed? That changes things," he commented. "The occasional body washing up in the surf happens from time to time. But not usually fully dressed."

He moved closer. The woman's body was mottled with sea grass and other beach life, her skin pale and glistening. Her clothing had been torn, with some of it missing. And she'd been exposed to the elements in a way that made it difficult to recognize her as being human. But then Jericho saw her hair, and alarm mounted inside him. A shoulder next, a place he'd kissed a thousand times on his way to the side of her neck.

"Stop!" yelled an officer standing over the body, his arms flailing in the air. But the warning only urged Jericho on, his shoes slapping against the rushing surf. "Hold him!"

Emanuel jumped in front of him. Jericho's expression filled with horror, a foamy wave having shoved the body enough to reveal the woman's face, bringing instant recognition. He pawed at Emanuel's chest, trying to take him on, but Emanuel's size was no match for him.

"Who is that?!" Jericho screamed, raw tears spilling down his face. His mind had driven him to ask the obvious, hoping for a miracle of miracles, hoping to wake up from a nightmare that had suddenly become his reality.

"Emanuel? Tell me who she is!"

But he already knew it was his Jessie.

"Casey?" Jericho said now, his eyes returning to mine, his voice bringing me back to where we were. The sound of the ocean's crashing waves and the boardwalk traffic rushed back to my ears. I could smell the popcorn and the sweets as families continued about their day while I struggled with what Jericho had described for me. "I don't remember very much after that. There was an investigation. Paige Kotes murdered my wife, but the initial investigation ruled the cause of death as drowning, and possibly suicide."

"Suicide?" I asked, confused and a little shocked that Dr. Swales would have made that call. "Was it the clothes?"

"The clothes," he confirmed. "Later, we learned Kotes was working with Geoffrey Barnes. Both of them fellow police officers. Both of them my friends. Or so I thought."

I let him fall silent then. I'd already known the facts of the case. Now I'd caused him to revisit his pain.

"They'd been behind a string of murders. Paige lured my wife to a remote location, telling her I was in trouble. It was a setup. She and Barnes drowned Jessie in a lake and then took her to the ocean, making it look like a suicide."

"I am so sorry you went through that," I said, holding his hand, hurting for him. "Thank you for telling me."

"I think that's enough about that," Jericho said, shaking off the memories like a bad dream, standing and leading me away from the bench. "We need a drastic change of pace. Something fun and sinful. What do you say?"

"I like the sound of that," I said, feeling a touch of guilt for having asked about Jessie's murder. I needed to follow up on any link with Ann Choplin's case, but it could wait until I was on shift again tomorrow. "What do you have in mind?"

The two of us merged with the tourists and headed south, nearing the ice-cream shop where Hannah worked. I checked the time: her shift had begun. "There's something sweet."

"Yeah. And salty too," Jericho answered with an agreeable nod. "Do you think Hannah would mind us dropping in on her?"

"Nah," I said. The boardwalk atmosphere outside the shop was like a gala, with children following a clown wearing wide purple pants. He circled around us in a comical dance, the children laughing hysterically and pointing to his blue velvet top hat, which spat bubbles like a fountain while he made funny faces at them. His broad yellow tie was riddled with green polka dots and his puffy pink sleeves disappeared behind a bright orange sign shaped like an arrow. He spun it in circles, the name of the shop, A Scoop for You, on the front. "I guess that's a good clue."

We opened the ice-cream shop's door, cold air spilling onto us, a bell above ringing our arrival. The counters with the long refrigeration bins were entirely blocked by rows of people, couples young and old and families, all wearing frowns and shifting impatiently. Behind the frosted glass and the massive tubs of ice cream, Hannah raced back and forth, her brown pants and bright yellow shirt a blur as she finished ringing up one customer and moved to the next. Her hair was pinned back, a green baseball cap sitting askew, her cheeks red with sweat speckling her upper lip.

"Casey," Jericho said into my ear. "I think she's working alone."

"On a day like today?" I sized up the waiting crowd. Hannah saw us at the door and gave us a reserved wave before shifting her focus back to the crowd. An idea struck. I needed to be up early to work the Ann Choplin case, but we had no other evening plans. "Jericho, would you mind if I helped?"

He put his hand on the small of my back, his lips near my ear. "You're a really good mom."

My heart melted as I leaned into him. "I'll bring some home with me."

"Promise?" he asked.

"Promise," I replied as he left the shop.

Hannah gave me a curious look, confused, as I made my way through the crowd and behind the counter. I eyed the faces as I took an apron from a hook on the wall. Next to it, I found a hat with the shop's logo and shoved it onto my head. Hannah joined me at my side as I told her, "I'll follow your lead."

"Really?" she asked, looking relieved, her dimples appearing with an approving smile. "Timmy flaked. He never showed up for his shift."

"Can we get some help, please?" an older gentleman asked, tufts of gray sprouting from beneath a tattered golf hat, his arm looped with his wife's, the two leaning against the counter.

"Certainly," I answered. "What would you like?"

For the next three hours, I followed Hannah, learning with each new order, her tip jar filling while we mixed malted milkshakes and scooped ice cream on top of sugar cones, and even made banana splits complete with whipped topping and cherries on top. When the crowds thinned, and the sunlight raced over the boardwalk, settling on the bay side of the island, Hannah and I dropped into seats to get off our feet.

"You saved my ass," she said, exhaustion on her face. She leaned back, dropped her hands toward the floor and threw her head back, blowing out a long breath. "I am going to wring that boy's neck."

"Don't be too hard on him," I said, mirroring her move, loosening every muscle, my feet throbbing with an ache I was sure would hurt terribly the next day. "He might have had a good reason."

"Well," she began and sat up, "it doesn't matter now. Thank you."

"Not at all," I said. "Just hope I did okay."

She cocked her head and put on a funny face. "I wouldn't quit your day job."

"I wouldn't quit my day job either," I joked, and shifted to search the tubs of ice cream. "Before I leave, I've got one more order to fill."

FIVE

The next morning, the station was quiet. Too quiet. During the late summer season, I'd become accustomed to the benches at the entrance being full—teenagers nestled between parents, barflies sleeping off drunken binges, petty criminals caught picking the wrong pockets, and destitute sad souls having no other place to go. Following the discovery of a body only a day prior, I'd expected to see reporters waiting for me, hands in the air, requesting a statement, eager to get a question or five answered before I reached my desk. But there was none of that this morning, the benches empty, the floor clear from the station doors to the wooden gate separating our desks from the public. I was relieved to have the place empty. But it wouldn't last. I wondered when news about Ann Choplin's death would bring the reporters, sure that it would be soon.

"Morning," I said to Alice, our station desk officer.

Alice glanced at her watch. "Morning to you, and thank goodness for it."

"Quiet night?" I asked, the desk's phone lighting and sounding a bell.

"You've no idea," she answered with a roll of her eyes, ending our small talk to answer the phone.

I swung the gate open, holding it for an officer leaving, my team coming into view behind him. It was good that some had arrived early. "Morning, guys," I said, meeting Tracy and Nichelle Wilkinson at their desks. Our cubicles adjoined, occupying the corner section of the station's office, the one closest to the conference room, which we'd adopted as our own.

"Morning," they grumbled, the early hour evident in their voices. Tracy's bright smile and dimples were absent, her face bathed in blue light from her monitor as she sat inches away from her screen. The circles beneath her eyes and the stack of open books on her desk told me she was finishing a paper for school. "Another report due?"

"I'm almost finished," she answered without looking up. "It has to be uploaded by eight this morning."

"I could tweak the server's time for you," Nichelle joked, her eyes telling me she was half serious about doing it too.

Tracy shook her head. "Not this morning, but I might take you up on the offer some other time."

"Anything good?" I asked Nichelle, motioning to her monitors. She was our resident IT genius, and with her light-brown skin and large brown eyes, Nichelle was about the prettiest nerd I'd ever met. Her desk was covered with computer screens, and stacked with monitors that towered above us. Each screen showed program activities, as though she'd stepped out of a science-fiction film.

"Just running some diagnostics," she answered, one of her favorite mugs in her hand: a pair of tortoiseshell cats sleeping on a red blanket, their bodies in the shape of a heart, the word *LOVE* printed along the bottom. The walls of her cubicle were entirely filled with cat posters and framed pictures, along with a calendar that showed cats in funny and awkward predicaments. She'd joined my team soon after I'd been given the lead position; like Tracy, she was also becoming an investigator, with a specialty in forensics technologies. If someone was attempting to hide their criminal activities in the cloud, Nichelle could find it.

My eyes went to one of the monitors, a familiar name on the screen. Tommy Fitzgerald. He'd been one half of the couple who'd kidnapped my daughter. A cold stone set in my gut.

Nichelle saw my glare and jabbed at a keyboard, changing the screen to a retro screen saver with flying toasters. "Sorry, I didn't mean to leave that—"

"Put it back," I said. I heard the sound of Tracy's chair in motion; she was up to speed on all the big cases and recognized the name. "What happened with Fitzgerald?"

"He's in the hospital," Nichelle answered in a solemn voice, showing me the news story. "A prison altercation."

"Status?" I asked.

"He's in bad shape, but he'll survive."

A silence fell, as though they were expecting me to cheer, but I didn't.

"Do you think about him?" Tracy asked, Nichelle flashing her a frown, the question out of bounds.

"It's okay," I said, Tracy's chair circling and coming into view.

"Him and his wife?" she continued, her expression inquisitive, almost naïve with innocence.

"Not so much about them," I answered, my voice weak. "More about what they did, what they took from Hannah and me."

"Sorry," Tracy said, her face pinched as she tried to find the right words. There were no right words. There never would be.

"It's in the past now," I said, ignoring the looks of pity that came from both of them, the kind I'd come to loathe in the days and weeks and months after Hannah's disappearance all those years ago. I put on a fake smile. "How about we get some real work done?"

The wheels on Tracy's chair let out a chirp as she returned to her desk, while Nichelle clicked on a mouse to rouse another of her screens. "I've been performing some searches on Ann Choplin too," she said, "and should have something prepared for our meeting."

"Sorry I couldn't be at the crime scene yesterday." A familiar baritone voice sounded from behind me.

"No worries. We had it covered." Emanuel Wilson was another recruit I'd picked up in the last year. He'd been promoted, trading in his police uniform for street clothes and a detective's shield. Standing head and shoulders above us all, a basketball star in a previous life, Emanuel was the team's muscle. He was a fine investigator, but it was also helpful to have him sitting in on interviews and questioning witnesses. Intimidation, when used strategically, could go a long way in this job. With Emanuel, there also came a history. He'd worked with Jericho for years, and had been at his side when Jessie Flynn's body was discovered. I'd never talked to him about Jericho's wife or her murder, but as a detective, my curiosities were always running busy. "Dr. Swales joined me and Tracy to help with the scene."

"We were at the doctor's again, and I had zero cell connection," he answered, a giant jug of coffee in one hand and a workout bag in the other. "Can't remember seeing the station so empty."

"Calm before the storm?" Nichelle asked. She shivered, adding, "It's eerie. You can almost feel it."

"Maybe you've been drinking some of Emanuel's coffee," I joked, poking fun at the jug.

"I'd have a stroke if I drank that much caffeine," she laughed.

Other stations I'd worked had had similar lulls, giving us time to catch up on paperwork and other office tedium we preferred not to do. And like other stations, the respite was temporary. I'd bet my badge on that. "Enjoy the quiet while it lasts."

"We will," Emanuel said, the rest of the team agreeing, nodding silently and taking in the stillness of the office, urgencies and emergencies abated for the moment.

"Is everything okay with Sherry?" I asked with concern. Emanuel had recently shared the news of his wife's pregnancy, and of some complications. I couldn't help but put myself in their place.

He raised a brow with a nod. "Doc said everything looks good. Sherry has gestational diabetes, but it's manageable." A broad smile appeared then, his face glowing. "We got to hear the heartbeat again."

"Really?" I asked, grinning, thinking how that'd be me and Jericho soon. The two of us in the exam room, the doctor using a fetal Doppler, our baby's heart on the black-and-white monitor, fluttering like butterfly wings, the speaker filling the room with a woosh-clop-woosh-clop. "If you need anything, just say the word. And don't hesitate."

"I won't," he answered.

"Promise?" I asked in a demanding tone.

"I promise," he replied. I couldn't help but want to break my own news to the team. But I didn't. It was still early, and I felt it would be bad luck. I wasn't one to be superstitious, but luck hadn't exactly been in my corner with children, and I didn't want to leave anything to chance.

Cheryl Smithson was the last of the team to arrive. The wooden gate slammed shut as she entered, Alice cringing at the sharp clap; she had repeatedly reprimanded us for letting the gate close unattended. Cheryl spun around, swiping her red hair from her face, and waved an apology. A seasoned detective, she was as tough as nails, often with a gruff and sharp attitude that went well with her freckles, which seemed to darken when team discussions got heated. It was common to butt heads with Cheryl, but her tendency to take an opposing position made her a positive addition to the team. It kept us honest and accountable, decisions made with thorough vetting.

"Just in time for the meeting," I said to her as she plunked her bag on her desk and yanked a phone from her back pocket. She held up a freckled finger while she checked her messages, Tracy side-eyeing her rudeness. Sometimes I wondered if it was intentional, a way of putting herself above us. Most times I thought she just hadn't a clue she was being rude at all.

When she'd finished with her phone, she looked up. "Meeting. Got you."

"As soon you're ready to get started," I said archly. We were all eager to dive into Ann Choplin's murder investigation.

"Let's do it," Emanuel said, his voice like a trombone, as he led the way to the conference room.

"Can I be ten minutes late?" Tracy asked softly, eyeing her watch, her paper's deadline fast approaching. "I'm having an issue with the formatting."

"Ten," I answered. "But no more. It'll give us time to set up."

"I'll get your photographs up on the monitor," Nichelle offered, following Emanuel.

Once they were gone, Cheryl asked, "Any chance I could take the lead on this one?" Her green eyes glimmered in the station's overhead lights. She put on a bashful expression, biting her upper lip. "I could use the experience... you know, for my career path."

I stared without an answer, unprepared for the question, somewhat gobsmacked. I had never had a detective on my team ask to lead an investigation. I wasn't even sure what the policies and procedures allowed and didn't allow. Unlike the city of brotherly love, Philadelphia, where I'd been a detective before, seemingly a lifetime ago, some other stations had many lead detectives and the caseload to support a much larger staff. The Outer Banks wasn't Philadelphia, and I could count on one finger the number of lead detectives at our station. There had been some recent rumors that Chief Peter Pryce and the sheriff, along with the district attorney, were putting requisitions together for two more lead detective positions. I could see Cheryl in one of those, but not just yet. She needed more experience. Maybe having her take the lead occasionally would get her there.

"Let me talk to Chief Pryce and get his take," I answered, feeling uncomfortable with any human resource dealings.

"So that's a no?" she said, crossing her arms in front of her chest.

"For now," I answered. "We'll get started on this case, and—"

"You know, I'm just as qualified," she said, cutting me off.

I raised my hands as Tracy looked over her shoulder, catching the aggressive tone of the conversation. "Cheryl, I'm certain you are, but I'm not in a position to offer the lead. Let me talk to the chief first, see if I can siphon off some of the role for you to manage."

"Fine," she answered, her expression relaxing. "I'll wait."

I hated her feeling disappointed or undervalued. "Listen. We'll work closely on this one so I can help sell the idea of another lead detective to the chief."

Her face brightened. "You'd do that?"

I dared a touch, my hand on her arm, reassuring her. "Of course I would. We need one or two more leads."

"Thanks," she replied. "That means a lot."

"Now, can we go solve a murder?" I didn't wait for an answer, coaxing Cheryl to follow me into the conference room, where a picture of Ann Choplin's body waited on the screen.

SIX

"Detectives," Dr. Swales said from behind me and Cheryl, the smell of lavender and peach following her. "How about that, it looks like I made it on time."

"Yes, you did," I told her, shuffling my coffee and laptop to shake her hand. "You came from the morgue?"

She lifted a file. "Completed the victim's report this morning." Her Crocs were purple today, and her oversized white lab coat was draped from her shoulders down to her knees. She appeared to have rushed to get here, her hair pinned back tightly enough to pull on her eyebrows, a bun standing off center and leaning to the left. "Early bird gets the worm," she commented as we walked.

"You're definitely the early bird," I said, having received emails from her at four and five in the morning on more than one occasion. "We were going to start with the scene, but since you're here, can you present?"

She gave a nod. "Certainly. We were able to finish up late yesterday, and even have the victim's tox report already." She moved to the end of the table, a rat's nest of cables in her hand as she fumbled with her laptop. "Please continue, don't mind me. I'll be ready in a few minutes.

"Right then," I said, taking her words as my cue to move on. "While Dr. Swales is getting set up, what do we know about Ann Choplin? Nichelle, how about you start?"

"Sure thing," Nichelle answered. "Ann Choplin was born and raised in the Outer Banks." A montage of pictures appeared on the conference room's monitor. "Age forty-five. Owned a home in the Southern Shores and also one on the mainland in Norfolk, Virginia, where she also ran a public relations firm."

"Married?" I asked, seeing a wedding ring in one of the photos. Nichelle paused the playback long enough for me to point to the screen, the victim's left hand. "Dr. Swales, was the victim wearing an engagement ring? Wedding band?"

Computer dongles in hand, Dr. Swales dropped a video cable, a look of defeat on her face, and paged through the autopsy report. "The only jewelry on the body was a necklace and a pair of earrings."

"Nothing else?" I wondered why the victim would have removed her wedding and engagement rings.

Swales stalled, wetting her lips, a pinched look of uncertainty on her face. I motioned for her to continue. "Well, there was also the 'Vote Flynn to Win' campaign button."

A dark notion flitted across my mind, Jessie Flynn's murder lurking like a shadow. *This feels like that*, Swales had warned, inadvertently connecting the Choplin case to a murder by Paige Kotes, Jericho's old partner. I stuffed the idea away, unsure of what to make of it, a knot in my stomach. "The victim's PR firm was handling Jericho's campaign, so it wouldn't be unusual for her to have it," I said. Understanding registered on the team's faces.

"I might know why she wasn't wearing her rings." Cheryl spoke up, the team's focus shifting to her. She spun her laptop around. "Ann Choplin had filed for divorce. I knew her name was familiar."

"How so?" I asked.

"When I was in uniform, before I was a detective," Cheryl began, "I was called to their residence a few times for disturbances. On one occasion I arrested the husband for domestic violence."

The beginnings of a lead scratched the detective part of my mind. "What else?"

Her eyes darted from team member to team member. "Well, on another call, I had to arrest the victim too. She'd hit him with a meat tenderizer, but claimed it was self-defense."

"Was it?" Dr. Swales asked, eyes widening, a Southern twang in her voice.

Cheryl considered the question, her mouth crooked. Then she nodded. "I think it was."

"Were there multiple calls?" I asked.

"Too many," she answered. "They were the kind of couple that should never have been together. Always clashing, kitchen littered with broken dishes and glassware, holes punched in the walls. The kind of house you don't forget."

"That sounds like a horrible way to live," Tracy commented as she joined us and went to help with the doctor's laptop.

"Sometimes it's impossible to see that there's a better way," Swales said quietly, with a knowing look that struck me as sad. Tracy stopped fiddling with the cables, the moment silencing the room. My mouth went dry with understanding. I hated thinking of someone I cared for being in that kind of situation. Sometimes we didn't know very much about the people we worked with.

"What else do we know about the husband?" I asked, clearing my throat.

Nichelle plugged in the name of the husband, Joseph Choplin, scouring through search results. "It says here that he was a real-estate investor; filed for bankruptcy when he lost a beachfront community investment."

"Beachfront in the Outer Banks," Cheryl chided. "How do you mess that up?"

"Oh, that's easy," Dr. Swales answered. She made an up-in-smoke motion with her hands. "When the beaches disappear, the property does too."

A memory came to me. We'd teamed with the FBI in a sting operation, a group of us on a yacht passing the southern edges of the Outer Banks. Miles of beach property had been consumed by the sea, the million-dollar homes abandoned, derelict, tidal surf rushing through the structures. "I think I've seen the homes. There was an entire development community ruined by rising seawater."

"The previous administration had a beach erosion and restoration project," Dr. Swales said, the details being of personal interest as she lived by that beach. "But every inch they reclaimed was eventually lost again."

"Bankruptcy and domestic violence," I said, scratching the itch of a strong motive forming. "What else."

"Any life insurance policies?" Emanuel asked, holding his hand in the air.

"I can dig into that," Nichelle offered, a peculiar glee on her face and a twinkle in her eye. She loved tech, and I loved that we had her on our side. "I haven't had to search for policyholders and beneficiaries before; this should be a fun challenge."

"While you're working that," I said, "also find out what state the victim's PR firm is registered in. It could be North Carolina, but I want to be sure. I need to know who stands to gain the most from Ann Choplin's death. And let's get a conversation with the husband. Estranged or not, they are still legally married."

"I'll work with Emanuel," Cheryl said. "Should we bring him in for questioning?"

I shook my head. "Not yet. Meet with him casually, outside of the station, somewhere he'll be comfortable—home or wherever he's working now."

"You want to join us?" Cheryl asked, tilting her head, a silent reference to our earlier conservation.

"Just the two of you first," I answered, giving her the lead and liking the idea of making it seem impromptu. "I don't want to make him suspicious and bind things up with a lawyer."

"After the meeting?" Cheryl asked Emanuel; he nodded agreement.

"Tracy, what do you have on the ropes used to tie the victim's wrists?"

Tracy jolted, her attention caught, her gaze blank. She tapped her keyboard and then picked up an evidence bag. "It's a nylon grade known as a three-strand rope, which is specifically used as a mooring rope and for dock lines."

"Availability?" I asked.

She mulled the question over and shrugged. "I suppose you could get it at any store selling marina supplies."

"Then find out which ones," I instructed, wanting to get her out from behind her desk.

"Which ones?" She seemed confused. "Should I narrow the search to specialty stores, or maybe just the general stores?"

"You make that decision," I answered, encouraging her. She was ready to take a lead on some of the investigation. I knew she could handle it.

"Road trip?" Emanuel asked excitedly, his hand in the air, offering. "I can help after we interview the husband."

"Perfect," I said, liking the idea of his presence. I motioned to the bag containing the rope. "The evidence stays with us, but take some pictures, multiple angles, including the ends, every detail, and walk them around every store. If that rope was purchased in the area, we want to know from where and when."

"I'm ready now," Dr. Swales said as she pushed her glasses into place. "A warning, though: these pictures are not for the faint of heart."

I cleared the floor at the front of the conference room, my head light and my stomach grumbling. My mouth tasted sour and I felt sweaty. I'd developed a bad habit of coffee in the mornings, black, no sugar, no cream. I'd been living on the stuff for years but had started cutting back with news of my baby. I was sure that its sudden absence had left me feeling woozy. When I reached the door frame, I clutched the metal, its touch cool as I carefully faced the screen. I'd never been queasy when it came to autopsy pictures, but I couldn't be sure that record would stand today. "Let's see what you've got."

"The rope bindings," Dr. Swales said, flashing the pictures of Ann Choplin's ankles and wrists, red-raw abrasions against gray skin showing a pattern. I held the evidence bag in the light, Dr. Swales catching onto the question coming. She added another picture, the nylon rope and its three-strand make-up matching the abrasions. "There are signs the victim struggled, which caused friction burns on areas of the skin in contact with the rope."

"I would have thought there'd be more," Tracy said as she took notes.

"Meaning?" I asked, encouraging her.

She tapped the end of her pencil on her chin. "Sailing, I've worked with this rope, or ropes very similar. If she'd struggled, there should have been a lot more damage to the skin."

"Good," I told her, wincing with a stomach flip. "We have a lack of struggle. But why?"

"Unconscious?" Nichelle answered, uncertain.

"Or it could be she was already dead? She'd already drowned?" I suggested.

"This will clear up the questions," Dr. Swales said, moving to a new image showing colorful plot lines and medical jargon with numbers I didn't understand. But one word stood out: *ketamine*. Our victim was drugged.

I went to the conference room's whiteboard, a fresh marker in hand, and jotted a newly assigned case number across the top in bold red. Beneath it I wrote Ann's name, followed by a description of the three-strand rope along with its colorful markings. Lastly I wrote the drug name. "Victim was rendered unconscious, tied up, then presumably taken out to sea and thrown overboard. Or did she die on land and was then taken out to sea, the perpetrator hoping to hide the body?"

"Your first theory is the more likely," Dr. Swales answered.

"She was alive when she went into the ocean," I said, a second question forming. "What about other marks on the body? Signs of assault or defensive wounds? Shins, forearms, the victim's back? Any post-mortem bruising?"

"Nothing," Swales answered. "Other than the friction burns. Aside from that, notably there was seawater in the victim's lungs."

"What if she went willingly?" I asked the team, my forehead damp and the sour taste relentless, as though I'd swallowed a penny. Their expressions were bemused. "No bruising. No signs of assault or struggle. Only minimal friction burns, indicating that the bindings were placed on her wrists and ankles while she was unconscious—"

"Or paralyzed," Tracy added. "Ketamine, when used in a low enough dosage, can cause dizziness, dissociation, disorientation, and impaired motor skills, but leave the person conscious."

"It's also known as a date rape drug," I said, feeling out our earlier theory about the husband. "But you found no signs of sexual assault?"

Dr. Swales switched her presentation, the autopsy findings now on the screen, reflecting much of what we already knew. "Correct."

"A working theory then—estranged husband in financial ruin, possible beneficiary, convinces his wife to meet him. Maybe he tells her he wants to reconcile."

"They meet on a boat, late afternoon, nearing sunset," Cheryl added.

"Stomach contents?" I asked, seeking another clue.

"The victim died before digestion took place; her stomach contained a small amount of food, possibly the remains of a protein bar, and nearly twelve ounces of water," Swales answered. "I believe the drug was introduced to her system through the ingestion of water."

"Roofied," Tracy said, her pencil spinning. "Someone dosed her water?"

"Her clothes," I said. "It looks like she'd been exercising."

"And might have had a water bottle," Emanuel added.

"The amount of water could suggest exercise," Swales agreed.

"The husband drugs his wife's water bottle, she falls unconscious—maybe whilst jogging or exercising—and he ties her wrists and ankles and drops her in the ocean, drowning her." Beneath the victim's name, I added *Joseph Choplin*, underlining it with red marker. Then I stepped back from the whiteboard, wiping my face, knowing I'd have to end the meeting sooner than I wanted.

"You don't sound convinced," Dr. Swales said.

"What if the husband had nothing to do with it," I said, wavering on the initial idea, finding it too easy. I wouldn't dismiss it entirely, though, having seen my share of insurance fraud and murder-for-money cases. I turned to Nichelle. "Can you look up jogging trails from her home?"

Nichelle pressed her back against her chair, the mesh stretching. She typed in the query, reading the results, "There are a lot. Some inland on nature reserves. And then there's the beach. Good news is, they may have security cameras we could review."

"What about the victim's phone?" Cheryl asked.

"No cell phone found with the body," Tracy answered. "We're presuming it was lost at sea."

"How about the carrier?" I asked. "If we know the cell phone carrier, could we identify the apps installed on her phone? Are there fitness apps for jogging, or even location services that show where the victim had been?"

"I'll visit the victim's PR firm, work with them to find out," Nichelle answered.

"The moment you have a carrier name, send them a preservation letter, noting that their customer is the subject of a murder investigation. We need all her records preserved." My voice was fading, a breeze from the open door turning cool on the back of my damp neck.

"We can follow up with a subpoena and court order, if required," Emanuel said.

"I'd like to participate in that," Tracy said. "I could use the experience."

I gave Tracy and Emanuel the okay, a short nod as I swayed and made my way to the table. Dr. Swales came to my side and gripped my arm as she guided me into a chair, her touch gentle yet firm. "Dare I say it, but you look a bit green around the gills." She laughed through her nose and then put on a serious face, the back of her hand pressed to my forehead. She checked my pulse too, pinching my wrist, lips moving silently, her gaze fixed on the face of an old watch, the second hand sweeping around. "Heart rate is a touch rapid, and you're sweating. If it's all the same to you, I think now would be a good point to break."

"It is," I answered, mind racing, words muddied. I fixed a look on the screen, on Ann Choplin's wrists and ankles, and tried to arrest a sickening spin that came from out of nowhere. I shut my eyes and took a deep breath, the air unusually hot, as though I'd opened an oven door. A shadow reared in my mind, a ghostly voice coming with it. It was Jessie Flynn, her decaying body and face much like Ann Choplin's, a *Vote Flynn to Win* button pinned to her skin, her words warning there'd be more.

*

Dr. Swales said I'd passed out. That I'd dropped like a stone, my forehead smacking the conference room table, the sound giving everyone a start. She also said I'd only been out for a minute, that I'd come to with eyes swimming wildly and mumbling about a baby. Of course, I couldn't recall anything after studying Ann Choplin's body.

The first thing I remembered seeing was concerned faces, wide eyes, pressed lips, and shared frowns. There was low chatter amongst them, asking each other if they should call an ambulance, and Jericho. A swig of cold water and some much-needed personal space was what I needed. A moment later I was back on my feet, my head clearing.

"I'm fine, guys," I said, trying to quell their concern and speculation about what virus or infection I might have. "I just need to take some time."

"Let us call someone for you," I heard Emanuel say from behind me as they helped me into my seat, Tracy adding, "I can drive you." Their words had me shaking my head, embarrassment spreading over me like a rash. I knew it was vain to think it, but I didn't like to show weakness.

"I'll be fine," I told them again, twisting briefly, a sting of sweat beneath my arms, the station lights needling. "Everyone has their action items. I've got some paperwork and mail to get through here."

The team let me be, Dr. Swales the last to leave my side after making me promise I'd take it easy. I knew for certain that I didn't have an illness. I'd always been one of those types who rarely fell ill—one of the lucky few who were oddly immune to rampant station stomach bugs and flu, the illnesses passing over me as though I was invisible. The only other time I'd ever felt like this was when I'd been pregnant. The first, a child Ronald and I had lost. And the second time with Hannah.

I sat still, afraid to move, scared of what was going on inside me. From my desk drawer, I pulled out a mirror, which showed that my skin was like ash and I had bags beneath my eyes. I dropped it on my desk next to a stack of mail, the envelopes a mix of junk and official county files I'd fallen behind filing. Flicking through, I noticed an unusual occurrence: an envelope with a handwritten address. While the world had transcended to the cloud and to digital forums with bits and bytes riding on Wi-Fi airwaves, receiving a handwritten letter held a charm I revered. I couldn't resist the distraction.

The paper-thin stationery showed that the return address was the North Carolina Correctional Institution for Women, the postmark stamped with yesterday's date, along with a collection time in the early morning. My name appeared on the front, the penmanship large and loopy and easy to read. The person who'd sent this letter had taken their time to make it neat and legible. But of course, in prison, they had plenty of time. The sight of my name gave me pause: I knew nobody in North Carolina outside of Jericho, our newly formed family, and my family at the station. Without giving it another moment, I tore into the envelope, finding two pages, the same handwriting as the front of the envelope. I went to the second page, flipping it over, my eyes searching to discover who'd contacted me. My skin went cold, a chill racing up and down my spine. At the bottom, I read, *Yours truly, Paige Kotes.*

SEVEN

Paige Kotes had been a cop—a very good cop, from what I'd read in her files and her past cases. She would later become a detective, working from the same station I worked today, perhaps from the same desk. I had walked the same steps, used the same computers, touched the same door handles and drunk from the same water cooler. She'd been here. She'd also worked closely with Jericho, formed an unhealthy obsession with him, and ultimately nearly destroyed him.

Somewhere in her journey, Paige Kotes had become a notorious murderer. A serial killer popular in the news, and with a level of notoriety like Ted Bundy, John Wayne Gacy and Jeffrey Dahmer. Notoriety aside, she was also the woman who had murdered Jericho's wife. Given the location of his wife's murder, and that of Ann Choplin, I couldn't ignore the timing of Paige's letter.

Her ballooning handwriting sat in a lean that indicated she was left-handed, a detail I could pick up later from her file. I studied it a moment, realizing that the hand that had written these words had also murdered Jericho's wife, and so many others. I was tortured by a mix of disgust and curiosity.

In her letter, Paige introduced herself, keeping the formalities to the opening paragraph, and assuming that I already knew everything there was to know about her. How did she know about *me*, though? Did she know I was with Jericho? She went on to comment about her day-to-day life in the women's prison, how it wasn't all that bad, how her hours were filled with making license plates. She split her time between isolation, and trial runs in the general population of the prison.

Once a cop, always a cop, and I suspected the other inmates knew who she was, who she'd been. No amount of prison credibility would change that, and I was sure they took shots at her every chance they could. If you'd asked the families of Paige's victims, if you'd asked Jericho and Ryan, they'd probably have said, *throw her to the dogs, let them have at her*. That wasn't how it worked, though. Paige Kotes was remanded to the state, and it was the state that had custody of her welfare.

Believing she might be joshing about the license plates, I looked that one up. It turned out the prison where she was serving her time happened to also be one of the largest license plate factories in the state.

She went on to say that she'd followed the story of Hannah's kidnapping, which answered the question of how she knew who I was. She also mentioned following some of my previous cases, and the letter ended with a request to meet with me. She didn't say why, and my mind tried to connect the timing of her letter to Ann Choplin's murder, and to the news reports broadcast yesterday morning. The letter had been sent yesterday, the island's mail moving fast. Was Paige Kotes hinting about an involvement? It seemed impossible.

That is, unless Paige Kotes already knew Ann Choplin was murdered. Sometimes I thought conjecture was half of our job, turning over idea after idea until one of them took root. I also believed Paige knew I'd be interested in a meeting with her. As a fellow detective, she knew that my curiosity would overpower me. She knew I had to visit.

I'd been to my share of prisons and had seen every shape and size and form—from the inside of a county jail cell to juvenile detention centers, and the hardest detentions found in a maximum-security prison. Today was the first time I'd ever been to the North Carolina Correctional Institution for Women—NCCIW. It was much like any prison, a mix of male and female guards, wearing hard expressions, emotionless and familiar. Outside, the walls were lined with red brick and guarded by towering fences topped with spiraling razor wire worn like a crown. Thick-tiled floors spanned endless halls, the corridors edged with heavy steel doors, the surfaces wearing layers of dark red paint. While I couldn't see the license plate manufacturing facility, I could hear the activity, feel it vibrating through the concrete and stone.

I was led to an interview room, not unlike the ones at our station, the walls bare and painted gray, a stainless-steel table at the center, fastened to the floor with a single pedestal stand. A pair of metal donuts were welded to the table's surface to sleeve the inmate's restraints, a safety measure for visiting officers. Being a detective, I'd been given the courtesy of using the interview room, forgoing the normal visitor facilities: rows of narrow cubbyholes with Plexiglas separator and telephone handsets.

The guards told me to wait, and for a few minutes I was left alone, the door shut and blank with the exception of a narrow window I could barely see through. The air was cold and damp. As the isolation became uncomfortable, I pondered the idea of prison, of life without a chance of parole. It had to be an agonizing experience, but I suppose that was the intent of serving time for a capital crime.

I jumped when a shuffling sound came from outside, a glimpse of dark-red hair appearing in the window. I was about to meet Paige. My mouth was suddenly dry and a ball of nerves was stuck in my throat. The door opened with a metal clack, reverberating through the room, and the guards reappeared, holding their prisoner arm in arm. She was taller than I'd expected, her face hidden beneath a veil of auburn locks. Breathe, I told myself. She's just another criminal. But she wasn't just anyone. She had taken Jericho's wife away from him. It wasn't lost on me that in a strange and awful way, if it weren't for Paige, Jericho and I wouldn't be together.

With an effort, my legs weak, I stood and made myself look busy, pulling a case file from my bag, her letter folded and tucked inside. As the guards led Paige to the table, sparkling emeralds appeared from behind her hair, the greenest eyes I think I'd ever seen. The chain linking her ankles dragged against the concrete, while another was draped between her wrists and clanked against the tabletop as the guards threaded the steel donut holes, ensuring my safety.

When Paige was seated, she huffed a deep breath to blow the hair from her face, revealing a beautifully freckled wonder, a combination of fair skin speckled with colors the same as her hair and large green eyes that drank in every detail of me. They were unblinking, mesmerizing, and frightening. But what I couldn't take my eyes from was a ragged scar that stretched from the top of her head, over her left eye, leaving it in a permanent droop, before traveling to her ear and then down to her chin. It was massive, as though her face had been torn open and haphazardly put back together with tissue glue and Band-Aids.

She saw me staring and pawed at the injury, the chains rattling as an odd giggle erupted from her lips, the sound breaking my stare.

"A gift," she said, her voice sultry and deep. "Jericho gave it to me."

I nodded and began my introduction. "My name is—"

"Detective Casey White," she broke in. "Paige Kotes." She reached across the table, extending her hand, chains sliding, her fingernails bitten to the quick.

A guard at the door gave a warning glare, but I nodded, taking her hand carefully. "Ms. Kotes." Her touch was warm and gentle, but left me revolted, knowing who she was and what she'd done. "I received your letter."

Paige tucked her chin in one hand and ran her fingers along the scar with the other. Her eyes remained on mine, following my every move, her lips tight as though hiding a secret that was desperate to come out. "I've been following your story. Fourteen years. That's a long time to be without your daughter."

"It was," I answered. "But that's changed."

Her eyes widened. "I know! I saw that she was back with you." Her fingers gripped mine in a swift motion, the chains locking her reach. The guard stepped toward the table, but Paige ignored him. "Congratulations. I'm so happy for you."

"Thank you." I retreated, letting go. "Why did you want to see me?"

"Isn't it obvious?" she said. "I'm a fan."

"Please." My voice dripped with disdain. I gathered my bag, stuffing the letter inside, making as though I were going to leave.

"Ann Choplin," she said. I had suspected her name would come up, and I sat down again, silently agreeing to listen. "She's the first."

"First what?" I said, repeating her words to play along. I turned to the guard. "Does Ms. Kotes have television access? The news?"

His double chin motioned in a nod. "Only the free over-the-air stuff."

"That was easy enough. You picked up the victim's name from the news," I said, showing the letter's postmark. "And then you sent me this."

"Are you sure?" she asked.

I smiled and waited.

"Sure, I had enough time to hear the news and then send the letter, but what if I already knew?"

"If you're implying that you knew the victim's name before it was released, then we'll have an entirely different conversation."

"I'll leave that to you to figure out, Detective," she answered in a mocking tone. She was playing a dangerous game, dancing around words that could be used to implicate her. I crossed my arms, remaining silent, hoping she'd say more. When I didn't speak, her sneer faded to frustration. "Fine, you're right. I saw it on the news."

"Okay. That's established. Now tell me what you're thinking." Paige's mouth twisted, annoyed that she had no control over our meeting. "That is why you asked to see me, isn't it?"

"You're looking for a male, early to mid thirties. A person with an abnormal psychology, but who contributes in the community. Career, possibly a spouse and family as well, appearing perfectly normal. They've practiced since they were young enough to recognize death and the power of it, their control over it. But I believe this is their first."

"What makes you think that?" I asked, trying to hide my surprise at hearing her describe a killer we'd yet to confirm even existed.

"Simple," she answered, turning her head. "You don't know, do you?"

"Enlighten me," I said, hating to have to ask.

"It's the display," she replied coolly.

"He wants us to find the body." I almost blurted it out. "For the recognition."

Paige winked, a coy smile appearing. "Now you're thinking like one of us."

My stomach rolled at the sickening idea of my thinking like a serial killer. But she was right. To catch a killer, I had to think like one. "This is his first, otherwise we would have had another body."

"Guard!" she said, the scar puckering in a sickening dimple as she requested to be taken back to her cell. "This isn't fun anymore. When the next body shows up, come back to see me."

Disappointment hit me: I wanted to continue the conversation. I held up her letter, hoping to coax her into staying. "You brought me all this way; don't you want to ask about my story?"

She didn't answer. Her hair fell in front of her face, but her eyes stayed with me. When the guards freed her chains, she lunged, slapping her hands on the steel table, splaying her fingers, a crazed spark in her eyes. The guards were on her, muscling her back onto the seat. "Vote Flynn to Win." She laughed then, almost maniacal. "Blow Jericho a kiss for me."

I was rattled, but I didn't back down; her scare tactics were a show I'd seen before. I squared my shoulders, then raised my voice. "What else do you know?"

Her face softened, her expression concerned, brow raised. "There will be more," she warned.

As I exited the prison, I knew I'd have to return. While Paige Kotes may have picked up the details about Ann Choplin's murder from the news, the *Vote Flynn to Win* campaign button discovered on the body was not public knowledge. Doubt entered my mind, thinking she might have seen news footage of Jericho's campaign. While she hadn't mentioned the button's existence explicitly, I knew what the comment implied. Paige had insight. But who had she communicated with?

EIGHT

Paige could smell the beach in Casey White's hair. She eased away from the detective, the leather of the guards' belts and shoes sounding an alarm as they moved to restrain her. Their hands came next, but not before she took in another whiff, her toes tingling in longing for the ocean, the sea spray, the sun and the sand. Who was this woman? This woman who'd lost a child and then lost much of her life trying to find her. Who was she to Jericho? These were not questions to be answered today. Later, perhaps. With careful planning. She must be cautious not to tip her cards and reveal how much she knew.

The letters, she thought wildly. I need to see the letters.

She raised her brow with a warning for the detective. "There will be more."

Not since Jericho's wife had another woman stirred such feelings in Paige Kotes. A memory flashed in her mind, two years old but as fresh to her as any that was new. In it she saw Jessie Flynn arriving at the lake, a look of fright plastered on her face. The image made her shudder with elation. Jessie had had no idea that the scene had been staged, Paige making her believe Jericho was in danger. Paige closed her eyes and swooned dreamily as the memory of Jessie's last moments of life washed over her. The woman's heartbeat had touched her, firing in rapid bursts. And those eyes, swimming beneath the lake's water, terrified in their blazing agony, her pulse slowing, becoming erratic as she died. After the murder, Paige had dumped Jessie's body in the ocean's surf, where Jericho would find her. Her plan had been a success. Now Jericho would be hers.

Only that wasn't how things had worked out, and now Paige faced the rest of her life behind bars. Prison had become a part of her, and she'd become a part of it.

"Come on, Kotes!" yelled the guard, shoving her, bringing her back to reality. "Let's get a move on!"

Her cell came into view. Like the interview room, it was damp and cold and felt like a cellar. She'd be cold forever if she didn't get moved or escape this place. Her gaze fell on the three bars splitting the sunlight; the sun rising and setting every day was the only indication to her that time was moving forward, that it hadn't gotten stuck when she was put in here. And there were the letters too.

"Turn," the guard demanded. She did as she was told, her arms out, a key entering the lock of her cuffs and spinning with a metal clink she felt in her wrists. Bruises would appear by nightfall—a ring of blue and green worn like bracelets. Her legs were freed too, as a prisoner across the corridor watched. There was a flash of orange and yellow to her left: two more prisoners, both watching like the first. She'd be the subject of discussion on the block today. A cop behind bars was often the subject of discussion, whether it was warranted or not. "Enter."

She retreated backwards into her cell, the door remaining open as the guards left. It'd be time for chow soon, but she had to look at the letter first. With the guards' footsteps fading, she faced her cell, faced her life today. A short cot on the northern wall, a combination toilet and sink on the southern wall, and a small table beneath the window. On the table were her sketchpad and pencils—short by design, but long enough to write with.

She picked up one of the more recent letters she'd received, its encoding a secret, his words a jumble only she could recognize. While she had many fans, and more than a few pen pals, his letters were the first to show promise. It had taken months after the first before she felt secure in writing freely. Their cipher had been determined and shared, memorized and then discarded. The guards reviewed all her correspondence, opening every letter and sometimes photographing them, providing only copies. But in the year since these letters had started, she'd never been questioned on their contents, which told her that none of the guards actually read them. Nobody cared. The envelope showed the same post office box as before, the folded letter containing a newspaper clipping: a picture of Jericho with Detective Casey White by his side, strengthening her suspicions that they were a couple.

"In time," she whispered, bringing the newspaper picture to her nose, the smell of ink rich. "All will be revealed."

Below her cell window was a bookshelf holding a dictionary and a bible, along with a few novels from the prison library she was never going to read. Amongst the books was her makeshift scrapbook, bits of cardboard strung together with threads she'd teased from the hems of a hundred or more prison uniforms during months of working in the laundry. It worked. And better still, she'd been given permission to keep it.

Now she opened the frail cover, carefully placing the latest clipping on one of the pages, adding to her collection of Jericho Flynn pictures, her work with him incomplete. On the next page, she found the newspaper photo of Ann Choplin, Jericho's arm around her, the *Vote Flynn to Win* button prominent on her business suit. Giddiness took her breath, her insides jiggling like gelatin, a laugh resonating. She covered her mouth, not wanting to draw any attention from outside, then ran her finger along her scar, touching where Jericho had creased her face like the book in her hands. His touch was forever, the skin raised and with a deep, painful tingle that was like an itch that could never be scratched. It drove her mad at times, the nerves partially severed, firing constantly, even waking her at night. He'd remember her soon, remember her work.

She'd write to her secret admirer this afternoon, thanking him for the latest clipping, asking for more, and questioning him about Ann Choplin too. She already knew, though. She knew he'd done this to prove himself worthy of her. This was the first, and there would be more. She now needed to write Detective Casey White a new letter and send the picture; throw fuel on the fire, start misleading the investigation, make them look left when they should be looking right.

She tucked the picture of Ann Choplin and Jericho between the pages of her bible, and then eyed the closed-circuit camera outside of her cell. It had been like a guardian angel to her, but not today, the glass dome hanging limp, its all-seeing eye blind. It'd be fixed by tomorrow, but tonight she'd make a shiv out of a piece of scrap metal she'd found during a shift in the license plate factory. While the edge of the metal warmed and occasionally sparked against her cell's concrete floor, she'd imagine how many ways she could use the prison blade. She'd imagine using it on Casey White.

NINE

Judy Granger chanced a look at the ocean, the bow slicing the choppy water and throwing sea spray into the air. The ride was exhilarating: the smell of the sea, and a hot wind gusting through her hair, pressing against her body as they flew over the waves. Her date glanced at her, a smile pulling on the corner of his mouth. She'd never seen him look so good before. When she'd known him in the past, she wouldn't have given him a second look.

A flock of seabirds rifled upward and circled overhead, their feathers white and gray, their bills pale red, their yellow feet tucked beneath them as they dived into the ocean. She watched a family of dolphins breaking the bubbling surface, their humped backs spearing the whitecaps. Her date pointed toward some rocky islands, the largest of them with a tiny beach, tranquil and remote. He steered toward them, driving the boat further from the mainland before the motors coughed with a gasp, the mechanical whine shifting.

With the wind settling, Judy tried combing her fingers through her hair, the sea spray mixing with her hairspray and causing it to stand out wildly. Her fingers turned sticky while she attempted to fix it, but it had a mind of its own.

"It looks great like that," he said, spinning the wheel, turning them into the wind.

"Thanks." Judy nodded, appreciating his being polite. She pretended it wasn't important to her and made herself look busy, rummaging through her bag as though she'd lost something. She fished out a breath mint. The ocean spot he'd picked was secluded and romantic, and she was unsure how far things might progress. She added a second mint, just in case. "I'm glad you looked me up," she said. "I was surprised you remembered me."

Without looking at her, he said, "Of course I remember you. You're hard to forget."

"That's sweet," she replied, his smile reminding her of a high-school crush she'd had, the dimpled chin a massive bonus. "You've done really well for yourself."

"That's nice of you to say," he commented, sunlight shining brightly on his face. He *had* done well for himself. And he'd also made an amazing first impression, making her laugh, picking her up in an expensive car, and filling the afternoon with a cruise on the ocean.

"What did you say the boat's called?" she asked, wriggling in the cushioned seat, trying to find a pose that would give him the best view.

"It's a bowrider," he answered, shifting the throttle, steering them into a sharp turn. "A Formula 310. It's faster than anything else in the Banks. It's my one vice, my most expensive toy."

"Well," she began, throwing her head back when she realized he was looking at her, "it's a hell of a toy."

His smile deepened as he wagged a finger at her, catching on to her flirting. A giddy laugh rose in her throat, lifting her spirits. He cut the motor, and the ocean around them fell flat and sedate. She looked around the boat, admiring the luxury: wrap-around seating, a cabin below deck, and a bed with expensive sheets showing just within her view.

"Some wine?" he asked, a bottle, two glasses and a picnic basket appearing from one of the lockers. She held the glasses for him as he uncorked the bottle, a gusty breeze blowing an ocean mist over them. The setting was surreal, like something out of a romance novel, the kind with tanned and chiseled bodies on the cover. "It's a Chardonnay, from a winery in Virginia."

"Sounds wonderful," she told him, beaming, her first-date nerves rearing in her belly.

"Did I mention how pretty you are?" he asked. Her insides warmed, a flash of heat on her neck. "A lot prettier than I remember."

"Thank you," she said, blurting a laugh even as it struck her that his compliment was a little backhanded. She politely accepted a glass.

The sun had dropped in the west since they'd left the dock, the angle catching her eyes and putting him in silhouette.

"I can take care of that," he said, working a canvas top, raising it above their heads. She looked him up and down when his back was turned, unable to stop smiling, feeling as though she had the stupidest grin stuck on her face. She gulped a mouthful of wine and grimaced at the bitter aftertaste. She'd drunk worse, and anyway, her interest was more in the effects than the taste.

Shallow waves lapped the side of the boat, the sound soothing, the rocking motion comforting. With the canvas top raised, they were completely isolated. She let out a chuckle, the wine going straight to her head.

Her host inspected the boat, moving swiftly from corner to corner. When he was satisfied, he nodded. "This is perfect."

"My thoughts exactly," she agreed.

He finished locking the canvas top, the sun disappearing behind it, the sudden shade giving her a chill. Continuing to be the perfect host, he laid a thick red blanket on the deck, the picnic basket pinning one corner. He sat on the other and invited her to join him. Judy lowered herself next to him. His eyes were a mix of green and dark blue, like grassy fields and the sky on autumn afternoons. She tried to swallow, but couldn't, her mouth dry, the tingle on her lips making her throat scratchy and uncomfortable.

She mustered her courage and touched his face, his skin smooth. They were the same age, but the years had had their effect on her, stroking the corners of her eyes and mouth. Her fingers blurred a moment, her vision doubling. She shook her head, remembering the seasickness pills, the dosage taken on an empty stomach. A stiff breeze rapped the canvas top, the sound grating her ears as a spin rushed into her eyes.

"Oh shit," she said, an itch swelling in her throat, a rush of nausea coming with a painful cramp. "I think I'm going to be sick."

She cupped her mouth and jumped up, but swayed and staggered, her legs clumsy, her feet seemingly detached. She clutched the air, her balance gone, the burn in her belly setting fire to her insides, her vision sparking with spinning colors, brilliant and sharp enough to make her squint. Then she dropped to her knees, her hands turning numb and her fingertips dead. The odd sensations climbed her arms, and entered her shoulders and chest, the feeling heavy like a blanket. She flopped onto her side, her breathing a wheezing gasp.

"What's happ—" she tried saying, but she never finished, as he put a finger to his lips and tipped his glass of wine into the ocean. He cocked his head a moment, and then dropped the glass after it with a watery plunk.

Picking up the wine bottle, he asked with a sneer, "Did you have one too many?"

"I—"

"You can't be too careful," he interrupted, dumping the bottle, along with her glass. Then he opened the picnic basket and dug out a handful of ropes. He plopped them next to her, his face empty of concern, the setting sun putting a nightmarish fire into his eyes.

Judy whimpered. How could she have let this happen? How could she have been so stupid? Fear seized her as his smile turned menacing. *Scream*, she told herself. There'd been a family fishing on a rock jetty, long poles in hand, their lines draped against the still water. It was possible they could hear her. Wasn't it? She urged the air from her lungs, but her tongue was swollen like a wine cork, drool wetting her chin.

He leveled his face with hers. "That stuff worked much quicker than I expected."

"Wha—"

"Tsk tsk," he replied. He blew air into a pair of plastic gloves, bright yellow, the kind she would buy to clean her oven. "Don't bother trying to do anything." Deathly fright raced through her as his moist breath touched her ear. "I'm not going to kill you. Not directly, anyway."

A warm tear ran across her nose, falling sideways, the red blanket stealing it. Whatever he'd poisoned her with had taken away her ability to move. She could breathe and move her eyes, but the muscles in her arms and legs were tightly locked. "Wha—" she tried asking again.

"No need to thank me," he said, placing three sections of rope in front of her, their cuts even, exact, the lengths measured. *Not directly.* She thought of the terrifying ramifications, her gaze shifting from the ropes to the ocean, a wave of panic mounting as swells rapped the side of the boat.

She strained to move, eyes bulging, fighting the poison. With a huge effort, her little toe brushed the blanket. Relief! It was the smallest of movements, but it was hers. *Now my legs?* But they stayed motionless, like a stopped clock, the springs unwound, the key lost. She wiggled another toe, and then another. Her mind exploded with dread as he caught the motion.

She whimpered again, a cry making its way past her lips, her voice returning. "Please! We were friends."

"Were we?" He checked his watch, alarm erupting on his face. "Damn, it's not lasting long enough."

"Please," she begged, sensations returning to her midsection. She thrust her hips, undulating briefly, squirming away from him, but he lassoed her knees and wrists with the rope, then tied her ankles, humming a melody while he worked.

Without warning, Judy was in the air, a breeze beneath her shirt, cold on her sweaty skin. He lifted her effortlessly and rolled her body so that his face was close to hers. "It's been nice."

"Wait!" she shrieked as she was hoisted over the boat's rail, the ropes cutting into her skin. But then she was falling, his arms gone, the boat slipping past her view. She hit the water like a stone, the surface swallowing her whole. There was no time to think, no time for anything. She had to swim.

Seawater rushed into her mouth and nose. She spat and forced herself onto her back, telling her legs and arms to kick. She was able to stay afloat a moment, enough for her to see the boat, see him watching her struggle, his gloved hands in a wave, the bright yellow a beacon in the dusky light. The sea planted salty kisses as a wave washed over her face, riddling her insides with a toxic level of panic. She could see him rifling through her bag, taking something out and shoving it in his pocket. The view was twisty and swirling, abstract, the spray stinging her eyes.

A breaking swell pummeled her head and shoulders, and she sank below the surface, the pressure on the outside of her body becoming oddly equal to the inside. White lights blinded her, and she convulsed and sank deeper, the seams of her lungs bursting, air replaced by a burning storm made of brine.

Her brain took over when her muscles went still, her senses accepting their last dance with life while the ocean's tidal currents carried her softly, like a butterfly floating on a breeze. There were memories, long corridors and ballrooms with half-remembered faces. There was her mother and father and her brother, who would be so sad. And there were friends, even the ex who'd tried for a time, even though the two of them could never get it right. She was floating, peacefulness finding her as the rush of images from her life passed in a blink. As death came, so did a single regret. She'd never told anyone about her date.

TEN

The victim was female, possibly in her late thirties or early forties from what I could tell, our flashlights beaming on the body, the sun beginning to break at the edge of the ocean. We'd see more soon. A lot more. And every instinct told me it was going to be as bad as Ann Choplin. A wave broke and sent a foamy surf around the body, sinking it, the tide whispering a threat that it would reclaim its treasure if we didn't hurry.

A beach patrol vehicle flashed its headlights, joining two others, their blue and red lights skipping silently into the early morning. A middle-aged vacationer carrying a metal detector stood with one of the officers; he had come across the body while hunting for lost jewelry and coins. The beach was empty, the early birds absent, a night of rainstorms keeping people inside.

"Long brown hair," I said. Tracy was by my side, her camera flashing, batteries cycling as she moved around the body and refocused for another picture. "Highlights. Checking roots to see if the addition was recent." I knelt, my knees soaking up seawater as a handful of crabs scurried from the brightness of my flashlight. They'd been clinging to the fabric of the woman's dusky blue blouse; her clothing showed no signs of struggle. "Victim's highlights are recent, and there is also what feels like hairspray or gel perhaps."

The sun offered some morning light, and I could see that the woman's skin was gray and shriveled, absent of bloat. I estimated that the body had washed up onto the shoreline sometime during the night, death occurring late afternoon, maybe the evening of the previous day.

"Tracy, get this," I said, shining my light on the victim's fingernails, her hands the color of clay but her nails painted a bright hot pink. "Let's check her toes also. I'm guessing a pedicure and the same nail polish."

"What are you thinking?" she asked, working around me, sea spray on her camera lens and her face.

"Given the estimated time of death, the victim may have been at work, or she could have been on a date?" I said, questioning. "She's wearing a blouse and makeup, her hands and nails done, and there's also hairspray."

"Manicure and pedicure appear recent," Tracy offered. "I'm thinking a date."

"I am too," I said, unsure why, sitting back on my heels. A blade of buttery sunlight touched the victim's face, skin bluish purple, her eyes half lidded and a cloudy brown color.

"There's no wedding ring," Tracy added, taking a picture, strengthening the idea of a date.

"Let's make a note of it, research and schedule interviews at her workplace once she's identified. That may also stir up some of her dating history." The sun chased the night and set fire to the ocean, putting a spotlight on the beach, on the victim and her murder, a stain against the beauty of it all. "We know she wasn't exercising like Ann, which excludes the jogging trails as a possible connection between the murders."

"Check," Tracy said. "I'm including Nichelle on the notes."

The surf rushed around me, but had eased some. The tide was going out, the sea wouldn't claim its prize just yet, allowing us to spend the morning working the scene rather than fighting to preserve it. The victim's body was partially buried, her middle stuck in sand while her legs, arms, and chest were free, showing bindings at ankles, knees, and wrists.

"The rope has the same color patterns seen with Ann Choplin," I said, Tracy's camera shutter snapping. "This establishes a connection to the previous murder."

"That'll free up any suspicions around Choplin's husband," Emanuel said, arriving breathless, shoes caked in wet sand, pulling latex gloves onto his hands, snapping the fingers to loosen the fit. He lowered himself slowly, reading the details the way we'd been trained to do. "That is, unless Joseph Choplin also knew this victim?"

"That's yet to be established," I said, but the thought had already crossed my mind. "We'll know more once we have an identity."

"Same rope," he said, the victim's hand between his fingers, rigor mortis sounded with a pop. "It's also the same three bindings—wrists, knees and ankles."

"Look at this," I added. Tracy hovered over my shoulder as I took hold of the victim's hand. Death had stolen the color from her skin, but on her ring finger, there was the faintest sign that the victim had worn a wedding ring at one time. "I believe she *was* married."

"I missed that," Tracy said.

"In this light, it was easy to overlook," I assured her.

"A broken marriage, like the first victim?"

"It's a hunch, but worth following up. There might be an ex-husband we can interview," I said.

"Hunches." Emanuel nodded, approving. "Those are some of our best leads."

"Let's hope one of them sheds some light," I said, Emanuel lending me a hand, my feet sinking into the sand. I shifted my position and prepared to move the victim. "Help me with her."

Emanuel worked one side of the body while I rocked the other, air bubbles surfacing in the packed sand as we rolled her until she was face up. "It wasn't a robbery," he said, his gloved finger behind the victim's ear, an expensive pair of diamond earrings sparkling in the sunlight.

"Smell that?" I said, lowering myself over the body, seeking the source. "It smells like oil, maybe gasoline."

Tracy joined me in the search, finding it on the victim's shoulders. "It's on her blouse," she said, taking a picture. With the seawater, there was no stain for us to see, but the smell of fuel was strong.

"Let's roll her again. Onto her side this time," I instructed. Emanuel braced the victim, giving me enough room to smell her hair. In among the mix of salt and hairspray, there was gasoline on the victim's neck. "More fuel," I told them. "Okay, we can lower her."

"Where did that come from?" Emanuel asked. I sat up and scanned the ocean, the morning light piercing, a sea of orange and red like liquid fire. He turned to face the same way. "What are you looking for?"

"I'm not sure. Fuel is less dense than water. If the victim has fuel on her head and shoulders, then she came from the ocean."

"I don't see any boats," Emanuel said, squinting and shielding his eyes.

"There's sand in her hair too," I said, lifting a lock of it. "That helps confirm that she came in with the surf, with the tide."

"If fuel is lighter than water, it would have floated on the surface," Tracy said, catching on.

"Exactly." I could see her mind working. "At one point, the victim was on the surface. Even with her hands and legs tied, she must have trod water. It may have been brief. And it may have been with her killer watching."

"That's sick," Emanuel commented.

"It is, but it also might have given us a clue." I sniffed the victim's hair again, confirming the gasoline's odor. "The victim was alive when she was on the boat, when she was dropped into the ocean."

"And the fuel came from the boat's motors," Tracy added, her face bright, eyes blazing in the sunlight. "Uncle Daniel used to talk about how unused fuel was expelled with the exhaust, especially if the motor had been flooded or was older."

"If we can identify the fuel," I said, "we can find the boat. And whoever did this."

ELEVEN

Paige Kotes had warned there'd be more. We finished processing the second victim's crime scene by late morning. It was the peak of low tide, the sea magically receding, the sun blazing in a cloudless sky, the packed sand drying around the body. The tourists came with the new day, smelling of bug repellent and sunblock, towels blanketing the beach, umbrellas propped for shade, and colorful plastic pails and shovels placed for children to play. The crime scene was cordoned off well enough, but crowds of gawkers pushed at the edges of the tape, hungry for a morbid look. When the victim's body was removed, a clean-up team shoveled and bagged the drying sand, removing what the retreating tide had failed to take.

I returned to the station with Tracy and Emanuel, putting together a folder with pictures of both victims. The fuel on the second victim's clothing led to us checking marinas and fueling points. If we were lucky, the marinas also included security footage, videos putting a face to each transaction. Tracy would continue her work with the rope, identifying retailers carrying the same type, including color pattern and materials.

My next stop was the prison. We had a second victim, yet to be identified, bindings the same as the first. Paige's warning wasn't part of some emotional outburst or theatrics. She'd given the warning because she knew. A part of me was seeking her help: before being caught and identified as a serial killer, she'd had a reputation as a brilliant detective. I was also curious. I couldn't help myself. I wanted to meet her again. Being around Paige Kotes was like watching a tragic accident on the road. I couldn't turn away.

The drive to the women's prison was long, but it gave me time to call ahead and request another interview. My request, being so last-minute, was immediately denied, and I was told to come back tomorrow. Disruption to the prisoner's schedule would be negative to her rehabilitation. I almost laughed into the phone. Having read her dossier, watched some of the docudramas and listened to podcasts about Paige Kotes, I knew there was no rehabilitation to be had. She was a killer passing time. At the first opportunity, she'd kill again. With my phone getting hot from the weak cell connection, Nichelle found me the warden's home phone number. I called her directly, making the request personally, explaining the open case, the potential of Kotes knowing more, especially with the warning provided. I was in, and Paige Kotes was officially a person of interest.

Person of interest is a telling label, the context giving it different meanings. From behind bars, nestled deep inside a prison, separated from the world by concrete and steel, it was impossible for Paige Kotes to have been directly involved in any murders. But she'd sent the initial invitation to meet, and then voiced a warning of the next murder. Indirectly, I was sure she was implicated.

At the visitor center, I veered to the left, where visiting law enforcement could securely cage their firearms. I'd only stood there five minutes and had already begun to feel it—confinement, being imprisoned, a sense of suffocation touching every cell of my body. From inside the prison, there was no telling what time of day it was, the windows far and few and barely big enough to let in light.

Paige Kotes was already waiting for me in the same interview room where we'd first met. Emerald eyes peered through locks of dark red hair hanging across her face, covering the ragged scar, the damage from her confrontation with Jericho. I'd still not received

Jessie Flynn's case file, but my searches online told of a disastrous struggle when Jericho discovered Paige had murdered his wife. Paige had attacked him, intent on killing him, crashing their marine patrol boat; he'd almost lost an arm, while Paige had lost her spleen and part of a kidney, the ragged scar on her face a lasting reminder.

"Detective," she said, pushing hair from her face, chains draped from her wrists dragging across the table's steel surface. "You took me out of my shop class."

"Shop class?" I asked, subtly bemused.

She picked at her scar, the deepest crevices, near her eye, being scabbed with welts. "That's what I call it—the floor where we make the license plates.

"Guard?" I said, getting the officer's attention and motioning to the restraints. "Can we remove these?"

Paige's face brightened. It was instantaneous and gave me a glimpse of a young beauty lost behind the horrors of who she was today. She held up her hands to the guards, snapping her fingers with a cheeky wide-eyed smile. "I promise to be on my best behavior."

The guard gave Paige a cautionary look from a round face with a chin that had more jiggle than jawbone. "Your best behavior, Ms. Kotes, I expect no less."

She crossed herself, chains clanking, then raised two fingers. "Absolutely. I promise."

As Paige stood to have the restraints removed, I sized her up. Caution and worry settled in my stomach. She was taller than me, and toned. I wasn't sure I could handle myself against her if she decided to attack. I'd worked with her type before and knew the fastest way to get answers was to make like I was her friend, to champion her, to be on her side—even if it was the smallest of details, like removing restraints.

"The legs too?" Paige asked, raising one foot, chains running up the side of the metal seat.

"We'll keep those on," the guard answered, while I removed a folder from my bag. I still had some reservations about showing her the contents. Paige turned her mouth down in a pout and then snorted a laugh, throwing the guard a middle-finger gesture when he'd turned his back.

"So, Paige," I said. "We don't have very much time."

"There *was* a second murder?" Her face turned serious, already knowing the answer, her tongue wetting her lips, her eyes fixed on the folder.

"Early this morning…" I began. I fought off the reluctance, the uncertainty of how Paige would respond, and opened the folder. Pictures of Ann Choplin and the latest victim glided onto the steel table as though floating. Paige's eyes grew wide as she organized them, placing them side by side.

"The victim was killed last night," she said, pinching her scar, a fingernail digging into it while her eyes drank in the details of the crime scenes. "Best guess, both bodies washed ashore within twelve to twenty-four hours. That's significant."

"It is," I agreed, but I wanted to hear her explain why so I could gauge if she was willing to help.

"Tick tock," she said, her fingers held like the hands of a clock. "Are you testing me?"

"I'd like to know why you believe it's significant," I answered flatly, not giving her anything more.

"The killer doesn't hold onto the bodies, not even for a minute. He doesn't do anything with them afterward or try to relive the moments before." She brought one of the pictures close to her face, sniffing it like a dog trying to pick up a scent. "Did Dr. Swales find anything on the bodies?"

Her mention of Dr. Swales surprised me for a moment. I'd briefly forgotten that Paige had worked with many of the same people I worked with today. "Nothing," I answered.

"So," she said eagerly, "that in itself is significant. I mean, your killer is organized. He goes to inordinate lengths to ensure his work is tidy, that it's clean. You're looking for someone who's very familiar with forensics, possibly trained and educated in the science."

I found myself repeating what she was telling me, my cell phone for note-taking stowed in the security locker along with my gun. "And they are aware of us," I commented, adding to the profile she was building.

"Definitely aware. The killer isn't just watching the news and reading newspapers either. They've probably reached out to the newspapers, the reporters." She slapped the table with excitement. "Might even have been at your station, working there just to be close to the case, to what they did, reliving the moments over and over."

"Mind yourself, Kotes," the guard warned. Paige settled down as distant prison sounds bounced around the room, the guard's head turning in their direction like an antenna honing in on a weak signal.

"What else do you see?" I asked her.

She straightened up, weaving her fingers together, her gaze focused on me. "Tell you what, I'll share what else I see if you promise to answer a question."

"What's your question?" I asked, intrigued now, Paige giving me a tick of interest, a tease to entice me.

She shook her head. "Not so fast." She leaned in, bringing her face close to mine, green eyes shiny, the beauty stolen by the scars. "You have to promise."

"Fine," I answered, despite having a dark reservation about the idea. Satisfied, Paige eased back and began. "Your guy isn't into a particular type—he's not targeting based on the victims being young or old or fat or skinny. He doesn't care about hair or skin color or whether the women are tall or short."

"That was one of the first things we noted," I confirmed, the two victims being different heights and builds and having different color eyes and hair. Having a similar look was a common trait for some serial killers, who often identified their victims with someone in their past, someone who motivated their selection. "The victims appear to be chosen at random, leading to the possibility of opportunity."

She shook her head. "You're wrong. These aren't opportunity killings. These women were selected. The question is why." She picked up the picture of the latest victim, parts of the woman's body submerged in wet sand like a sunken ship. "This woman is dressed for someone. She's dolled up too, from the looks of the nails." She glanced at the picture of Ann Choplin. "And this one is wearing exercise clothes, like she's been jogging. You're checking the trails?"

She's talking about security cameras. I tried not to show my reaction to the quick study Paige was making of the pictures. "What are you thinking?" I asked.

"Please," she answered with a frown. "Don't insult me. You've already got someone working security footage, maybe the victim's cell phone too."

"We do," I confessed. "But what else do you think?"

"Okay," she said, shifting to stand, fingers splayed, pressing against the table, her lips pinched in thought. "There's something common to both victims."

"Care to share—" I began to ask, before a prison alarm interrupted me, the sound deafening.

"Let's wrap this up," the guard said, rapping the door frame with his knuckles.

"Would you listen to that! Saved by the bell," Paige laughed, and then turned serious, perching her face in her hands, elbows propped on the table. "My question now. Are you and Jericho… ya know, a couple?"

"That has nothing to do with—"

"Hold on, you promised to answer my question," she said in a low voice, eyes threatening. Remembering her history with Jericho, my arms instinctively moved to my front. It was only a split second, an instinctual moment, before I moved them back again. But the damage was done: I'd given myself away. Paige's eyes followed my arms, catching what I was protecting. Her mouth gaped open, eyes pivoting with shock and revelation, and her voice shot high like a giddy schoolgirl. "You're *more* than just a couple?"

Pulse racing, mouth dry and heart walloping, I was suddenly afraid for both myself and my baby. "Guard!" I called.

"Oh come now," Paige said loudly, pasting on a forced smile, her gaze never leaving my belly as I quickly gathered up the photographs. "Give Jericho big hugs from me. Tell him Auntie Paige sends her love."

She blew me a kiss that turned me cold and stole my breath. I couldn't get out of there fast enough and stumbled while gathering my things. Paige's laughter bounced off the cinder walls and followed me down the corridor, accompanied by the sound of the guard yelling for her to quieten down, warning she'd lose privileges if she made him late for the shift change.

When I exited the front gates, I left the prison dampness and the chill of the concrete and steel and jumped into the first band of sunlight, standing there until the icy fear had melted some. I was shaking, and it wasn't just from the cold. I'd gone inside the prison with authority, a determination to advance this case. But in a single exchange, Paige had got me running, fear sweeping though me.

Hormones, I thought wildly, swiping a tear and making a stupid excuse. She was the most dangerous person I'd ever met in my career, and I'd taken who she was for granted, letting my guard down, letting myself work with her for the sake of the case. She was vicious and murderous, a frighteningly cunning criminal. I was doing my job, but I could never forget who Paige Kotes was, not for a single moment.

I sat in my car long enough to begin sweating in the heat. It was also enough time to settle my heart rate and consider the constructive aspects of the meeting. Paige had said the victims had something in common. It was highly unlikely that she knew them personally. That meant her comments could only have referred to the pictures. My window rolled down, a hot wind sweeping my hair, a summer storm rumbling in the distance, I leafed through them again, looking deeper into the details, trying to see what it was that Paige had seen.

"The knots," I said at last, making a wild guess. I'd overlooked them before, believing them insignificant. Tracy's pictures included multiple angles of every subject area, which let me identify the knot used in each of the bindings. There were six bindings, three for each victim, and the exact same knot had been used in all of them. While it might have been the only knot the killer knew, it might also give us a clue into his background: a previous job perhaps. Maybe he worked on a ship or at the docks?

As I drove east, the newest summer storm chasing me, Paige having identified what was common across the victims continued to bother me. I didn't want to believe she was a better detective than me. I put my free hand over my belly. Like the storm, there was a new threat coming after me: Paige and her knowledge that Jericho and I were going to have a baby.

"I'll never let anything happen to you," I whispered.

TWELVE

Paige Kotes entered her cell. Any change in the monotony of her day-to-day was apt to be fun. A person could go insane if there wasn't some kind of break now and then, a blip in the daily schedule, a hiccup in the stagnancy of prison life.

She was relieved of the metal restraints cutting into her ankles and wrists, the guard muttering something about the hour, about the schedule and the inconvenience. Paige half ignored it, knowing full well that when guards were out of sorts, they'd often take it out on the inmates. She needed time alone and didn't want to risk a cross word with them. There was work to do before dinner and lights-out.

The letter, she thought excitedly, biting her lip and holding her breath, dirty fingers pinching the edge of her scar. A laugh slipped out, her guessing about the victims having something in common, and Detective White buying it. Her puppet was still a work in progress. She had given him good directions, guided him in how to select his victims. Today's letter would confirm if he had followed through, confirm that he was behind the latest murder and that the victim was the one she'd wanted him to pick. She pushed through the pile of fan mail stacked on her small table, seeking out the envelope with his post office box. *Where are you?*

Eventually she found the letter, the envelope showing it had already been opened and reviewed by the prison officials, and then resealed. But of course they were only looking for contraband hidden between the pages. They never looked at the pages themselves, or read the encoded words. Their secret gave her freedom, him doing for her what she couldn't do for herself.

She slipped her finger beneath the flap, swiping across and breaking the prison seal, the edge of it slicing into her skin and making her wince. She tasted blood, her finger on her lips, the smell of a memory, of murder, the cut surprisingly deep and miraculously timed. His words came easily, their cipher memorized. She could decipher whole sentences in her head now, and no longer needed to map the letters and words on paper.

The name she needed to see came a third of the way into the letter, along with the time and place and how he was going to do it. He'd done the same with Ann Choplin, mirroring the details, building his profile, his modus operandi just as she'd instructed him. Her belly warmed, giddy excitement gushing through her entire body as if the sun had poured delight into her soul. She sat back, panting, brushing her hands across her arms and chest and middle, the sensation raising goosebumps.

"How good are you, Detective White?" she asked, looking sharply over her shoulder, making sure nobody was at her cell door. "How long before you figure this one out?"

THIRTEEN

Warm sunlight bathed the guest bedroom walls, the sun setting over the edge of the bay as scraps of clouds lumbered steadily east. The windows faced west, bringing a bright sunset for me and Hannah to work the day's last hours, making a new bedroom for her.

"We can use these," Jericho said, plunking down a ream of folded cardboard boxes.

"Are you sure this is okay?" Hannah asked, sizing up the room, spinning to face the windows, warm butter light making her face glow. She hopped up and down on her toes, giddy with excitement. "This is an amazing room, it's so much!"

"It's just sitting here," Jericho answered, sweeping his hand across the bureau, stacking magazines.

"Any packing tape?" I asked, delighted to see Hannah so happy.

"I sent Ryan into the garage to get some," Jericho answered, his phone abuzz, an all-too-familiar distraction in his eyes.

"Is the campaign calling?" I asked, the abruptness coming with disappointment, our family evening interrupted.

"Sorry, guys," he said, cupping the phone. "It's my new campaign manager."

"Go," I said tersely. He paused at the door, arms lowering. I put on a fake smile. "Go be political. We'll be fine—" And he was gone before I could finish. I turned my attention back to the folded boxes, the blue-printed instructions showing how to assemble them. "Tab A goes into slot B?"

"It's like practice for baby furniture," Hannah laughed, joining me, knees creaking as she knelt. "Let me take a look. I'm good at these."

"You get that from your father," I said, slipping mention of him into the conversation, curious as to how things between them had been going. Hannah continued as though she didn't hear me, her lips moving as she recited the instructions. "Hannah?"

She plunked down, sitting on her feet and crossing her arms. It became immediately obvious that something had happened. "He's a dick."

"Hannah!" I said, voice raised, trying to sound parental while attempting not to laugh. She caught the laughter in my tone and burst into a roar. "I mean, I've called him worse. Many times, in fact. What happened?"

"He wants me to take a test," she answered, the laughter fizzling as her annoyance toward her father returned. "A DNA test."

"A DNA test?" I asked, raising my voice, shocked. The idea had never crossed my mind. The confessions of the man and woman who'd kidnapped Hannah years ago left zero doubt that she was my daughter. "Did he say why?"

She shrugged, her lower lip pouting, one tear falling, another standing. "I guess he doesn't believe."

"Baby, I am so sorry for this." I took her in my arms, my nose in her hair, wrapping her in a hug, remembering what it was like comforting her after skinned knees and hurt feelings back when she was just a toddler. We'd missed so much. "He's not ready."

"It's fine," she said. "I'll take the test."

I took her face in my hands, lowering mine to hers. "You don't have to do anything you don't want to."

"I know," Hannah answered. The floor vibrated with Ryan's footsteps as he ascended the rear stairs. She moved away from me, her focus returning to the boxes and the task at hand.

"I couldn't find any tape," Ryan said, and dropped a rolled bundle of rope onto the floor. "But I found this in the garage."

I froze a moment as he left the room, Hannah's concentration stolen by the cardboard puzzle. I stretched my arms outward as if making room for a bomb squad. Six feet from me lay a type of rope I'd seen twice now this week—the nylon braid a shiny white, the weaves threaded with specks of green and blue—a marina rope, the same as the one used on Ann Choplin and the latest victim.

"Hannah," I said, voice crackly, throat scratchy and dry. "Get my bag from the bed."

She glanced over at me. "Is there a bug?"

"I can't explain. Just open my bag, and inside you'll find a roll of clear plastic bags."

Hannah did as I asked, retrieving an evidence bag from the roll I always carried. "What is it?"

My mind was scattered with too many answers to single out any one of them, my instincts kicking in like a firefighter's reaction to the scent of smoke. I had to secure the rope, regardless of whether it was evidence or a mere coincidence. I heard the low drone of Jericho's voice rolling in from his bedroom, and felt a stab of pain in my chest as though I were betraying his trust. But I followed what I'd been trained to do, turning the evidence bag inside-out and using it like a glove to handle the rope as though it were ripe with contagions. Once I'd sealed the bag, I turned to Hannah, answering her. "I'm hoping it's nothing at all."

FOURTEEN

I'd bagged and tagged the rope from Jericho's house and sent it to the forensics lab for analysis. The lab techs would compare it with the ropes retrieved from the victims and determine any likeness or match. Since the rope was common around the Outer Banks, I was certain it was a coincidence, but that didn't stop the needling questions in my head. I shook off the taunting thoughts, needing to concentrate on the case and my presentation to the team.

"Victim's name is Judy Granger," I announced, thunder rumbling, fat raindrops smacking against the conference room windows. The team remained quiet, absorbing the details of the murder and Tracy's photographs on the screen. "Age forty-four, resident of the area, single, no children. Immediate family is her mother, who lived with the victim."

"There were no missing person reports from family members or co-worker," Emanuel added.

"That means she wasn't missing long enough for anyone to worry?" Cheryl asked.

"Death may have been less than twenty-four hours prior," he agreed.

"The cause of death is assumed to be drowning," I said, motioning to Nichelle. She advanced the presentation, landing on the pictures from the beach, and the restraints. "The rope is the same type and style used on the first victim. We have one additional detail: the knot. The same knot was used on both victims and across all bindings."

On the conference room table I'd placed segments of rope, a clothes-line variety I'd picked up at a local dollar store. Each of us had one in front of us. "What are we supposed to do with these?" Cheryl asked.

"Learn the knot," I answered. Her face twisted into a scowl. I indicated the screen. "This isn't a typical knot, not one you'd use to tie your shoes with. It's intricate, which means it was learned, practiced, rehearsed, maybe even timed. My thinking is there was training involved. A vocational school, or military—"

"Or law enforcement," Tracy added. Without looking up, she continued, "If we know the knot, we'll find the questions to ask."

"That's right. There are thousands of knots. Why does the killer use this one? I want to know if they were an Eagle Scout, or are currently in the military. Maybe they work on a crabbing boat?"

"I got it," Cheryl said, waving understanding.

"That's the first thing. Secondly, Nichelle, where are we with the cell carrier for Ann Choplin? Location services? Jogging or fitness apps installed?"

Nichelle looked up from her monitor, her hair loose, her brown eyes large with concern as she shook her head. "I'm still working on it. There's an assistant with Choplin's PR firm who's been really difficult to get anything out of."

"The ex-husband is on his way in for an interview," Emanuel offered. Nichelle welcomed the interruption.

"Could be they still share the cell phone accounts?" Nichelle asked, fingers poised, unsure.

"We'll get clarification in the interview. I'd like you and Emanuel to join me."

Tracy raised her hand. "Any room for one more?"

I gave her a nod before shifting to our latest victim. "We need to add Judy Granger to our search for cell phone service providers.

She had no phone on her person, and there was none found at the scene, but we can be certain she had one. Let's find out the carrier so we can get a list of locations and apps installed." We were early in the investigation and putting feelers in every direction.

"Any thoughts on whether the victim was working or on a date?" Tracy asked. On cue, Nichelle flashed the monitor with pictures of Judy Granger's fingers and toes, along with her clothes.

"I'm not sure," I answered. "She does seem to be dressed up. Could be she was at work, and went out after. There's no real knowing until we interview co-workers. How are we on the fuel from the victim's clothes?"

"I'm working that one," Emanuel said. "We've sent portions of fabric to forensics to determine the type, and anything else usable."

"What does the fuel tell you?" Nichelle asked.

"She came from the ocean, not the beach," Tracy answered.

"Correct," I said. I explained our theory for Nichelle's benefit. "The killer took the victims out to sea and dumped them overboard. The boat's motors expel unburned fuel, and the victim's clothes came into contact with some of it when she was in the ocean."

"That's awful," she said, her fingers moving across her keyboard. "Is there a possible angle with the motors? One type over another that we could derive from the fuel samples?"

"Not really," Tracy said, tapping her chin, eyes wandering. "Unless two-stroke versus four-stroke makes a difference."

"But that'd cover nearly all boats in the Outer Banks," Emanuel said. "I like the idea, but it won't help narrow anything down for us to use."

"It's a thought," Tracy said.

"It's a good one too. We have to keep thinking out of the box, so review all your ideas," I said, trying to encourage them.

"Was she drugged?" Emanuel asked. "Like Ann Choplin?"

"I'm waiting on the toxicology report, but given the number of similarities we've seen already, I'd expect to find ketamine," I answered.

Nichelle refreshed the presentation with pictures of the victims. A sharp light brightened the room, an immediate thunderclap rolling over the station.

"They don't look alike at all," Cheryl said. She picked up the photographs I'd shown Paige. "There isn't anything similar other than that they're both white and female. Different hair, face... there's no resemblance at all."

"You're right. Nothing similar in looks, but they are the same age," I answered.

"And they're both locals," Nichelle added, flipping the screen to show a young Ann Choplin. "It was one of the first things I checked once we had a positive identification."

"Same age and local. Any chance they knew each other?" I asked. Perhaps the women's past held a clue. "Maybe they grew up in the same neighborhood?"

"I found some newspaper clippings, pictures from football games, Friday nights, cheering squad, that sort of thing."

I waved for her to present what she had, excitement building with the small break. A newspaper picture showed on the screen, the black-and-white paper yellowed, the text and photograph fuzzy. It was a picture of a picture, but there was enough to read names across the bottom and put faces to them. Four girls wearing cheerleading outfits stood at the center, stringy pompoms held in front of them, their faces bright in the football stadium lights, signs of teenage adolescence evident—braces and blemishes and awkward hairstyles.

"Judy Granger," I said, pointing out the first name beneath the photograph. "Ann Stewart? Could that be a maiden name?" I asked.

"I believe so, but will confirm," Nichelle said.

"We'll verify in the meeting with her ex-husband," I told her. I pointed to the second girl. "This could be her; the chin is the same, as are her eyes."

"The next in the photo is Lisa Wells," Cheryl said, reading the names. "And then Jessie Cooper." The last girl's face looked surprisingly familiar to me, but I couldn't work out where I'd seen it before.

"I know her," Emanuel said, coming to the front of the conference room, He towered over me, the monitor's blue glare shining on his face as he looked closer. "She became Jessie Flynn."

My stomach sank instantly as my eyes registered the woman's face, the image striking a memory like a blacksmith's hammer on burning steel. Sparks flew in wild directions as the case that had put Paige Kotes in prison surfaced in a sudden gush. "You're sure?"

His head bobbed up and down, a sorrowful look telling me he was certain. "I was the responding officer. I'll never forget it." His jaw slack, he continued, "I was on the beach when we recovered her body, when her husband arrived on scene."

"Wait," Tracy said, eyes on me and then shifting to the monitor. "You're talking about Jericho Flynn's wife?"

Emanuel nodded, his shoulders slumped. He shook his head and put his hands to his hips. "An awful thing to see. There was no consoling him."

I held my breath and didn't speak. It hurt hearing what Emanuel said, listening to what Jericho went through the day he came upon a murder scene and discovered his wife was the victim. Tracy fished out a folder from her endlessly overstuffed bag of study books and old case files. A hundred sticky notes sprung wildly from it, like a patch of bright dandelions, her fingers sifting through them to find the one she wanted. "What is it?" I managed to ask, the strength gone from my voice.

"I have a copy of Jessie Flynn's case file. I've been studying it, along with Paige Kotes."

"Kiddo with the extra-credit homework," Cheryl said. "Do you think you've got something in there?"

"I'm writing a position paper for school… here it is!" Tracy said, pinning the page against the table with her finger.

"Ma'am," an officer interrupted from the door. "We have Joseph Choplin in interview room two for you."

"Thank you," I said, welcoming the break. I turned back to the team. "The victim's phone service, I want to know more. Also, everyone grab a piece of rope and learn the knot like you were a scout working to get your badge. I want full reports on what it is, where it's taught, and how it's used, particularly on boats." I went to the monitor, tapping the yellowed newspaper clipping. "And Lisa Wells, who is she? Where is she? Could she be the killer's next target?"

We had a photo showing four smiling high-school girls. Now three of them were dead: two our recent victims; the other killed at the hands of Paige Kotes.

"And Jessie Flynn?" Tracy asked, still holding the file, intent on including Jericho's wife as part of the investigation.

My breath was hot and short with concern, an unwillingness in me growing like a cancer. I felt the team's stares, and answered abruptly. "For cross-reference purposes only. Were the girls close? Did they remain in contact? Who did they all know? That sort of thing, but not until you've finished compiling the list of stores that carry and sell the rope."

One by one I acknowledged each member of my team, each with instructions in hand, before turning my thoughts to Ann Choplin's estranged husband. He'd come to us willingly, and I felt no sense of urgency around him being a person of interest. Initially there'd been a possibility, but now, with a second murder—both victims the same age, both discovered on the beach, and especially with the new evidence of the photo—I knew this case wasn't about a husband

and wife and their irreconcilable differences festering into a heinous act of murder. It was about a killer targeting a very select group of women. I didn't know why, but I'd find out. And Paige Kotes was going to help me.

FIFTEEN

I'd seen men grieving. Men who'd lost mothers and daughters and wives and girlfriends—faces sullen and shadowed with gloom, whiskered with damp cheeks and creases and folds beneath puffy eyes, the faint smell of bourbon or vodka on their breath.

Joseph Choplin showed none of these things. Our first victim's husband sat in the interview room with one leg crossed over the other. On the table was a leather-bound briefcase along with two energy drinks. His suit was pressed with sharp pleats, face glowing with a fresh tan, slicked black hair with thin streaks of gray. A cell phone was glued to his ear, his voice pitched with excitement as he discussed a real-estate development project.

When we entered, he said, "Listen, I'll call you back with the details." He tapped in a message, then put the phone down on the table.

"Sounds to me like business is on the rise," I said, taking a seat opposite him along with Emanuel and Tracy.

"Steady enough," he answered, flashing a nervous smile while studying the three of us. "I got a call to come in, answer some questions?"

"It's with regard to the recent passing of your wife, Ann Choplin," Emanuel said. "For the record, this meeting is being recorded."

"Recorded?" Choplin asked, gripping his hands together. "Should… should I have a lawyer?"

"Do you feel you need a lawyer?" I asked, answering his question with one of my own.

"No—" he began, and then shrugged. "I mean, you tell me."

"It's your right to have representation," Emanuel told him. "We've only got a few questions, but we could reschedule?"

Choplin shook his head. "I'm traveling a lot. Can't reschedule."

Deciding to move forward, I cut to the chase. "You have our deepest condolences on your wife's death—"

"Ex-wife," he interrupted, eyes shifting to each of us. "I mean, if this is being recorded, let's get that established."

"Officially, you were separated," Emanuel corrected him.

He half nodded. "Officially. Legal separation is a requirement before filing for divorce."

"Tell us about your separation," I asked.

Joseph glanced at his phone, the face of it lighting up with a text message. "What's there to say? Fell out of love, irreconcilable differences. Never had children, so the split was kind of amicable. I could give you a dozen more reasons."

"Was the decision mutual?"

"Amicable, like I said, but since this is being recorded, Ann left first," he answered sharply, his eyes pinched with hurt. "Got dealt a bad hand with those houses, and she wanted out."

"I'd say your wife was dealt a bad hand." I opened a tablet and brought up the case file, including all the crime-scene pictures. "Mr. Choplin, do you understand that this is a case of murder we're investigating?"

"I thought I was just here to answer some questions," he said, shifting uncomfortably as I flipped through the photos.

"Correct," Emanuel said. "Some of our questions will be difficult."

"I understand," he replied, more engaged.

I was tempted to show him the photograph of his wife's remains, her middle partially buried, her arms and legs jutting awkwardly, her face ash-gray like driftwood. A picture like that might shock him enough to give us an angle to explore. I studied him, hesitating, and decided to swipe the screen instead, keeping the pictures hidden. "Any reason to think someone would want her dead?"

"No," he answered. We said nothing, and his eyes darted around. "I'm telling you, I really don't know."

"You stand to receive a lot of money with your wife's death," Emanuel said, putting the man on the spot, declaring our team's suspicions without outwardly stating them.

"Life insurance policy, and her company," I said. "So maybe the hand dealt has a few aces in it for you. That money would go a long way in your new business venture. Correct?"

"I don't like what you're implying," Joseph said, his voice raised. "Are you referring to my business in Florida?"

"Florida?" I asked, homing in on a new detail. "Tell us about that."

He let out a sigh, then pulled out a stack of business cards and peppered the table with them, throwing one to each of us like a dealer at a casino. "I'm opening a new business to sell and manage beachfront condominiums. If you're looking for a good deal—"

Ignoring his business card, I asked, "Why Florida?"

"Business doesn't sprout like flowers," he said. "I've been spending my days and nights the last month in the peninsula state."

"We'll need receipts, travel, lodging, food, everything you have," I told him, making a note.

He held up his phone. "Every dime spent is recorded, all electronic for tax season."

"That's fine," I said. "We'll be calling each establishment to confirm." Switching topics, I swiped the tablet's screen, landing on the newspaper picture. "Do you recognize these women?"

His expression warmed as he sat up to take a closer look. "We were so young," he said. "That's me in the background, along with Flynn and Ashtole. Hard to believe three of the people in that picture are dead now." I flipped the tablet around and searched the background, the field behind the cheerleaders showing a handful of boys in football gear. Joseph seemed to be quietly reveling in the moment. Picking up one of the energy drinks, he chugged half. "We were the group back then," he said with pride in his voice. "All the kids wanted to be us." His face went sad then, turning grim with disappointment. "It's a terrible thing when you peak in high school."

"You and your wife were a couple at the time?" Tracy asked; she'd moved to look at the picture, her late uncle being one of the boys on the field.

"Uh-uh." Joseph shook his head. "We didn't get together until a month, maybe two after that picture was taken."

"Could you elaborate on your relationship back then?" I asked, more out of curiosity than any relevance to the case.

He shrugged and stuffed the deck of business cards back into his suit jacket. "You know how it is at that age, small groups, the popular kids, everyone dating. We traded teenage crushes about as often as the weather changed."

"It wasn't just a crush, though," I said. "You got married."

"Eventually, yeah," he answered, taking another swig of his drink. "But we dated other people too. If I remember right, for a while I was dating Lisa Wells, Ashtole was dating Jessie Cooper and Flynn was dating Ann."

"How long for?" I asked, curious to the extent of Jericho's relationship with her.

He glanced at the picture and waved his hand nonchalantly. "If a crush lasted more than a week, then you were a couple."

"So you and your wife got together shortly after this photo was taken?" Emanuel asked, his curiosity piqued.

Choplin smacked the table. "That's right. I remember now, 'cause there was a big blow-up between Ashtole and Flynn when

Jessie broke it off with him. She had a crush on Jericho, so the two of them started dating, and I broke up with Lisa so I could date Ann. We hit some rough patches in college, but made it through and then got married."

Out of nowhere, emotion slammed into him, his skin turning bright red, his eyes glassy, lower lip trembling. He jabbed his cheek with the heel of his hand, drying his face as he took the tablet and stared at the photograph. "I'm sorry," he said, addressing his dead wife, apologizing for their torrid past. "I could have treated you better."

He was clearly distressed, but I had to explore every angle. Thinking of what Cheryl had told us, I moved the conversation on from their school days. "You have a history of violence toward Ann. You've previously been arrested for domestic disturbance."

Tears puddled and fell, the sobs coming, his first taste of mourning a loss. "Sorry, what?"

Emanuel spun his laptop around to show the paperwork, the court filings.

"We both were," Joseph said bitterly, telling us what we already knew. His gaze fell back to the picture. "We could have been kinder to each other."

"With a record, you know how it can look," I said. "How was your relationship before your wife's death?"

He frowned, the tears drying. "We were separated. How do you think it was?" He sat squarely and finished his energy drink. Sliding the tablet closer, he pointed at one of the background figures. "This guy, Jericho Flynn, you should talk to him."

From the corner of my eye, I saw Emanuel and Tracy shift in their seats and glance briefly at me. Choplin was creating a distraction, reaching for anything that would pivot focus away from him. By now, though, I'd heard and seen enough. This man wasn't a killer.

Within a day, maybe two, every receipt from his business in Florida would corroborate his story.

"Why is that?" Tracy asked.

"He's not the nice guy everyone thinks he is."

"Decorated officer, elected sheriff, and soon to be mayor," I pointed out, feeling the need to defend Jericho's name.

"Yeah, that's all well and good," Joseph answered. "But I've seen who he can be first-hand. That man has a violent side."

I swiped the tablet, clearing the picture, the man's words stinging like poison. The interview room was stifling hot, making me feel claustrophobic. I knew the tactic he was using but couldn't stand to hear any more of it. With the tablet in hand, I said, "You'll get us those receipts to establish your whereabouts the night your wife was killed."

"I will," he said. "I'll send everything I've got."

He stood up to leave, taking the cans from the table, stuffing his phone in his pocket. As he moved toward the door, Emanuel asked, "What do you mean, a violent side?"

Joseph looked at his shoes as he answered. "There are rumors. About Jessie and how she died."

My body went stiff, not wanting to move until he'd finished.

"I heard Ann and her friends talking about it. They suspected Jericho was in on it, that he persuaded Paige Kotes to kill his wife. When she threatened to tell the truth, Jericho tried to kill *her*."

"These friends. You have their names?" I asked, voice heated.

"You already know them," he answered, his hand on the door, making to leave. "That newspaper picture. My wife was Jessie's oldest friend. She was sure something was off about her death. Judy Granger and Lisa Wells thought so too."

Tracy wrote down every word while Emanuel and I listened. "And why should we believe this?" I asked.

"You can believe whatever you want," he said, eyes shifting from mine to Emanuel and Tracy. "But ask yourself who has the most to lose if that rumor got airtime with reporters. Sounds a lot like motive to me."

"This doesn't add up," Emanuel said sharply. "If there ever was such a rumor, then why would your wife's PR firm work with Flynn's campaign?"

Joseph shrugged. "Who's to say? Maybe Ann had some notion of bringing justice for Jessie's death, working undercover on her own to find evidence that'd help build a case."

"And Paige Kotes?" I added, challenging the man's accusations. "She's got all the time in the world to talk, so why not say something now?"

He shook his head, opening the door. Before leaving, he answered coldly, "That's for you guys to figure out."

He was right: it *was* for us to figure out. Joseph Choplin had successfully diverted our focus on him by burying a time bomb in our investigation.

I excused myself and exited the interview room. With my desk in my sights, I put on blinders and avoided the men and women in the station needing a few minutes of my time. I had to sit and think and understand what the implications would be if Jericho's name was brought up during this investigation. If the press heard it in connection with *any* case, old or new, it would torpedo his campaign. I plunked into my chair and cradled my head in my hands, my thoughts erratic as Paige's words rang in my head: *There's something common to both victims.* It wasn't the rope's knot she'd been referring to at all. It was Jericho.

A sliver of doubt reared its ugly face, knifing the pit of my soul, casting a shadow on the man I was in love with, the man who would be father to my child. It was impossible to fathom, but I was a cop, and diversion or no diversion, I was compelled to investigate.

SIXTEEN

With every investigation, particularly murder, there will always be troubling developments to tackle. It comes with the job, a detail many detectives struggle to manage. It was our responsibility to make sure such developments never derailed the case. But then there were the crushing disruptions, the kind that rose to dizzying heights and threatened to obliterate the investigation altogether.

I'd hit the crushing kind when Joseph Choplin mentioned his wife and her friends and their belief in Jericho's involvement in Jessie's murder. In one brief moment, he'd turned my questioning about his wife's murder into a conversation about something else entirely. I'd hit similar before, particularly in prison interviews, two inmates tattling, one turning on the other as part of a plea deal. It was common, but in my experience, it also usually meant there was guilt carried by both individuals. Joseph's words had found their way inside me, nestling deep like a pebble in my shoe, causing a relentless pain I couldn't ignore.

It was the motive he proposed that struck true like a newly forged bell. I'd searched for the unreasonable but found none. As much as it pained me, he'd spelled out a motive that made sense, and left me with the burden of dispelling it. Our victims had been friends with Jericho's wife—long-time friends, the kind of friendships born in childhood, fostered through corner lemonade stands and sleepovers and hanging out after school. They'd endured adolescence together, carried their friendships through prom and college acceptances, all of them attending the same college. If I looked hard enough, I was sure to find a trove of memories and keepsakes captured in videos and photographs. And like the newspaper picture, I'd find their husbands on the fringes, including Jericho.

What I told myself, kept telling myself, was that with every high-profile case came a mountain of speculation and rumor. Nobody knew how it started—an eager reporter dreaming of a book deal, perhaps? Gossipy talk at a hair salon? A drunken story told over half-smoked cigarettes and sloppy whiskey shots at the local drinking hole? Maybe that was all this was. Maybe Joseph Choplin was simply telling an old story, passing it along for the hundredth time, a tale he'd heard between the sheets during an intimate evening with his wife.

I couldn't discount the rope, though, or Paige's comments. Surely Paige would have heard the rumors about Jericho too. In prison, telling tall tales was a popular way to pass time. Prisoners often spun stories, trying to gain enough credibility to warrant a discussion with an attorney, or even a court hearing. They'd say anything if it meant a break in the monotony. But since her incarceration, Paige Kotes had never met with an attorney regarding her original case. There had been books and movie documentary deals, the courts awarding all proceeds to her victims, including Jericho and Ryan. But at no time had she ever approached anyone about Jericho's supposed involvement. This small factoid grounded me, gave me something to cling to as though it were a life vest and I'd been abandoned in rough seas.

Unfortunately, most of my team had heard what Joseph said. They'd left the interview room with a nugget of an idea about Jericho having a motive. From this point forward, regardless of what I thought or what I said to them, there would be little I could do to quell their curiosity. Like me, they were detectives and had investigative natures. There was only one way to clear Jericho's name. I had to do what we'd originally set out to do. I had to find who had killed Ann Choplin and Judy Granger.

Jericho slept soundly, our legs woven, our bodies naked and warm beneath a thin sheet. Summer air stirred through the bedroom window and carried the sound of the waves lapping against the shoreline while tree frogs and crickets chattered among the trees. The moon was nearly full, turning everything steely gray. On the far wall, the moon shadow of tree branches danced with the steady breeze.

This case had become a thorn in my side, and if I didn't say something soon, I was sure to burst. The ideas coming alive in my head fed my imagination like black coal to a hot stove and took me to horrible places the way we often entertain our worst fears. I decided I'd have to talk to Jericho before my team did.

I silently lifted his arm and held it in mine, tucking it against my skin, the knobby scars of his past showing horribly bright like a string of shiny beads. Only these weren't jewels. They were memories of a true nightmare, one he'd barely survived. Along with his wife's murder, the surgical scars riddling his shoulder and arm would forever connect him to Paige Kotes.

So much pain, I thought, tracing them, running my fingers over each smooth bump, my thoughts snapping back to Joseph Choplin.

"What are you doing," Jericho asked, half-lidded, voice crackly.

"Just looking," I said hesitantly. He always hid his arm, embarrassed by the scars. His eyelids fluttered open in recognition and he tried rolling toward me to tuck it beneath him. I tightened my legs around him, saying, "Don't."

"You know I don't like it when people stare."

"Yeah. I know," I said, continuing to touch him. "I'm not just people, though. I love you, Jericho." I lowered my head, brushing my lips against the largest of the scars, a half-moon nearly a foot long that stretched from the top of his shoulder down to the crook above his forearm. "I love every part of you."

I expected he'd wrangle himself free of me, turning over to hide, but he didn't. The room's window faced east, the curtains drawn, the moon at its peak. I could see pale saucers floating in Jericho's eyes, a brief smile forming, allowing me the indulgence. A moment passed, then he asked, "What are you doing awake anyway?"

"I couldn't sleep," I replied, desperately wanting to ask him about Paige, and about his wife. A salty gust blew into the room, the cool draft rushing over my bare neck and bottom, turning my skin prickly with bumps. Jericho tugged on the sheet to help cover me. When we were both back beneath the linen, sharing comfortably, his hands went to my middle, to our baby. "You know, in a few months, we won't be able to get this close," I said.

"I won't mind," he murmured, his lips on mine, his hand finding its way around me.

"Can I ask you something?" I asked.

"Mm-hmm," he hummed, closing his eyes.

"Tell me more about Joseph Choplin?" Jericho rolled onto his back, his eyes open again. "How well do you know—"

"I know Joseph as much as I need to," he interrupted. "I've known him as long as anyone I grew up with. Grade school, high school. We also played football together."

"Yeah, he mentioned football."

He rolled to face me. "Are you guys investigating him for Ann's murder?" he asked, propping himself onto an elbow. "Do you think he had something to do with it?"

"They've got a violent history," I said. "Even arrested, both of them."

Jericho frowned and dug his fingertips into his whiskers; with no camera interviews scheduled for the next few days, he was letting his beard grow. "I knew they had some troubles. Ann mentioned it a few times."

"Did she?" I asked, covering my chest with the sheet, the fabric cool. I sat up, having opened the door to ask more questions. "What else did she share?"

He shrugged. "Most of what I learned, I got from Jessie. They were close."

"And Judy Granger too?"

"Gosh," he said, eyeing the walls as if watching old memories play in the dark. "It's been years since I've thought of them. I mean us, our little group, kind of a clique. We were the popular kids in high school. Daniel too, and a few others."

"Lisa Wells?" I dared to ask, trying not to show how much I already knew. Jericho's expression changed instantly, the name ringing more than a memory.

"Uh, yeah," he answered, surprised. He sat up, the sheet falling from his lap as he turned to sit on the edge of the bed. I felt tension coming from him, a wall of it mounting. "Casey, if you've got something on your mind, or you've been digging through the town's high-school yearbooks, then tell me what this is about."

There was no coasting through a response, making it sound like innocent curiosity. I had to tell him. I moved toward him, feeling uncomfortable, wanting to remove any barriers. With his back to me, I put my arms around him, my body pressed against his, bracing for what I was about to ask. "He told me that Ann and Lisa and Judy had raised questions about Jessie's death."

"What?" he exclaimed, his voice rising. He stood up, his body in full moonlight, his looming shadow on the wall mirroring his motions. He gave me a cold look, brow furrowed and mouth twisted in a grimace, and I moved back to my side of the bed, my knees up to my chest, tugging the sheet to cover me. He saw my reaction and raised his hands. "Sorry. I just—I haven't thought about those rumors for a long time either."

"Rumors?" I asked, lowering my voice to a whisper.

"It was awful," he answered, voice breaking. He pinched his forehead. "It was bad enough losing Jessie like that, but then to have Joseph Choplin do what he did…"

I lowered my knees and raised my hand, urging him back into bed. He took my fingers and eased his legs beneath the sheet until they were paired with mine. "I didn't mean to stir things up and make you mad," I said.

He let out a huff, his lips pinched. A moment passed, then he said, "That guy tried pulling this shit the day of Jessie's funeral."

"What do you mean?" I asked, beginning to think Joseph Choplin might have been playing an old hand, trying to make something out of nothing, stirring up trouble like a catty gossiping witch.

"There was press everywhere. News crews from all over the country following the story. They couldn't get enough. It was huge," he said. I understood, having experienced similar with Hannah's kidnapping. "And it was disgusting."

"Where did the Choplins fit in?"

Jericho's eyes widened, showing a look of bewilderment, something I'd not seen before. He pointed toward the front of the house. "Right out there, on the street, out of nowhere, Joseph calls this press conference with Ann standing behind him. I thought they were paying some nice tribute to Jessie, since we'd all been so close."

"But they weren't?"

Tears stood in his eyes, glistening in the moonlight. "It was nothing but lies. He made these accusations, talking about things Jessie had supposedly told Ann—which she hadn't."

"About you?"

He shook his head. "About me and Paige, working together." He wiped his face and ran his fingers through his hair. "The DA shut it down, finding there was no merit in their accusations."

"Why would the Choplins do that?"

"Money," he answered flatly. "I'd heard there was a book deal. Joseph Choplin was bankrupt, and he was trying to cash in on Ann's friendship with Jessie."

A question came to me. "After all that, you worked with Ann Choplin's PR firm?" I added quickly, "I mean, if it were me, I wouldn't have given them the time of day ever again. Who needs friends like that?"

His face softened, the anger fading, the corners of his mouth curving. "I know. I thought about it. But it really wasn't Ann's fault. She and Jessie were close, and Jessie would have hated it if I held what Joseph did against her. I think Joseph forced her into the press conference. I also think maybe that's why they were getting divorced."

"Yeah, but still…"

"Don't get me wrong. It took a long time before I'd even look in Ann Choplin's direction."

"What about Joseph?"

He shook his head firmly. "Uh-uh. Since that press conference, I haven't said a word to him. I thought about suing for libel and defamation, but never followed up on it. I doubt I had a case."

"I'm sorry I brought this up," I told him, lying down and turning toward him with my leg draped over his middle and my arm on his chest. Jericho followed my lead, propping his pillow, his face near mine. "I know you have a long day tomorrow."

"It's okay," he said, his voice already heavy and groggy; he had an enviable ability to fall asleep in an instant, as though he had an internal light switch. As his breathing deepened, he murmured,

"Casey, the next time you have follow-up questions from an interview, let's do it when the sun is up. Okay?"

"Okay," I said, kissing him on the lips, my face in the crook between his chest and neck. "Love you."

"Love you too."

We had a few hours remaining of the night, and I told myself I should sleep, rest being a must-have for me and the baby. I couldn't, though. When I closed my eyes, I saw images of the green and white rope, the bloodied knots, the dead women lying in the surf. I knew I couldn't rest peacefully again until the forensics report on the rope found in Jericho's garage was cleared.

SEVENTEEN

I woke feeling groggy, the sun ushering in a new day, the moon still high in the sky, the two meeting where the night and the daylight were one. Jericho snored through the sunrise, while I kept my movements soft and silent, wanting to get to the station and follow up on a text I'd sent Nichelle. I needed her to pull up any old news footage showing Joseph Choplin discussing the death of Jessie Flynn. She'd replied with a thumbs-up, but I didn't expect to see anything immediately. One could hope, though. Nichelle had a heavy presence on crime boards, the online world of amateur sleuthing of criminal cases old and new. I'd asked her to nose around the boards and podcasts and blogs, see what the community's opinion was about Jessie's murder.

I made my way to the car over grass coated with dew, checked on badge, gun, and all the essentials, and set off. It wasn't until I'd rolled to the end of the street, the right-hand turn signal winking with a thump, that I realized my heart was pounding. I was agitated and anxious. Being home with Jericho shouldn't leave me feeling this way. But it had, and I didn't like it.

I was first to arrive at the station, sacrificing my early-morning routine of home-brewed coffee for a watered-down cup of tar purchased at the local gas station. It tasted nasty, but it had the octane kick I needed. I was watching my intake, limiting myself, grateful that it was about my only vice. On my desk was a length of the clothes line I'd bought for the team to learn about the knot. I was a bad teacher, I thought, having given them my instructions without doing the homework myself.

My inbox was full of the usual trash, emails I'd read a line or two of and quickly dismiss, sending them to the digital heap of discarded letters from human resources or pension planning. Amongst the pile, though, there was a message from Tracy to the team, the subject reading: *Knot identification.*

I clicked to open and scanned the rows of text. She'd found the knot to be a taut-line hitch, popular with fishermen and sailors, and included instructions on how it was tied. With my chair eased back, the nylon rope segment in my lap, I gave it a try, making two loops and threading the end of the rope through them, alternating outside-in and inside-out. When I was done, I coiled the loops as though I were tying shoelaces, the knot I'd seen on the victims beginning to form in front of my eyes. When the last twist was in place, I pulled the ends per the instructions, the knot tightening with a vicious cinch. I let out a hot breath, immediately understanding why the killer had used this knot—the more the victims struggled, the tighter it became.

"They may as well have been dead when they hit the water," I said, flinging the rope onto my desk, disgusted by it.

"You got it?" Tracy asked. She'd arrived early, probably wanting to follow up on the emails. Her hair contained an abundant number of highlights, and her usual indoor book-work complexion was showing a light tan—signs of spending a little more of her life outside.

"I did," I said, picking up the rope and tossing it to her. "Great instructions. Do you know why the killer used this knot?"

The corner of her mouth curled, a dimple showing while she regarded the question. Tugging on the rope's ends and plugging a finger where the victim's wrists and ankles would have been, she shook her head. "Maybe because it gets tighter?"

She was right, but her voice sounded unconvinced. I didn't say anything, but stood up instead, scanning over the cubicle walls to make sure we were alone. When I was certain it was just the two of us, I said, "That's the correct answer, but if I were a district attorney, I wouldn't be convinced by your explanation."

She frowned, perplexed. "But if it's the correct answer..."

This was a teaching moment, my opportunity to pass along some of what had been taught to me. "It isn't always about the answer being right. It's about how you present it too."

"Present it?" she repeated, shaking her head, nerves showing. "I... I don't know what you mean."

"Watch," I instructed, and took the rope. "We believe the killer used a taut-line hitch knot because of the way in which it restrained the victims."

Playing along, Tracy asked, "And what way is that?"

"Continuous binding. That is, the knot tightening as more load, such as pulling, is applied." There was immediate appreciation, a bashful smile, her dimples popping. I couldn't help but smile with her, hoping it helped. "See what I mean. It's the confidence in the way you answer that really helps tell the story."

"You're so good at this," she said, her hands suddenly on mine, gripping them warmly.

Her touch was unexpected, and a spark flicked with instant connection. I never had favorites when it came to working with a team, but Tracy was special and I'd do anything to see her succeed. Emotion struck me. "Well, you're a joy to teach, and you'll be an excellent criminal investigator."

"A few more tests and a couple more papers to write," she answered, letting go and returning to her desk.

My warm feelings left as quickly as they'd arrived. She'd been scouring the history of Jessie Flynn's case for her paper. Had she included Joseph Choplin's recent interview and the rumors about Jericho? "Mind if I ask about the paper you're working on?"

Her keyboard rattled and the tempo of mouse clicks eased as she peered over her shoulder. "Which one? I've got three due this week."

Hesitantly I approached her cubicle, glancing at her overstuffed book bag, denim blue with a patchwork of oddly colored fabric, thick green stitching sewn in places to mend the holes. The front zipper was undone, her books and folders jutting. I saw Jessie Flynn's folder with the bright yellow Post-its and answered, "The Flynn case."

Tracy bit her upper lip. The look on her face told me she'd worked Choplin's interview into her paper and had possibly found out more about the rumor. She swallowed dryly, rifling through the bag. "I've got a first draft written—"

"What's the position?" I asked, interrupting, her nervousness putting me on edge. "You mentioned you were writing a position paper. That means you have to put forward evidence to form an objective discussion." Tracy didn't answer, her fingers sifting through pages. Frustrated, I insisted, "What's the position?"

"It's just a paper," she answered, the summer color draining from her face. I raised my hands, urging her tell me more. Voice wavering, she continued, "It's titled 'The Second Accomplice'."

I shut my eyelids with a heavy sigh and squeezed them hard enough to hurt. On record, Paige Kotes had had a single accomplice: Geoffrey Barnes, a deputy she'd befriended a year before her murdering spree. Before the two were caught, she'd executed him in an attempt to pin the murders on him.

"Jericho Flynn?" I asked, my stomach rolling, sickened by saying his name in connection with the murders. I braced against the cubicle wall, the back of my neck damp, my knees weak. Tracy's eyes were wide, their light-blue color glistening wet. "He's your second accomplice?"

She shrugged. "It's just a paper—"

"It isn't, though," I argued, raising my voice, the station's morning shift filing inside. I took to the closest seat, my elbows on my knees, Tracy's face within a foot of mine. "You took an old rumor, a story, the same one Joseph Choplin talked about, and put words to it. Do you understand the damage it could do?"

Tracy shrank back in her chair, her lips dry and the corners down. Without a word, she fished the paper from her book bag and handed it to me, the pages curled and creased, with penciled notes lining the margins. I sat bolt upright, my hands falling to my sides as though the pages were radioactive. She shoved them in front of me, insistent. "Please. Read it. I don't think it's just a rumor."

Cheryl passed us and entered her cubicle. I snatched the paper, rolling it so nobody could see the title page. Then I went to my desk and shoved it deep into my bag, the ugly rumor about Jericho's involvement in his wife's death alive in the young, imaginative mind of Tracy Fields.

The pages were like kryptonite. I could feel their presence, the powerful words that threatened to dismantle Jericho's world, sweep away a life he'd worked hard to build. I dared a look toward Tracy, her chair facing away from me. She was smart enough to avoid latching onto useless rumors unless there was solid evidence to back them. What had she found? What had led her to believe in the rumor? And if she believed it, who else would?

EIGHTEEN

A *Vote Flynn to Win* banner rattled above the podium, a sign with *JERICHO FLYNN FOR MAYOR* in broad capital letters hanging below the microphone. Gulls glided effortlessly amidst towering cloud plumes, edges crested in gold sunlight, while a mix of locals and tourists gathered around us. The smell of the ocean carried on a stiff breeze as I stood off to the side of the press conference, reporters and techs with cameras and lights gathering at the front.

A last-minute town-hall-style conference for Jericho's campaign had been pulled together by his new public relations firm. They'd staged it next to the Outer Banks' busiest boardwalk entrances, the fishing piers to the south of us, downwind of course, and the priciest vacation homes behind us. The ice-cream shop Hannah worked in was less than ten minutes' walk from here. Her shift ended in the next hour, and I planned to stop off there to see her.

A politician's wife, I thought randomly. We weren't married, but still, the strangeness of the gathering felt impossible to get used to. I didn't think I could ever become accustomed to the crowds, the press and being the center of attention. It was only the second time I'd been able to stand with Jericho while he campaigned, our schedules never quite aligning. The woman he was running against, Julia Stiles, always had her family at every press event. If there was a microphone or a camera, her two sons and husband would be with her. By contrast, Jericho almost always stood alone. I felt the need to apologize to him, thinking I'd let him down somehow by not being there. *I should do more.*

"Thanks for coming," he said now, his voice shaky with nerves. "I'm not a fan of these last-minute rallies, but the new guy thinks we can piggyback on the latest tourism numbers, respond to the downward trend with a solid position for ratcheting them up."

"Of course," I said, bracing his arm, straightening his collar. "Listen to you, sounding all political." Beads of sweat sat on his upper lip, his forehead damp, the sun feeling like a heat lamp whenever the breeze slowed. "Jericho, can I ask, would it help you if I came to more of these?"

"How do I look?" he asked without answering, hands steady, eyes clear and confident. He scratched the stubble on his chin, adding, "I didn't shave."

"I think you look better with the stubble," I answered softly, close to his ear, the crowd growing.

"You're on," the new PR man said, his voice low enough so only we could hear him. A short man with thinning hair that made him look older than he was, he wore a suit and round spectacles and spoke with a slight lisp. He moved us close together, positioning us like a wedding coordinator preparing a couple for their big reveal. "Okay now, nervous?" he asked with a brief smile. He didn't wait for an answer, instructing, "Stick to the agenda, the numbers, talk about tourism dollars. Don't stray, and only give boilerplate answers when it's an off-topic question."

We approached the reporters and gathering voters, Jericho's hand in the small of my back, moving like ballroom dancers as camera flashes and shutters snapped fresh pictures for this afternoon's online press releases. "Any time you can come to campaign events is a gift," he answered, offering a positive without actually answering.

"I can make more time—" I began, but was interrupted by the first questions, a barrage of them rolling in like thunder.

Jericho addressed each reporter by name. He knew most of them from his previous time as sheriff, but had memorized the rest using index cards he kept stuffed in his jacket pocket. He answered the tough financial questions clearly, his voice stronger and more confident than I could have ever imagined. He looked handsome and charismatic, and kept the crowd engaged. He was good at this. Really good. I eased a step away, leaving him on the podium, the sun reaching the peak for the afternoon and stealing all the shadows. At one point, he stepped down into the crowd, taking questions from everyone, including tourists who'd happened to pass by.

"Can you tell us what you know about Ann Choplin's murder?" a reporter asked, shocking me, the question seeming louder to my ears. I recognized the young man as having been around since I'd arrived in the Outer Banks. Jericho said nothing, a gull calling sharply over the crowd making his silence more obvious. He peered across to his PR manager and then back at the reporter, uncertainty showing, his mind working up a response to the off-topic question. This was what he had been warned about—political snares hidden like landmines.

"Ann Choplin's death is very unfortunate. My condolences go to her family and friends," he answered steadily. I could tell he was rattled as he eagerly sought to take another question.

"Is there any connection to Judy Granger's murder?" the reporter continued, stepping closer.

I pushed up onto my toes, wondering if I should field the questions, deflect them from Jericho. I clutched my bag, Tracy's paper inside, the danger of it slung from my shoulder.

Jericho made his way back to the security of the podium, bracing it and answering. "The deaths of these women are tragic. I'll also add that they're under investigation and I'm not at liberty to comment."

Jericho's answer was short, but he'd said enough to satisfy. The reporter returned immediately, firing back, "And what of the connection to the murder of your wife, Jessie Flynn?"

Jericho glared at the reporter, his grip on the microphone turning his knuckles white. The sun's heat was blazing and seemed to have been turned up, baking us all. Stomach twisting, I was horribly uncomfortable for him. I could only guess the reporter must have been digging into Jessie's past, possibly uncovering her friendships with the two recent victims.

Jericho's composure returned, a calmness coming over his features. He cleared his throat, scowl softening. "Any questions regarding the case should be directed to the investigating officers." He bit his lip, taking a moment before continuing with a smile. "I'm here today to discuss tourism in the Outer Banks."

"So you don't deny the women were friends?" the reporter asked, moving closer to the front, cameras trained on him and Jericho as though this were a showdown. I glanced at Jericho's PR manager, my eyes bulging, urging him to take control of the press conference. He tried catching Jericho's attention, but to no avail.

Jericho didn't budge, didn't flinch, his focus locked, his expression fixed. Then he raised his brow, and answered, "We were all friends."

"Including Paige Kotes?" the reporter countered. Jericho shut his eyes and reeled, the sound of the name making him wince. I stopped breathing, every muscle tense. "Is that why Kotes has been questioned by the investigating officers recently?"

He was referring to me. I froze, my hands like anchors dangling from my arms. *My visits?* I questioned, a cold spear driven into my gut. The prison log, my visits recorded. I stood motionless, knees locked, feet planted, wondering if I should speak up.

"I can't comment on an open case," Jericho replied. "However, I want to say that the Outer Banks has the finest team of detectives on the East Coast." He took a breath, glancing subtly in my direction without making eye contact. I'd never told him I'd been talking to

Paige, but now he knew. "I'd like to discuss a platform to help restore the beachfront properties lost in recent years due to erosion..."

The reporter sank back into the crowd. The rest of the questions were all good campaign fodder, but I feared that the only segments to air on television would be about Paige Kotes and Jessie Flynn's death.

I had no idea how Jericho would react now that he knew about Paige's involvement in the murder investigation. I squeezed my bag beneath my arm and sighted the reporter who'd asked about the murders. He glanced at me as though knowing I was watching, catching me in the act as I turned away. If he was nosing around the investigation, how long before he questioned Joseph Choplin? As much as I hated to do it, I'd have to read Tracy's paper. It was the only chance I had to stay a step ahead of what might eventually get published.

Jericho regrouped with his PR manager while the press conference disbanded, the regular foot traffic resuming, vacationers coming and going, some destined for the boardwalk, others with their sights on the beaches and the rest returning to their hotels, motels, and rental properties.

"That wasn't all bad," the PR man said, starting off the discussion, the tension thick like the air's growing humidity.

And like the humidity, I could see a storm brewing on Jericho's face as he answered sharply, "It wasn't all great either."

The PR man cupped his mouth, a fingertip pushing between his lips. He chewed on it for a moment, the habit an old one from the looks of his stubby fingers. "I'll reach out to the reporter. Maybe we can trade favors."

Jericho shook his head. He faced the boardwalk and the sea, a salty gust sweeping over his hair. "Leave it," he said. "I don't want to start trading favors." His brow furrowed. "Can you give us a minute?"

The PR manager collected his things and left us alone. I didn't know where to start, and said, "I thought you looked and sounded—"

"What are you doing?" Jericho asked, interrupting. The anger I expected wasn't there. The color was gone from his face, and the look in his eyes was one of fear. He was afraid. Terrified.

A chill raced over me. I took his arm with concern. "What is it?"

"Please tell me you haven't started working with Paige Kotes in your investigation." I chewed on my lower lip, wanting to tell him everything, but also not wanting to disappoint him. He groaned, my lack of response an answer. He braced my arms tight. "Casey, do you know what you're doing?"

I straightened my shoulders, taken aback that he was questioning my ability. "Of course, I know what I'm doing."

He took a deep breath. "Everything that woman says is a lie. She'll do and say whatever she can to mess with your mind."

There was a hard concern in his voice I'd never heard before. It was the kind that stole my words, but also made me question if he might be overreacting. "Jericho, I can handle Paige Kotes."

He shook his head. "Please, no. Please don't go anywhere near her."

"Jericho," I said, insistent, my fingers on his chin, lifting it so I could look him in the eye. "She's in a maximum-security prison. What's she going to do?"

His lips pinched, eyes glassy. "You don't know her like I do," he said. "She'll get inside your head, and that's where she's free, that's where she'll do whatever she wants."

"I'm stronger than that," I argued.

"Casey, I'm begging you," he pleaded. "You should see the letters she writes me." He gulped, skin like ash. "They're morbid. Sick."

I could feel him trembling, his reaction scaring me. I took him in my arms, his heart pounding against my chest. "Babe, it's okay."

"Please. I can't lose you too."

NINETEEN

It was quiet today, none of the usual chaos: the yelling, the cries of daily heartbreak, guards stirring prisoners, cell doors clanking. Instead there was the distant murmur of conversation, coming from the common area maybe. The quiet put Paige Kotes on edge. She peered out of her cell to the one across the corridor, the inside dark, a ray of dusky light eking through the matchbox window, a figure snoring beneath the sheets. The neighboring cells were all empty.

She followed the sound of voices. A fight might be brewing, the guards taking favors to look the other way for a spell. She glanced at the ancient clock on the wall, the second hand sweeping seconds from her life, and her legs felt heavy with unease, knowing she could be the subject of interest, other inmates in wait.

She was right about the voices: they were coming from the common area at the end of the block, the place where prisoners gathered for classes and reading and television privileges. She slowed a moment, thinking to return to the safety of her cell, but the gathering crowd had their backs to her, their attention taken by something else.

There was good reason not to frequent the common area, good reason for her to be wary. On the outside, she'd been a notorious serial killer, and she'd also been a cop, a detective. On the inside, the inmates feared the former, but they'd never forget, or forgive, the latter. Paige could handle almost any one-on-one attack, having proven herself a few times already. But against two or more opponents, she knew she'd lose.

Her temples throbbed with a hastening pulse, the excitement adding some of that heat, that fluttery zest she'd experienced when murdering those women. She felt for the outline of the shiv she kept tucked into her sleeve, its point nearly buried in her skin. If this was a ruse for an attack, the blade would help, and might even save her life. She wasn't ready to die yet. There was too much to do, Jericho still a free man, the work with her puppet incomplete.

With one eye over her shoulder, caution coursing through her veins like steam racing through pipes, she sat down at one of the tables. The metal seats and tabletops were rooted in the concrete floor, the televisions behind a metal mesh showing years of abuse, bent, broken and pitted.

"Ain't he a looker," one of the inmates said.

"Mm-hmm," another replied. "He could turn down my sheets anytime."

The group laughed.

Paige heard his voice then. Jericho was speaking. She moved to get a better view of a screen. Her heart skipped as his face appeared, the television's age blurring and washing the image of him green, her memory correcting the mistaken details. She hadn't seen him since her sentencing.

Heart pounding, a giddiness steeping, she forgot where she was, who she was with, and pawed at her scar, picking at the scabs. It was the closest thing she had to him, her obsession like a drug, her enduring an endless withdrawal, an emotional pain she both savored and hated. She picked harder, the oddly mended nerve endings firing an electrical pulse straight into her chest, naked and raw, stabbing sharply enough to make her groan.

"It's Jericho's cold touch," she whispered wryly to herself. All her letters to him had gone unanswered. But there were those other letters, the encoded ones, her puppet doing her bidding. The mystery of who was behind them was always on her mind. Dreamily, she thought of Jericho and the idea of her protégé being him. But she knew it was a fantasy. "Just you wait. I won't be ignored by you. By anyone."

"Including Paige Kotes?" a reporter on the screen asked, the camera panning to Jericho and then back.

The shuffle of clothes, the movement of bodies. The group's focus swung from the television toward Paige. Her muscles tensed, her spine going rigid, the attention unwanted.

"They talking 'bout you, girl," someone chided from the back. "Ain't that the guy you were in love with? Killed his wife?"

In prison, any kind of attention was bad attention. Some inmates wanted it, craved it, even needed it. But mostly it only invited trouble. "Can't say," Paige mumbled, acting uninterested and easing away from the crowd. Movement again, eyes shifting toward the televisions.

"Is that why Paige Kotes has been questioned by the investigating officers recently?" the reporter asked, his voice tinny and static through the cracked television speaker.

She needed to leave, get back to her cell, where she was protected. Without another word, she left the common area. She ignored the muttering and the questions, jerking her arm free of those brazen enough to paw at her, risking retaliation from a nearby guard. The eye in the sky, she thought miserably, welcoming the sight of the domed closed-circuit camera mounted high on the wall. She was safe inside her cell, the guards keeping a constant eye on her. No inmate would dare an attack as long as she was being monitored.

When she got back inside, she shook herself with a scream, her frayed nerves shedding like dead skin, then picked up the latest encrypted letter. The cipher loaded in her brain, the taste of salt coming from the sweat on her upper lip, she sat down, scanning the page, then glanced at the newspaper clipping she kept in her scrapbook. A young Jessie Flynn stood with Ann Choplin and Judy

Granger. *He* wanted to go after the fourth girl in the photo, Lisa Wells, but that would be too easy for Detective White.

"We can't hand her the investigation," Paige said with an abrupt laugh, her voice bouncing off the cell's cinder-block wall. She cupped her mouth, carrying on the conversation as though not alone. "The detective needs a challenge." And Jericho needed to be afraid. He needed to feel as though his world was coming apart.

Instead of Lisa Wells, Paige had selected another woman connected to Jericho. She'd sent her puppet the details, telling him to leave the Wells woman alone. For now. His reply confirmed her instructions.

She brought the letter to her nose, sniffing the ink and paper as though holding a murder weapon. She'd never be free again, but this was close. Toying with the detectives was a bonus. Their simple minds lacked the sophistication to make the necessary leaps. Except for Detective White. Would she figure it out? Would she make the connection before they got to Lisa Wells?

Laughter erupted, spilling maniacally from Paige's mouth, but now she didn't care about being heard. "Let them listen," she yelled, fearing little as long as the guards watched her. She considered giving them a show later, after the lights dimmed, something that'd bring their noses close to the monitor. Another laugh.

"And after this one?" she said, the lone conversation carrying on, her eyes widening, her mind fixed on Detective Casey White. "But she's with child," she countered, debating with herself. She shook off the argument. "Child or no child, Paige, you've done far worse."

TWENTY

Pamela Levine couldn't wait to get out of her scrubs. Her single shift had turned into a double, a co-worker being a no-show and taking the day off. As usual, Pamela covered for them, working the extra hours, working the taut muscles of her patients. Their bodies were riddled with injury, and they often yelled from the pain of the physical therapy they endured. They had names for her—some nice, some not so much.

A bottle of Chardonnay, she agreed with herself. To wash the day away. She turned up the tunes on the radio, rolling the windows down, winding along a back road—dark, remote, sparse traffic, with the beaches and cresting waves less than a half-mile east. A Queen song blared over the speakers, and she tapped her foot and sang along, glancing up at the sky, the moon near full and slipping between thin clouds. *Although I should probably just have the one glass, and then straight to bed—*

The steering wheel suddenly lurched from her grip, the passenger side dipping as the front tire erupted with an explosion. Tire rubber beat against the underside of the vehicle as she sucked in a breath and tried to recall what to do. The front of the car cut sideways, and she eyed the sandy shoal on the beach side of the road, and the asphalt lip edging a thicket of woods on the other.

Steer into it, she remembered. She snagged the wheel, a hard lump in her throat, her breath held tight, not letting it go until the front of the car straightened. She released the brakes, the car moving entirely under its own momentum and crossing the double center lines, putting her in the path of oncoming traffic.

A pair of headlights winked through the trees, the road winding around a hillside less than a quarter-mile away. *Gas*, she thought, punching the pedal. The car lumbered forward like some of the injured people she worked with.

"There you go," she yelled, encouraging herself more than the car as she steered onto the shoulder. The shredded tire vibrated against the floor and shook every cell in her body. Through the passenger window, she heard plastic and metal crunching, the front of the car being torn open like a tin can. "Shit!"

She jabbed the hazards button, and the car's flashers started blinking, casting yellow light. As she opened her door and planted her feet on the sandy pavement, hot booming air shoved her backward, a big-rig truck barreling past suddenly, its horns blaring and making her scream. Still, while the truck had given her a start, she'd at least made it safely to the side of the road, her car limping onto the shoulder.

Her Crocs grinding against the asphalt, she knelt to look at the damage. The moonlight dim, but enough to work with. Her shoulders slumped with disappointment—the flat tire wasn't just a blowout; a thick board, a two-by-four, had splintered and lodged in the wheel well. It might have come from a construction vehicle, a bump in the road jarring it over the lip of a truck and tossing it onto the road. Not that it mattered. It was part of her car now.

She surveyed her options, remembered the full spare in her trunk and contemplated changing the tire. She nudged the board, carefully gripping an end free of jutting nails. It wouldn't move, the nails lodged sturdily in the tire's rubber, the board shredding her car's front quarter panel. She picked at part of the bumper, the corner dangling limp, her doubt mounting. She was strong for her size, but for this she'd need a tow truck.

She wasn't far from home, and if needed, she could take a shortcut through the woods and make her way on foot. She glanced at her shoes. The brush and grass were teeming wet, and the Crocs wouldn't protect her feet from the brackish water. The custom shoes had been a special order from her college, and featured Virginia Tech's popular mascot the HokieBird, an odd-looking oversized turkey. They were also the only shoes that could withstand the punishment of sixteen-plus hours on her feet.

Headlights beamed from behind her, throwing her shadow onto the road, the sight lifting her hopes, but with strong caution. She was in a remote area, and utterly alone. Relief came with the sight of blue flashes, the light erupting like sheet lightning, skipping off the road's surface as a patrol car slowed onto the shoulder behind her, tires crunching. She shielded her eyes.

"Evening, ma'am." She heard a man's voice, the car door opening and closing. "Got some car trouble?"

"I do," she answered, squinting, hoping for a familiar voice; she knew a few of the patrol officers. The patrolman appeared in front of the car, his silhouette showing no detail other than the outline of his body, his utility belt, and his hand draped over his gun and holster. "I think maybe a construction truck lost some boards back a ways. I ran over one."

"Any damage?" he asked, coming around the front of the car, his face flickering white and blue with the patrol car's lights.

"Sheriff?" she asked, thinking she recognized him; Jericho Flynn had been her patient for months following a terrible injury to his arm and shoulder. No answer. The patrolman knelt down, his face hidden in the car's shadow. "Sheriff Flynn?" she asked again, then recalled that he'd moved into politics and wasn't in law enforcement anymore. The patrolman stepped into the light, his dark slacks and slate colored uniform different from what she knew. "Sorry, I thought you were someone else."

"I can be whoever you want," he said, his voice riding on a soft laugh as he tugged at the wedged board. "This worked really well. Better than I thought."

"What?" Pamela's guard was suddenly up, her jaw clenching with fear. Then she noticed the badge and uniform. It was like nothing she'd seen before, nothing from the Outer Banks.

She spun around, one foot landing on the grassy shoal as the patrolman lunged, his hands taking hold of her other leg, his grip strong enough to make her scream.

She fell onto her back with a crashing thud, the man's face horrifically bright in the patrol car's headlights. A knee driven into her chest silenced her scream, collapsing the air in her lungs. She squirmed and kicked and fought until the next strike blinded her with a flash.

Pamela opened her eyes, her understanding of time and place lost. Her mouth throbbed, her tongue and lips split, her gums bleeding. She gasped and spit, her head heavy and groggy, her arms behind her, wrists tied tight; then tensed, fear striking every muscle as recollection slammed into her mind. She lifted her chin, finding the patrolman holding her by the ankles and dragging her to his car.

"No!" she screamed, fighting the rope on her wrists, the knot tightening as she struggled against it. She clawed randomly, a handful of dirt coming up in one hand, her nails striking asphalt with the other, chipping and breaking. Tears sprang from her eyes, her moans lost in screams that went unheard. She kicked at her attacker then, her right heel nailing his lower back with a hard thud, dropping him and freeing her legs. As she scrambled to her knees, a pair of headlights needled through the trees. It was another car, the same winding turn; they'd surely slow when they saw the blue lights flashing.

But he was on her fast, smashing her body against the road, knocking the air from her, his muscled arms, roped with sinews, tightening around her head and neck. She gasped, unable to breathe, her vision fading, her strength going with it, his chokehold unforgiving as he finished dragging her behind the patrol car. He dropped her like a sack, her face striking dirt, and she sucked in a breath filled with road dust and scanned the vehicle, the logo on the passenger door unrecognizable like the badge her attacker wore. She was hidden, out of sight, her hopes of rescue dashed.

A woman's voice singing hit her ears, the approaching car's windows open. Pamela scrambled again to escape, scraping at the road, kicking and clawing. But her attacker was quick, his treaded shoe pinning her against the asphalt lip. She peered up as the car slowed and the patrolman waved it on. His leg was like a steel girder. She batted at it until she couldn't move, until the darkness came and she heard bones break. Then she fell unconscious for the last time.

TWENTY-ONE

I arrived at the beach, the site of another dead body. A foamy surf ran over the half-buried corpse, the sun rising and casting its first light on the gruesome death. The location being a connection to the other murders, and to Jessie Flynn, was immediate, turning my insides tight, fearing the worst of possibilities. The wind shifted and hit me with a thick smell of sea salt and rotting death, the stench coating my skin as though the guilt upsetting me had seeped from my pores. We had another body. A possible murder. Proving that we were no closer to catching the killer.

With the rope, Joseph Choplin's interview, and Tracy's damaging report about Jericho, cold fear had silenced me, and maybe that was for the best. Adding another connection, no matter how indirect, would overwhelm the investigation, not to mention what it would do to Jericho. In my head, a wall of denial was forming, but it was futile. I had to address this carefully, but I'd do so only when the time was right. That was not now.

"Morning," Tracy said arriving next to me, sizing up the scene, fiddling with her equipment.

I waited a moment for her to register the location, but she said nothing. "Ready to get started?" I asked.

"Look at that," she said, making small talk. The morning was young, the sun just a small sliver in the east, and the sky warming with orange and pink, giving us a sailor's forecast for summer storms to come in the afternoon. "Red sky in the morning, sailor's warning."

I nodded, my shoes sinking in the sand, nerves ebbing like the waves.

"It's beautiful," she said, bringing her camera to her face and focusing on the brilliant horizon, capturing it for a digital eternity.

"Not quite the crime-scene photograph I'd expect," I exclaimed, secretly wishing I had creative and artistic talents of my own.

"True," she answered, glancing at me before turning away. I sensed the tension from our last meeting, as I'm sure she did as well. The bond we'd formed had hit a bump, a big bump. "It's for my journal. I like to—"

"That's nice," I said, interrupting rudely and ditching my decaf coffee in a garbage bin, the taste unpalatable. I handed her booties and gloves, leveling the conversation, keeping it purposely curt. "We better move. The tide's rising and there's work to do."

"Yeah, sure, okay," she said, her face pinched with disappointment.

I slipped a pair of booties onto my own feet and sleeved my fingers in gloves. As we walked, a family of seagulls circled us, wings batting the air, believing we had food to offer. Blue light glistened in the wet sand, patrol cars remaining on scene since the discovery was phoned in. I held my phone over my shoulder to show Tracy the tidal app. "High tide in three hours."

"That'll get us started," Tracy said, walking briskly behind me, feet shuffling, kicking sand as she tried to match my pace. Her breath choppy, she asked, "Possible suicide was the call."

"That was the call," I agreed, continuing to answer short and direct. An emotional pang stirred in me, making me sad. I was better than this. With a deep sigh, I slowed until Tracy caught up. Her cheeks were ruddy, her brow sweaty. I waited until she'd got her breath, then asked, "To rule it as a suicide, what should we look for?"

Relief came to her face at my testing her with a question, challenging her as part of her learning to become a crime-scene investigator. "A note?" she answered.

We continued walking, the beach patrol's blue lights flickering brightly. "That'd be one thing," I said. "But what else?"

Tracy knelt to take pictures at beach level, the first glimpse of the scene showing greater detail. The orientation of the body looked peculiar, unnatural, and I suspected it hadn't washed ashore. "We'd look for all evidence supporting suicide," she said. "That is, the ability of the individual to have performed the act entirely on their own."

"That's good," I told her, realizing she'd memorized the words from one of her textbooks. "We have to rule out all possibility of another person's involvement."

"Got it," she said under her breath, the visual of the body stealing her interest from the lesson.

The waves were breaking with a roar, their size unusual, cresting as high as the patrol cars. The body was clothed, wearing what looked to be medical scrubs, maroon in color, the figure slender, toned and fit, possibly a woman in her late twenties. She had been positioned so that she was kneeling facing the ocean. Her face was buried, as were her knees and lower legs, the evening tide flushing sand ashore and covering parts of her like a seashell. Her arms were extended perpendicular to her body, hands open, the skin pale, the fingertips absent of dark discoloration, telling me death was recent, possibly occurring during the night.

"If there's a note, I'd expect it to be in her pocket."

Tracy went to work immediately, kneeling in the packed sand, foamy surf racing around her as she captured the images of the body. "Suicide by drowning?"

"I have my doubts," I answered. I went to the woman's head, her ears exposed, her hair pinned back, thick strands loose and floating with the rise and fall in the surf. "Brunette and Caucasian."

"Is it her? Lisa Wells, from the photo?" Tracy asked.

The question was already in my mind. Tracy had registered the location, but had said nothing. She was being careful too. "I don't believe so." The hair color was right, but the shape of the victim's body had me thinking it was someone younger. I glanced at the wrists and ankles, shaking my head, my knees wet as they sank. "The body position is too formed. It was purposely placed like this. There's no rope on the ankles or wrists, but there may be evidence a restraint was used. Look at the wrists; the skin is raw with abrasions."

The medical examiner's vehicle pulled up next to the patrol cars, a white wagon with red lights on the hood. Nichelle and Dr. Swales exited from it, the two working together in a cross-team knowledge share. Derek, Swales' autopsy assistant, also climbed out and went to the rear to extract the gurney and prepare to recover the body. They were familiar with the tides and understood that our review at the scene would have to be short.

"Guys," I said, greeting them.

"We were just discussing Lisa Wells," Tracy said, continuing with the idea.

Dr. Swales approached, using Nichelle's shoulder to support her as she sleeved booties over her crocs. With the brisk wind blowing steadily against us, her hair had gone wild, tight curls tossing errantly, her glasses speckled with sea spray. She said nothing about the location, but focused entirely on the woman's body.

"That's not Lisa Wells," Nichelle said, her brown hair blowing wildly too. "I found Lisa on social media. She's married with a family, living on the mainland and working as a schoolteacher."

"I guess that answers that," Tracy commented.

"Another body washing up on the beach doesn't necessarily connect it to the other cases," I said, feeling relieved. If this wasn't Lisa Wells, it could be an unrelated murder. It could still be a suicide, the body's position entirely a chance happening.

As the sun began to peer higher, the blades of light came on like a switch, the buttery color turning the dank gray scene into something alive. Sharp light danced on the ocean's surface beyond the waves, and gave the dead woman's skin an eerie lifelike color. But the sunlight was only a mirage, the exposed skin showing the avenues and roads where blood had once flowed but then stopped dead.

"This woman didn't wash up on the shore," Dr. Swales said, her assessment matching my first thoughts. She knelt down, her face next to the woman's head.

"Is it possible to drown yourself kneeling in this position?" I asked, briefly returning to the idea of a suicide, ensuring that we covered all possibilities. At this point, I was almost wishing it, though it was awful to wish something so horrible.

Swales peered at the body, her round eyes magnified by the lenses in her glasses. "A person could drown themselves with a spoonful of water if they knew how."

"That's a troubling thought," Nichelle said, joining Tracy and taking notes.

"It's the sand. Rather, it's the lack of it," I said.

"What do you mean?" Tracy asked.

"The body is far enough from the ocean that even at high tide, the surf only touched it. The waves are like a washing machine, especially with ones like this morning." I ran my hand over the woman's back, the shirt completely free of any tidal grime or sand. "If she had come from the ocean, there'd be sand, and there'd be sea grass, but there's none of that either."

"Good," Dr. Swales said. "If this body had been washed ashore, she would look entirely different. Especially the positioning."

"So if it was suicide, she came to the beach and then knelt down," Tracy said.

"Knelt down and put her head in the sand like that?" Nichelle asked.

"Or she was brought here. There's evidence of restraints used on her wrists," I pointed out, scanning the beach, searching for signs of struggle, a trail, but finding nothing but windswept sand. Sunlight stung my eyes, piercing, but revealing more of the woman's body, and my heart sank. I moved the hair from the back of her neck to show the team. "I believe there's significant trauma here."

Dr. Swales held up her hand, finger raised as though pointing to the sky. "Careful." I moved to give her access, and she dug one hand into the sand, feeling beneath the woman's neck while inspecting the area of bruising. When she found what she was looking for, she sat back on her heels and plunked her hands into her lap. "This woman's neck is broken. It may have occurred while she was being held down against the sand."

I thought for a moment. "Let's look at her fingers."

The team followed my direction, inspecting the victim's hands, the nails torn and ripped from the beds.

"Definite signs of a struggle. The killer brought the victim here, but wherever she was abducted is also where the struggle took place."

"We'll want to figure out where that is," Nichelle said.

"Exactly." I nodded. "Victim is wearing her work clothes, possibly in the medical field. Best guess is she was coming from or going to work when the abduction occurred. A struggle took place, she lost consciousness, was brought here, and in an attempt to drown her, the killer broke her neck."

"Very possible. We'll know more at the morgue." Dr. Swales moved around the body, lifting the woman's bare foot and stopping when the ankle was exposed. "We've got bruising and what might possibly be a handprint. Could be that the victim was dragged."

"Or the killer grabbed her to prevent an escape," I suggested.

Tracy responded at once, taking pictures, the camera's flash catching Dr. Swales as she and Derek dug out the victim's other leg, the wet sand packed hard and dense like clay. The woman wore one shoe, but not just any shoe. It was a clog similar to Dr. Swales' Crocs, but this one was colored for a college, Virginia Tech, its mascot on the face and sides in colorful orange and white. I recognized it. I'd seen one other person wearing shoes just like this.

I said nothing, standing abruptly. If I was right, the victim was a local physical therapist. When I'd first become involved with Jericho, he had visited her regularly, three times a week, while he was in rehab following his last surgery. I was suddenly nervous and queasy, the connection overwhelming. A hard lump in my chest shot into the back of my throat, and I turned away from the team, trying to breathe through a sickening wave.

"We can take it from here," Swales said quietly, her hand on my shoulder.

"I'm fine," I said, uncertain if this was morning sickness or the result of pure emotion going into overdrive. I wiped a swath of spittle from my mouth and chin and braced against what I couldn't bear to think, forcing myself to rejoin the team. I motioned to the rough ocean and said jokingly, "Waves. They've got me feeling a little seasick." I caught a look from Swales; she knew full well that seasickness didn't work like that.

"So," she said, scanning the beach, her balled fists plugged against her hips. "This is the exact same place where Jessie Flynn, Ann Choplin and Judy Granger were found." She knelt down next to the body, her face upturned, her focus on my eyes, shaking her head. "That can't be a coincidence."

TWENTY-TWO

We made it back to the station having completed as much of our investigation in the field as possible with the tide rising. The team convened inside the conference room as the first crack of thunder exploded over the station, the sailor's warning ringing true, a storm arriving earlier than expected, dousing the early afternoon and breaking the thick humidity. Nichelle, Emanuel, and Cheryl were already in their seats, the conference room monitor showing the victim from the beach, and her name: Pamela Levine. The window curtains were half drawn, the storm clouds darkening the sky enough to allow us to use the projector to throw a map onto the front wall, a myriad of digital thumbtacks strewn across the familiar outline of the Outer Banks.

As I made my way to the head of the table, Tracy joined, rushing through the door, her face sweaty and flushed, her book bag draped from one shoulder, the weight of it causing her to walk on a slant. "Sorry I'm late," she announced to the room.

"You're good?" I asked, concerned. Tracy's eyes brightened, assuring me she was okay while taking her place at the table, laptop plugged in, notebooks open and camera at the ready. "Okay then, let's get started."

"Fuel for boats," Emanuel said, crossing the projector's light, which threw his shadow onto the wall as he took a place in front of the map. "The orange thumbtacks are all the gas stations within five miles of boat ramps."

"And the purple ones?" I asked.

"Gas stations on the water," he answered. "They're everywhere. Any boat can pull up to these and get fuel."

"And how about surveillance cameras?"

"I'm working with the owners, collecting whatever we can get," Nichelle answered, turning her laptop around for us to see a checkerboard of video surveillance footage feeds, each showing boat owners and station attendants at work. "Some of the stations have no surveillance, or it was never maintained and is just there for show, to scare off thieves."

"Brilliant," I said sarcastically, disappointed with the hole in the coverage, the idea as a lead feeling weak. This was the Outer Banks and there were far too many fuel places for us to cover. "Go ahead and review the footage, but make it less of a priority. How about the other thumbtacks?"

Nichelle flicked her mouse, clicking to reveal a legend on the map, each series of colors assigned a victim's name. She took a turn at the screen, her shadow growing as she stepped around the map. "I've finally managed to get access to the phone company records of the first two victims, and have listed all the locations visited the days before their murders."

"The phone company came through," I said, crossing my arms, satisfied by the progress. Some of the thumbtacks were adjacent to roads, while some were in fields and other places no one would visit. "I'm guessing these are cell tower locations?"

"Exactly," Nichelle said with a wide smile. "Ann Choplin's privacy settings didn't allow for her locations to be recorded, so we used cell tower pings to her phone to generate coordinates and map them."

"And Judy Granger?" Cheryl asked.

Nichelle motioned to the yellow thumbtacks. "Her location services were enabled, giving us exact coordinates to map."

"Any crossovers?" I asked, studying Judy Granger's yellow thumbtacks along with Ann Choplin's green ones, each series entirely different, seemingly random, with only one point of connection. "From this, it looks like the two of them met at this one location." I pegged the projection on the wall with my thumb. "Zoom in, let's see where that was." Nichelle returned to her laptop, mouse clicks firing up a magnifier, the map enlarging with the details flying toward us fast enough to make me unsteady. "And also get a date and time—"

"One sec. When it's magnified, the time stamp will display."

"Good," I answered, studying the details as they came into focus.

"It's a restaurant," she said, changing over to the satellite view. "They met the day before Ann Choplin's murder."

"But the thumbtacks aren't together anymore," Tracy said, her hands apart to show distance. "Does that mean they *didn't* meet?"

"Uh-uh," I said. I tapped on Choplin's thumbtack, the satellite view showing a group of trees next to the restaurant where Granger's marker was pegged. "It just means Choplin's phone was pinged at a cell tower we can't see. It's probably hidden behind this tree line."

"The phone companies use fake tree limbs to dress the towers up, try and make them natural," Emanuel commented.

"Is it possible to find out how often they met?" I asked, directing my question to Nichelle. "This may have been a casual lunch. The two women have history and could have been meeting regularly. Let's make sure it isn't anything beyond ordinary."

"By beyond ordinary, do you mean like discussing Jessie Flynn?" Nichelle said.

I stifled a gasp, the room suddenly hot, the subject becoming a third rail I'd hoped to avoid. "What makes you say that?" I asked. Nichelle didn't respond, her face frozen, her big brown eyes turning a gray-blue in her laptop's light. At the end of the table, I saw Tracy shrink into her chair, leading me to realize she'd given Nichelle a copy of her paper. The muscles in my arms and legs went taut, frustration stirring. I didn't want to battle the team on this. "You read Tracy's paper?"

"I read it too," Cheryl said, her words robust, her shoulders squared.

"And you?" I asked Emanuel.

He side-eyed Tracy before answering. "It's a good paper, but it's completely speculative." He shifted uncomfortably, adding, "I'd never buy into it."

I took to my seat, fishing the paper from my bag, laying it flat on the table. "I didn't read it," I said, pausing a moment, the conference room remaining stuffy and uncomfortable. When the moment's tension had weighed on us long enough, I continued. "But since everyone else has read it, you can explain it to me. Make your case."

"Can we speak freely?" Cheryl asked.

"Of course," I replied. "In here, we can speak openly and without bias. We can explore all ideas and theories objectively. Understood?" Heads nodded, with the exception of Emanuel's, his face like stone as the team muttered in agreement. I tried not to show my nerves, afraid of what was coming. "Now, talk to me."

"There is a theory that Jericho Flynn seduced Paige Kotes, convinced her to kill his wife, and promised her he would marry her," Cheryl said. It was not so far off the worst thing I could imagine being in Tracy's paper.

"Absurd," Emanuel said, rolling his eyes as he poked at the corner of the report.

Cheryl leaned into her chair and pushed a pencil through her hair, a bundle of red rolled into a twist, pinned into place. "Casey said we could speak freely."

"I did," I assured her, raising my hands. "What else?"

"There were reports that Jessie had told her friends about the affair between Jericho and Paige."

"Why wouldn't she leave him then?" I asked, challenging the theory. I'd investigated spouses involved with murder before, and found that it wasn't always the green-eyed monster, jealousy personified, that reared its ugly head to do the deed. There was almost always another reason. "What's the motive in this theory?"

"Greed," Emanuel answered, his voice low and gravelly, the afternoon storm whipping the rain against the windows, distant thunder rolling. "There was a prenuptial agreement in the marriage."

"Do you have details?" I asked, wishing I'd read Tracy's paper. I knew about the money going to Jericho and his son for all earnings awarded to Paige Kotes in film, television and book rights. But I'd never known about a prenuptial agreement.

"Sure do," Tracy said, coming alive from her quiet corner, standing to open her copy of the report, blasting it onto the wall. "Right here."

I glanced over my shoulder into the station, taking an inventory of who might be able to see inside the conference room, catch sight of what was on the wall. It was clear that nobody but us could see. Tracy's report listed family and estate names—Jessie's parents, the Coopers, and the Donnellys from the mother's side—along with numbers including a lot of zeros with commas next to them. "Is this a trust fund?"

Tracy nodded. "Two million dollars. During the marriage, the fund would remain in the control of Jessie Flynn, her decisions final about its use and any distributions to dependents such as her children."

"But after her death?" I asked, growing concerned by the surfacing motive.

"The trust fund is turned over to her spouse," Cheryl answered, her tone abrupt. She was enjoying this, and I think I might have hated her for it in that moment. She motioned to Tracy, telling her to scroll the page. "This is the kicker. There's no money awarded in the event of a divorce."

I tried to find some rational or simple explanation. There was none. "What about the original investigation?" I said, my voice weary. "This would surely have come out and been questioned."

"There was questioning," Emanuel answered, frustration in his words. He was visibly upset with the discussion. "Guys, this is Jericho we're talking about."

"And?" Cheryl asked, excitement rising in her voice.

"There were confessions signed; the district attorney worked the case direct to sentencing, meaning there was no trial. Only Kotes and Barnes were named as being involved in the murders," Emanuel answered. "Including that of Jessie Flynn."

"That should tell you enough," I said, forcing my voice, trying to remain objective but finding it a challenge. I picked up Tracy's paper. "I'm sure this is convincing, but with enough information, any story can be sewn together and made to sound legitimate. That's why people listen to rumors."

"What about the money?" Tracy asked. "That's a solid motive."

"Money is always a powerful element," Cheryl added.

I didn't know how to answer. I thought of Jericho's house, the work it needed; he'd let it go since his wife's death. Sharing more than I had to, I said, "If there's money, I can't say I've ever seen it."

"Television spots like that aren't cheap," Cheryl said, motioning to the station monitors, their reflections bouncing off the conference room windows. On them, I saw Jericho, a new television commercial he'd been talking about. Along the bottom of the screen, *Jericho Flynn for Mayor* in bold lettering. "How's he paying for the campaign?"

"Cheryl." Emanuel objected, voice grating. He'd known Jericho professionally longer than any of us, and had heard enough. He picked up the report, waving it. "Do you truly believe this?"

Cheryl shrugged, her gaze bright and filled with ideas. The sight of it scared me. She wasn't going to let this go. "There's a connection to Pamela Levine too," she said, eyes shifting to each team member and finally landing on me.

"What connection?" I asked, fearing she'd mention what I already knew and moving on quickly to the physical evidence. "There's no rope. Based on the bruising we found on the victim, the abduction was forced. When the toxicology screening comes in, I have strong doubts we'll find any ketamine as was found with the other two victims."

"Pamela Levine knew Jericho," Cheryl answered smugly.

"That's weak," Emanuel said, annoyed, his expression filled with irritation. "Everyone in the Outer Banks knows Jericho."

"Yeah. I suppose you're right," Cheryl conceded, sitting back in her chair.

"We're still treating Pamela Levine's case separately?" Tracy asked.

"We don't have enough to say yet. We need the toxicology and the autopsy results." I felt exhausted, the meeting seeming to drag on. "But we can explore ideas. That's what we're supposed to do. It's our job."

I dropped Tracy's paper with a slap against the table and hung my thumb over my shoulder, pointing toward the front of the station, where reporters hung around waiting for the next story. "Guys, I appreciate the honesty and the candor. I just want us to be careful. What's said in here as we explore ideas can be extremely damaging out there."

"Understood," Emanuel said.

"Agreed," Tracy and Nichelle added in unison. "Jinx," Nichelle directed toward Tracy with a broad smile.

"Cheryl?" I asked. She picked up Tracy's paper and began leafing through it, the act purposeful, her way of telling me she was going to continue investigating it. Surprising her, and even myself, I offered,

"You can carry on working it if you feel there's enough to substantiate the investigation."

"Okay," she answered. "As a courtesy, I'll bring any findings to you immediately."

"As a courtesy," I said, repeating her words, the idea of it sickening. "And I don't need to remind you that all lines of enquiry remain in this room until evidence is substantial enough to make arrests. Understood?" My tone was demanding, and the team stared wide-eyed, then nodded in agreement.

Laptop lids were closed and chair wheels and seatbacks sounded as the team stood to leave the conference room. I made myself busy, hands moving in a blur, focus wandering, my face blank, showing no emotion whatsoever. But inside, my mind chased ideas of how to protect Jericho from this investigation. My relationship with him could be misconstrued as my having a bias. And of course I *was* biased. This was the man I was in love with, and now there were two million spotlights suddenly shining on him.

When the room emptied, I braced the table, conflicted and feeling weak. The position I was being put in was unlike any I'd ever faced. My job was to pursue justice over all other things. I owed that to the victims. That meant I might have to turn this case over and remove myself from it entirely. Doing so would also remove my ability to protect Jericho. Could I do that?

TWENTY-THREE

I'd come to enjoy the family meals at Jericho's place, our time together sacred. I especially loved when they were last-minute and impromptu, Ryan fetching three large double-cheese pizzas from our favorite eatery, along with a beach pail of seasoned boardwalk fries and a box of candied strawberry sweets. The afternoon's soaking rains had let up. Now the gutters were dripping, tree branches hanging low, their leaves coated and showing their white underbellies, while the roads slowly dried in the low-setting sunlight. It was all the ingredients for a beautiful Outer Banks sunset.

Voices from the team meeting were in my head, Cheryl's particularly. I had to let it go for the evening, and tried to distract myself with the food and the view. Jericho's kitchen and den offered the best view, with its windows facing west. The bay was glass-calm and mirrored the sky with an endless swirl of orange and red and purple. I peered toward the tops of the trees to see the first signs of evening appear, the moon hovering over our house. Twilight would be upon us soon, that brief moment when we were between daylight and darkness and the Outer Banks glowed as though touched by magic. I loved this time of day. I only wished the team meeting wasn't eating me up.

"Fries?" Ryan offered as I bit into my first slice of pizza, filling my mouth with the taste of cheese and sauce and chewy dough. I masked what was bothering me as he passed the beach pail around, our hands shoving playfully, fingers jumbled as we grabbed at the fries. "Better eat 'em fast!"

My gut was filled with too much ache to squeeze in any more food. "Thank you for picking this up," I told Ryan, putting my slice away for later. I saw Jericho watching me.

"Nothing yet," Hannah said as she came in, referring to the DNA test her father had ordered. The idea of him needing a lab to verify that Hannah was our daughter struck me as profoundly, almost painfully silly. I mean, surely, he could see his parents in her face, especially his mom. He was being obtuse, annoyingly stubborn, causing trouble for the sake of it. It made me sick inside. I wouldn't show how I felt, though, fearing it would upset Hannah even more. She gave us a half-grin, the corner of her mouth curling enough to see one of her dimples. "All we can do is wait."

"I'm sure he's only siding with caution, making certain," Ryan offered, patting Hannah's back. "Don't read too much into it."

"Time takes time," I said, borrowing one of Jericho's favorite sayings. "Your father just needs time." I eased my arm around her middle and felt her tense and become rigid. She sidestepped my touch just enough to remain apart. I'd read article after article about victims of abuse, about what she might have endured. I understood, and patted her arm instead, making space so she'd be comfortable.

"I know," she answered, flashing a forced smile, her shoulders slumping. "I think I just want it all to be over."

"Over?" Ryan asked, filling his mouth with a handful of fries. His face stuffed, he continued, "You mean what happened?"

Hannah gave him a nod, a laugh coming with it as Ryan spoke through his mouthful of fries. The smile was good to see, and their joking together even better. Jericho reached around me, pulling me close. He liked the family get-togethers too. I felt our unborn child inside me, and found myself dreaming of what it would be like this time next year. I leaned into Jericho, bringing one of his hands around my middle, holding him. For the sake of love and family, I tried to let the day drain out of me so I could enjoy their company.

As we retreated to our bedrooms, I was glad the day was ending, wanting nothing more than to strip and stand under a hot shower. The door closed behind me, the metal clacking with the sound of the handle locking. I turned to find Jericho at the foot of the bed, looking at me oddly.

"What is it?" I asked, fearing that he had horrible news to share—the death of a friend or co-worker perhaps. His face was pale, his eyes shifting around unfocused as he hunted for the right words to say. I went to him, taking his arm and finding his fingers clutching papers like a rolled-up newspaper. He unfurled the pages, the words *The Second Accomplice* showing at the top. My first thought was that he'd gone into my bag and found Tracy's report. Only these weren't the same pages. They were copies, photos from a phone that had been printed out. Tracy's report had been leaked. "Oh shit."

"When were you going to tell me about this?" he asked in a gruff voice, tempered just enough to keep the kids from hearing us.

"Where did you get that?" I asked, knowing the question was meaningless. Nothing I could ask mattered now that the report was out there. Not even the truth would matter when facing public opinion and the press. I shook my head, understanding that the damage to his campaign would be catastrophic. "Do the reporters have it?"

"Damn right they do," he said, freeing my hand from his and plopping onto the bed, the anger toward me brief, the pages falling to his feet. He covered his face with his hands. "How long have you had it?"

"A few days," I answered, my insides shredded, my mind torn by the idea that someone from my team had deliberately leaked the report. "Tracy wrote it as a college assignment. It was never—"

"Never!" Jericho belted, startling me. "The moment it existed was the moment that meant it would come out."

I wouldn't be able to reason with him, but I had to know how the pages got out there. "Did your PR guy pick it up from a reporter?"

Jericho nodded. "One of the favors he traded." He pinched his eyes, his knuckles white. "I guess the trading was a good idea after all. Still, we only bought about twelve hours." He waved his hands above his head dramatically. "And then it's kaput."

I didn't know what to say. Could his campaign survive a paper that implied his participation in his wife's murder, while also connecting him to two other murders? Doubtful. "I'm sorry I didn't come to you when I first saw it."

"Dammit, Casey, I wish you'd said something… anything," he said quietly. "I might have been able to get ahead of it."

"Jericho, I'm so sorry," I repeated. Tears stood in my eyes. He'd put everything into the campaign, and I could feel the disappointment coming off him in sharp waves. I eased onto the bed, unsure if he'd accept me. After a moment, he held his arm out. I put my head onto his chest and wrapped my arm around his middle. We remained quiet for a long time, a breeze softly lifting the window curtain, Jericho's phone pressing against me, blowing up with text messages. My own phone sat on the nightstand and remained quiet, telling me the team hadn't heard the news yet. I thought of what the next morning was going to be like; imagined Jericho walking outside, a sea of reporters waiting to pounce, their questions honed like a blade to cut his campaign into pieces. "They're going to ask about the money."

"My motive." Jericho nodded. "Jessie's trust fund."

I pressed my hand against his heart, feeling it beat steadily against my fingers. "What are you going to say?"

He covered my hand, pressing down. "It's not my money." His heart rate remained steady as he took a deep breath and focused on my eyes. "When Ryan turned thirteen, I bumped my life insurance as high as we could afford. I didn't want to take any chances, leaving him and Jessie without money to live on if I died."

"But didn't Jessie have her own money?" I asked, confused. "She wouldn't have needed yours."

"The trust fund is old money," he answered. "Given to her by her grandparents. Now it's Ryan's. I had Jessie change the paperwork so it would go to him on his twenty-fourth birthday."

"So you never had any of it," I said, seeing a hole in Tracy's paper, the largest part of the motive dismissed. "How are you paying for your campaign?"

My question caught him by surprise. "Are you and your team investigating the paper?" he asked, sitting bolt upright.

"It was just a question that came up—"

"I would never use Jessie's money," he answered with a snap, picking up the pages and crumpling them in his fist. "And I'd certainly never take money from my son."

"Jericho, please—" I began, my hands raised, trying to calm him down.

He pointed toward the window. "It's bad enough what the press is going to do out there."

"I know, Jericho, I do—"

"But I never expected to be questioned in my own house," he said, his voice low. There was a deep hurt on his face as he tossed the pages down. "I'm going for a walk to cool down."

"Come to bed," I pleaded, his expression scaring me.

He tried opening the door, but the handle stuck. Anger came then, and he rattled it until the wood around it groaned and the door shot open. "Guess I better fix that before the bank takes the place."

"What do you mean?" I asked.

"Campaign donations were light, but we needed television coverage," he said, his voice dry as he looked around the bedroom with an empty stare. "I borrowed against the equity on the house, borrowed every penny."

I sank onto the bed as though a blanket of dread covered me. Jericho's home was collateral. He'd gambled it on winning the campaign. "The Marine Patrol," I blurted encouragingly as he started to leave. "Your old job—" but he was already gone.

Alone in our bedroom, I cried and cursed myself for not having done more when Tracy first handed me those damn pages. I should have demanded she bury the report, delete it, burn it, do anything to prevent this very thing from happening. Now Cheryl and the team were working the paper, investigating. Jericho's innocence didn't matter. Any investigation would be viewed negatively. He wasn't just going to lose the campaign; he was going to lose his home.

TWENTY-FOUR

Our pleasant family evening disrupted, Jericho left the bedroom in a heated rush. I couldn't blame Jericho for storming out, and although I considered following him, I decided to give him space. Deep inside, I felt that I'd failed to protect him. I lay on the bed staring blankly at the ceiling and listened to him checking in on Ryan and Hannah playing a board game in the den. He sounded pleasant enough, but his tone was gruff and his comments unusually short. Afterward, I heard the rear sliding door open, the metal rollers yawning, then Jericho shutting it hard enough to rattle the house. I heard one-sided conversations with his PR firm, talking about damage control and mentioning another press conference. All the while, I remained awake and wide-eyed, troubled by festering anger, a toxic mix of hurt and betrayal. I didn't have to think too hard about who on my team had leaked the report. I knew it was Cheryl.

Jericho came to bed eventually, but he tossed and turned and punched his pillow a hundred times or more. I tried soothing him, holding him as he spoke the saddest words I'd ever heard: about what it was like the day he saw Jessie's body washed up on the shoreline, and the newspaper stories and television reports that followed. He was distraught at having to relive her murder, her death becoming a story for the reporters to feast on in an attempt to sell newspapers and rack up online clicks. I hadn't thought of that aspect, the horror of his past and what the reporters would do with it. But it was Ryan that he was most upset about; the prospect of his son having to relive every detail as well.

Two hours passed, possibly three, sleep coming fitfully as I glared at the bold digital numbers on the clock and wished there was a way to roll them back a few days. It was daybreak when I finally gave up and got out of bed, Jericho warning me to avoid the reporters until after his press conference. I tried to think of something encouraging to say, anything that could shed a promising light, but few words were spoken as we made our way through our morning rituals and headed out in separate directions.

The beauty of an Outer Banks sunrise was lost on me as I drove to the station, my foot heavy on the gas pedal, my car tightly hugging the street corners. I'd already guzzled one cup of coffee, hitting the caffeine, and switched to decaf by the time I entered the station. The clock had barely nudged past eight a.m., but the reporters were waiting for me with copies of Tracy's paper in their hands and questions tumbling from their lips, asking about the mayoral candidate's connection to the open case.

Keeping my focus on the floor, I got to my desk unscathed, a deep hurt like cold metal pinching my heart as I regarded the reporter's words, and thought about the type of day Jericho and Ryan were about to have. I glanced toward the conference room, where my team were already in place, going about the morning as though nothing had happened, set to discuss the preliminary findings on Pamela Levine from Dr. Swales, her still working the autopsy.

My neck was hot with anxious sweat, the familiar nerves of conflict rising as I considered Cheryl, making me feel unsteady. As a cop, I'd learned to face confrontation, trained to stay grounded and level-headed. This was different. This was about someone I'd thought of as more than just a colleague; I'd considered all of us as friends. All that training went out the window. I could only hope to do my best and keep my composure. I glanced over my shoulder toward the reporters, the crowd blocking the line of sight to the conference room. Now would be a terrible time to add fuel to the fire by losing all self-control.

Tracy and Nichelle were huddled in one corner, Emanuel standing behind them, busily reviewing the preliminary autopsy report from Dr. Swales. Cheryl sat alone, laptop closed, pushing a pencil through her hair, which was a bundle of red rolls. She was dressed more formally than usual—a white blouse and slate-gray slacks, and a dark belt to match her high heels. The station had followed up on the requisition to hire another lead detective, and from the looks of it, Cheryl was going for the position. Leaking Tracy's paper was a strategic move, a tactic to position herself as the right candidate for the job.

I closed the conference door behind me, swiped the video cable from the table and plugged it into my laptop, bringing up "The Second Accomplice" on the screen. All eyes were on me, pivoting to the screen and then back, my jaw clenched, teeth grinding, while I tried my best to remain as professional as possible. Cheryl looked up from her phone and saw the monitor, recognition washing over her face instantly. She knew that I knew it was her, and in that moment, I thought I could have vaulted the table and plucked her eyes from her head.

Breathe, I warned myself, and asked calmly, "Anyone talk to a reporter today?" Nichelle and Emanuel took their usual places at the table. Silence. Cheryl turned away, burying her face in her phone. I raised my voice. "Nothing? Nobody?"

"How do you mean?" Tracy asked, unfamiliar with why an investigation would use reporters, or the practice of trading favors with them.

"Sometimes it's a way of indirectly communicating with the assailant, or in this case, the killer," Emanuel told her.

Tracy crooked her head, palms up. "I don't understand. Why would you do that?"

"Cheryl?" I asked, and bumped the conference room table hard enough to shake it. "We have a teaching moment. Do you want to take this one?"

Cheryl didn't answer. Emanuel shifted, chair legs scratching the floor, his height working to his advantage as he checked the front of the station and then looked at the monitor. Glancing at Tracy, he said, "The reporters. They have your paper."

"No," Tracy said, voice dying to a whisper, color draining from her face. "That's not possible."

"Cheryl? I said again, her phone's screen reflecting in her eyes. My legs were rubbery and weak from the rush of adrenaline. I braced the back of my chair, wanting to sit but forcing myself to remain standing. "Go on, explain to the team why we would leak information to the press."

She surprised me then, standing abruptly, her heels giving her a few inches over me. Before saying a word, she eased close enough to me that I could smell her body wash, her eyes locking on mine, a challenging gleam in them. "I leaked the report," she admitted coldly, her words flat and unemotional.

"You said you wouldn't!" Tracy rose in her seat.

"It's okay," I said, motioning for her to sit. It wasn't okay, but I wanted to hear from Cheryl.

"Like I told you, kid, your paper is good," Cheryl said. "We sometimes leak information, knowing the press will publish it and the killer will read it or see it on the news. It's a calculated move to elicit a reaction that can work favorably for us. A suspect's response can help us move a case forward."

"You think leaking Tracy's report is going to help?" Emanuel asked reproachfully, standing and towering over Cheryl. "It implicates Jericho in a crime he had nothing to do with!"

"Maybe not," she said.

"Explain," I demanded.

"This killer wants recognition," Cheryl answered, staging a defense of her actions. "If the reporters post the story about Jericho, the killer is going to make a move. They'll come forward with new evidence to take credit for their work."

"But the cost!" Emanuel said, fixing Cheryl with a hard stare. "Do you know what this is going to do to him?"

"What if it's true?" Cheryl argued, sticking her chest out. "What if the kid's paper is deadly accurate and Flynn *is* an accomplice, killing those women to cover up the murder of his wife?"

"Impossible!" Emanuel shouted. "I was there. I saw Jericho's reaction when he saw her body!"

"You believe money is the motive?" I asked, clutching the chair as hard as I could, burying my fingers into the vinyl until my knuckles ached. If I let go, I was going to strike.

"Yes! Jessie Flynn's trust fund."

"Jericho can never touch a dime of that fund," I said flatly. Cheryl's expression emptied. "It's set up for their son, Ryan Flynn."

There was a moment of silence, broken after a few seconds by Tracy. "My paper is wrong," she said in a small voice.

Cheryl shifted, eyes darting, then regained her composure. "So what if the trust fund is only for Jericho's son? It doesn't matter whose name is on it. It was a calculated move, and—"

"You're off the case," I said, interrupting her. Cheryl spun on her heel, a look of shock appearing, eyes glaring with fury. There was no room on the team for someone who undermined my orders. She'd left me with no choice but to cut ties. "You're also off this team." A wave of relief came with my words, pouring out of me like a vase emptying. I found the strength to leave the safety of my chair and approached her until we were standing toe to toe. "This is *my* team. We can't work together without loyalty and trust. And that's the door."

The room went silent again, Emanuel, Tracy and Nichelle like statues. Cheryl's lips pursed and her cheeks flushed with a burn. She said nothing as she gathered her things from the table, heels clacking against the floor. When she reached the door, she said, "Not that it matters, but I already put in for a transfer."

"You're right," I answered. "It doesn't matter."

She scowled with a brief look of hurt that slid into a sneer. "And by the way, you might be interested to know that I've also talked to the district attorney. We're old friends."

"I'm *not* interested."

"Well, I gave her a copy of the report and discussed my taking over the case." She cocked her head. "She's considering my request. She agrees with me that you're too close to it. That there's a conflict of interest."

She was gone then, making her way to the front of the station, Tracy and Nichelle's mouths agape while Emanuel and I remained still. Questions rolled into the conference room, punctuated by the sound of camera motors. Cheryl could have struck me with a sledgehammer and I would have felt less pain. I needed this case. If the district attorney followed through with her request, she would take away my only means of finding the killer and clearing Jericho's name.

TWENTY-FIVE

The conference room had never felt so hot, so suffocating. I'd never fired anyone before and was suddenly overcome by the heaviness of it. I wanted to collapse into one of the chairs, fold my arms and rest my head on the table. But there were eyes watching and needing me. It was my team, and it was time to lead.

"Give me a minute," I said, voice shaky.

"We can take a break," Emanuel suggested, coming to my side, offering a chair. I must have looked worse than I felt.

"Thanks," I said, going to a window instead, opening it to let the morning breeze inside. A salty gust blew my hair around my face and I closed my eyes. "A minute. I just need a minute before we continue."

Footsteps. Soft and reserved. It was Tracy, and I could only imagine how she must be feeling, her school paper taking off the way it had. She joined me while Nichelle and Emanuel exited the conference room, their empty coffee mugs in hand and at the ready for a refill. I said nothing as Tracy leaned a shoulder against the wall opposite me, sunlight gleaming in her wet eyes, her chin trembling. I was sick with worry, sick for Jericho and sick about the district attorney and Cheryl taking the case.

"What did we learn from this?" I asked, deciding against a scolding or reprimand. As much as I wanted to yell and shout until I saw her cower into a corner and cry herself hoarse, I couldn't bring myself to do it. The breeze coming off the ocean caught her hair, twirling it in front of her face, the color shining with sunlight and matching mine. Her skin was splotchy. As though she were my own, a motherly instinct coming over me, I tucked her hair behind an ear and gently wiped a tear from her cheek. Tracy didn't back away, welcoming my touch while continuing to look apologetic.

"I honestly don't know," she said, a frown forming, hating to disappoint me further.

"I'll tell you what *I* learned." Her eyelids fluttered, her eagerness to learn engaged. "There is always a point in time, a point in every case, where the only thing you can do is move forward. It's what you have to do if you're going to survive in a career like ours."

"Move forward?" she asked, chatter and the smell of fresh coffee entering the room.

I braced her shoulder and gave her the best encouraging look I could muster given the circumstances. "Manage what is in your control. In this case, moving forward means continuing with the investigation, picking up on a new lead, working the autopsy, finding something, anything. It doesn't mean doing nothing but dwell and sulk."

"Okay," she said, looking restless, clearly wanting to say more.

"Go ahead."

"If I'd known what Cheryl was going to do, I would never have written—"

I shook my head, interrupting. "And never compromise. You worked from your gut, which is a gift. Not every investigator has your level of insight. You're able to see more than most of us. And you're able to conceptualize and then convey it well. It comes naturally to you, so use it."

"But look what it did," she said with a hard frown.

"Your paper didn't do anything," I said, taking a discarded sheet from the table and ripping it in half. "Alone, it's powerless. It's what Cheryl decided to do, which has nothing to do with you."

She marshaled a look of understanding. "I heard she's following up on some of Joseph Choplin's interview. I'm afraid that what I did… I mean, what Cheryl decided to do is only going to make things worse."

"I expect she'll follow up on everything, including Ann Choplin and Judy Granger's meeting." The women's lunch could become something more, might even become critical in the case they were building against Jericho. Or it might have been nothing but a regularly scheduled meeting between old friends. "Ready to get back to work?"

"Yes, ma'am," Tracy answered, her formality making me wince. She caught my look, and rephrased. "Yes, Casey."

My head clearing, I left the comfort of the open window, a fresh cup of decaf coffee waiting for me at the head of the conference room table. Nichelle had brought one of her cat mugs from her cubicle, featuring an orange kitten holding onto a clothes line. Beneath the picture, the caption read *Hang In There!* I picked up the mug with a quiet laugh. "How fitting."

"It was Emanuel's idea," Nichelle said. "I thought it might be too soon."

"Nah, it's good," I assured them, taking a sip, forcing myself to get used to decaf, letting the warm roasted taste sit on my tongue. I was about to propose a huge shift in the investigation. It was Jericho who'd given me the idea without even knowing it. My eyes sprang open and I looked at the team. "How would you like to read Paige Kotes' mail?"

"Paige Kotes' mail, as in actual letters?" Emanuel asked.

I nodded. "It was something Jericho mentioned. He told me about Paige sending him letters from prison. Serial killers are notorious for racking up a lot of fan mail. What if there's one fan she's working with?"

"Like a copycat?" Nichelle asked.

"This is a lot more than that," I answered. "I think we're being played."

"By Kotes?"

"After Ann Choplin was found, I got a letter from Paige, an invitation to meet her."

"You met with Paige Kotes?" Tracy asked, surprise flashing across her star-struck face.

"Don't get too excited," I warned. "She wanted to talk about the Choplin case, offer her opinion. She also warned there'd be more killings."

Emanuel shook his head, wiping his brow. "Inmates will suck every minute of your time dry if you let them."

"I know," I said. He was right. Behind bars, time passing was a horrible reminder of what a prisoner had lost. Each second. Each minute. Each hour of every day. It must be excruciating. That was why they latched onto outsiders. "And I know when to be cautious. But she did offer some insights."

"Well, at one time she *was* a cop," Nichelle offered, trying to put a positive spin on it. "Maybe she's trying to pay it back."

"I doubt it," Emanuel muttered, leaning heavily into his chair, the frame groaning. "That woman is a cold and remorseless murderer. She's up to something, and having seen first-hand what she can do, it can't be good."

"Exactly," I agreed.

"What did she say?" Tracy asked, raising her hand to speak, a habit I wished she'd stop. I gave her the usual motion to lower her arm. She obliged, adding, "In your meeting, what else did she say?"

"She gave me a profile of the murderer. She was careful about it too, offering nothing that could connect her with the case; she's too smart for that. But it was *how* she said things, her interest in the case, following our progress like she was testing us." Paige's voice was stuck in my head.

"I'm not sure how we can review her mail," Nichelle said.

"It's sorted," I answered, having cleared the path for my idea. "I've been in touch with the warden, explaining that the mail review is part of an open case."

"Really?" Nichelle looked at each of us. "Isn't there some rights or privacy law?"

"Not in prison," Emanuel said. "Every piece of mail is searched before an inmate receives it. That goes for outgoing mail too. You'd be surprised at how creative people can get when it comes to sneaking money, drugs and weapons into prison."

"Someone from the prison will be in touch with you," I said to Nichelle. "At NCCIW, they scan every letter, which is what the warden is offering us."

Tracy's hand shot up faster than a bullet as she thumped the table with her other hand. Nichelle glanced at her and nodded. "Yeah, kid. You can help." Tracy's arm returned to her side, a smile brimming.

"I want a short profile on every person sending mail to Paige Kotes," I instructed. "The context, how often, where they are, and most importantly, whether they have a record."

"And the letters Paige sends?" Nichelle asked.

"Absolutely review them too. Those are to be your top priority," I instructed, a twitch pinching my gut at the thought of what Paige might have been mailing Jericho.

Shifting focus, I said, "Now, let's talk about the latest victim. What do we know about her?"

"Pamela Levine," Emanuel began, taking my cue. "Physical therapist. She recently turned thirty and has worked in a few practices local to the Outer Banks, as well as the hospital."

"Cause of death?" I asked hopefully, though I knew it was still too soon for anything official.

"According to Dr. Swales, the suspected cause of death is suffocation in combination with a broken neck," he said, reading from his phone. "She'll have more for us by tomorrow."

"Tracy, bring up the pictures of the victim's ankle, as well as her hands," I said, raising my voice over the traffic sounds drifting from the open window. As the images appeared, I pointed to the bruising on the ankles. "At the scene, we were thinking this could be a handprint."

"Or she could have rolled her ankle?" Nichelle suggested. "We can't tell from this picture if it's an injury or not."

I motioned to Tracy. "The hands." She swiped, showing images of pruned fingers, the skin pale gray like the belly of the crabs we'd shooed away from her body. On the fingertips of the right hand there were cuts and bruises and chipped fingernails, with one nail missing entirely. I made a circle around the damage. "These injuries are consistent with an attack, the victim fighting back, or clutching onto something while being dragged."

Nichelle agreed, her voice sick with understanding. "Yeah, I guess they are." She sat up, facing the team. "I tore my ACL playing frisbee football on the beach last summer. Since then, I've been in physical therapy—"

"You've been working with the victim?" Emanuel asked.

She gave a heavy sigh. "Anyone injured in the Outer Banks and needing physical therapy has worked with her. It's a small town. The point is, when you're rehabbing an injury, you tend to talk, and Pamela Levine loved to talk."

"What about?" Emanuel asked. Sensing we might have some insight into who the victim was, I took a seat at the table, turning the meeting over to Nichelle.

"First, there was the running. Pamela was always running," she said, and rolled her eyes. "You know the type, physically fit, working out all the time, making you feel self-conscious about yourself."

"Understood," I said, encouraging her to continue.

"Well, when she wasn't running, she was at the gym."

"Which is why you introduced the possibility of a rolled ankle?" I asked.

"Correct." Nichelle fluffed her hair, a tic I'd come to recognize when she was nervous. "Next to working out, the girl liked to gossip, and I mean gossip like she was writing a trashy romance novel."

Tracy perked up, leaning in Nichelle's direction, eager to hear every word. "Do tell."

"Mostly it was about the staff at the hospital: who was sleeping with who, that sorta thing. That place is a real soap opera."

"Is it possible that her gossiping could have led to murder?" I asked.

Nichelle shrugged. "I mean, it could have."

"Do you have names for the people she was gossiping about?" Emanuel asked.

"She never used real names. She'd call them fictional names, like from that board game—Dr. Mustard, or Nurse Peacock."

"Clue," Tracy said. "I love that game."

"I guess she thought she wasn't really gossiping at all, as long as she didn't use their names. For all I know, she might have been making it all up."

"Could be she talked about the wrong person," Emanuel suggested.

"And that would mean we have something to work with," I said, though I was unable to gauge its strength as a lead just yet. Tracy and Emanuel stood as I considered where to take the discussion, their focus stolen by the station's monitors. I circled around the table,

Nichelle following, the four of us peering through the conference room's glass walls. "What's going—"

On the monitor closest to the room, Jericho's face appeared, a banner scrolling beneath him colored in brilliant blue and white with bright red edging the words: *Breaking News… Flynn Suspends Campaign!*

"Oh no," I heard Tracy say, my body turning numb with dread. "This is all my fault."

I exited the room, my feet heavy, the speaker's tinny voice stabbing my ears with words I didn't want to hear. Jericho came on, his tone flat as he directed responses to the press, telling them his reasons for suspending the campaign. He stared into the camera long enough for me to see the flair in his eyes die, the excitement driving his plans for the Outer Banks extinguished. He went on to explain that, with his wife's murder case potentially being reopened, his full attention was required.

"What's this about Jessie Flynn's case being reopened?" Emanuel asked. "There's no way! Not unless it was already in the works."

He was right. I realized that Cheryl's work with the district attorney had begun the moment she read "The Second Accomplice". A reporter spoke up, asking about the trust fund. Jericho's gaze fell to the podium, and I bit my lip, a scream born of rage perched on my tongue. I swallowed it dry and told the team, "We have to move fast."

TWENTY-SIX

Hours slipped, the morning long. I texted Jericho a million times, an endless flutter in my chest, my voice stuck in my throat, my head throbbing with a never-ending stream of painful questions. His answers were short, telling me we'd talk more at home. I told him that I loved him, and would support him, my mind racing with how to blow through this case and deliver the real killer to the district attorney.

One bit of good news came from the forensics team, who had finished analysis of the rope found at Jericho's place. While it was a match on type, this was not the same rope used in the killing of Judy Granger and Ann Choplin. I was also told it was very common and we were apt to find it carried by every store on the island. There was one additional finding: the rope had been cut, the blade possibly serrated, the end of one binding from Granger a twin to one from Choplin. The forensics lab sent pictures showing that the two segments paired nearly perfectly.

While working analysis of the rope, I ignored calls from the district attorney, who then texted me telling me we needed to talk. I decided I'd avoid her for as long as possible, making the excuse of being at the morgue as the reason for the delay in returning her calls. I already knew what she was going to do—she was giving Cheryl the case involving Judy Granger and Ann Choplin, citing my involvement with Jericho as a conflict of interest.

In return for playing along with the arrangement, I would hold onto the Pamela Levine case, which Cheryl and the DA did not believe was related. They might have been right, but the location of the scene gave me pause, hinting strongly that there was a connection. What bothered me most about the DA's decision was the sudden shift. Citing conflict of interest meant indirectly identifying Jericho as a person of interest. Jericho must have known this, had maybe even heard the news as a courtesy, which was what had led him to this morning's decision. It hurt thinking about it, feeling what he must be feeling. Like I'd told Tracy earlier, the best thing to do was to move forward. That meant that the best I could do for Jericho was to work this case until the DA peeled it out of my fingers.

Dr. Swales greeted me at the morgue. I'd already changed into a lab coat, gloves and booties. Cleanliness was paramount in her world, eliminating any possible trace of contamination. I could appreciate the level of attention and was apt to oblige her every request. The lab coat was optional, but it helped guard against the cold.

"This is a bad business," she said, hitching up onto her toes, the bottom of her Crocs squelching against granite as she gave me a hug, brief and light. She shook her head, curls swaying, and continued, "Poor Jericho. Such an atrocity."

"Jericho will work it out," I said, trying to reassure myself as much as her, though my words were spoken with uncertainty. Swales wasn't convinced, and I teared up almost immediately. We were alone, and the morning news finally caught up to me, the ache driving through like a stake, the hurt I felt for Jericho overwhelming. "He worked so hard. It's just not fair."

"There, there," she said, her lips pinched. She offered me a chair.

"No," I said, wiping my eyes vigorously, and shaking the moment from my body. "Let's work. I need to work."

"Are you sure?" she asked, her thick glasses nearing the tip of her nose.

"I'm sure," I answered, re-gloving my hands and pushing on the heavy resin doors.

"Whatever you say." She followed me into the autopsy room. The chilled air bit my skin and stung my lungs immediately, my breath a cloudy puff. She led the way to the wall of refrigeration units, some empty, their doors open, the coffin-shaped spaces dark and spooky-looking. It was always better to see fewer of them occupied. The doors to the other units were closed, three of them containing the bodies of Pamela Levine, Judy Granger, and Ann Choplin. "Ready?"

"I am." I was preparing myself mentally, telling myself that what I was going to see was not as bad as Pamela's body on the beach. But my thoughts dwelled on the physical signs of the autopsy—the massive stitching crisscrossed over her chest, a line around her head too, the top of her skull having been removed, her brain weighed. "Doctor, give me a second," I pleaded, the back of my throat sticking. I turned around, hands on hips, eyes closed, annoyed by the way I felt. "Not sure why I'm having such a problem today."

"Oh, I think you know," Swales said. I peered over my shoulder, finding a sly smile on her face. "And I think it's a wonderful thing."

"You know?" I asked, my hand on my belly.

"I do," she said, her smile broader.

"Since when?"

"I've known since the beach. Jericho knows?"

"Yeah," I said, unable to stop grinning. "We haven't been sharing the news, though. Not yet."

She pinched her fingers in front of her lips and made like she was tossing away a key. "I won't say anything." She motioned to the refrigeration unit. "Deep breaths through your nose, slowly. It'll help settle your stomach."

After a minute, I gave the okay, and Swales jerked the refrigeration unit's handle, the hinges groaning as the door glided open. Frosty air thinned to reveal Pamela Levine's feet, the color of snow at dusk, light blue and gray. The skin remained pruned from the time on the beach, but the soles showed evidence of what Nichelle had told us: worn blisters on her big toes and calluses on her heels speaking to physical activities, running and workouts.

I took hold of the body tray, helping Dr. Swales to extract Pamela Levine from the locker, an evidence sheet covering her head and torso. Without warning, the doctor threw back the sheet, cold vapor spiraling above our heads before disappearing. As expected, the victim's chest had been opened, her skin peeled back, her insides removed, inspected, weighed and returned. Large nylon stitches dressed the place where young, beautiful skin had once been. It was sad to see, but it was also part of what happened during an autopsy.

"This bruising?" I asked, motioning around Pamela's face. "Struck in the face multiple times?"

"We recovered a broken tooth," Swales said, lifting a clipboard, reading from it. "Poor girl swallowed it. And there were three others broken as well."

I let out a sigh while envisioning the attack—a morbid exercise, but necessary to help me find the questions I needed to ask. I circled the area around the victim's breastbone, where oval-shaped bruising was evident. "Struck in the face, likely done so abruptly, an attempt to knock the victim unconscious. She falls onto her back, and the killer plants his knee on her chest?"

Dr. Swales nodded in agreement. "Although we found bruising there, the pressure wasn't forceful enough to do additional harm."

"That's because he wanted her alive," I said, concluding that this was intended to be an abduction; that he'd meant to kill Pamela elsewhere; in the ocean, like the other women. "But that's not what happened. Blood work?"

"Clean," she answered. No ketamine then, to connect Pamela with the other murders. She held up an evidence bag, the bottom of it lined with tiny black and slate-colored pebbles. "We did find these burrowed into the victim's skin."

At once, I knew what they were. The victim's car had been found abandoned at the side of a road, one front tire missing entirely, and evidence of severe damage to the wheel well and the front bumper. "Pieces of asphalt." I tilted the bag, the small debris tumbling into the corner, a mix of sand in its company. "The road where her car was found was close to the beach."

"That explains the sand," Swales said. "But of course, the stuff is everywhere."

"Let me guess. These were recovered from the knees, elbows, and maybe her palms?"

"Mostly. We also found some of it in her shoulder, a significant scrape like road rash where she must have fallen," Dr. Swales said. She lifted the hand with the missing fingernail, the tips blackened and raw. "She fought back."

"She didn't fall," I corrected her, and went to the ankle with the bruising. The handprint I'd hoped to find had become a blood pool of green and purple and black, indiscernible. "She was dragged, shirt torn open, scraping her shoulder against the road."

"Possibly," Swales acknowledged.

Thinking through all the various scenarios, I spoke aloud as I recreated the scene. "Pamela struck the piece of wood we found on her tire, damaging her car enough to disable it and force her to pull off to the side of the road. The killer showed up and offered to help, and then attacked her. His intent was to take her elsewhere, but she fought back. And after he'd dragged her to his car, he had to kill her there. Was it an accident?" I paced around the body, the cold, wispy air floating above the victim's skin. All at once it hit me, and I blurted, "They weren't alone!"

Swales' eyes grew wide as she listened.

"She would have been screaming as she fought back. And he couldn't let her be heard. There was traffic. And what do you do when passing a car on the side of the road?"

"You slow down," she answered, playing along, understanding where I was going.

"Correct. Another vehicle slowed down, maybe thinking it was an accident." We went to the victim's head, the dark ring around her neck the source of her death. "When she screamed for help, he held her down, pinned her with his shoe."

"We did find scrape marks on the neck; pressure from the sole of a shoe could be the source," Swales said as I made a note. "There was enough force to break bone and crush the larynx."

"That would mean she was on her back." I motioned to the front of my own neck. "His foot here?"

"That's consistent with these marks." Dr. Swales ran her fingers around what could have been a footprint, but the markings lacked the detail needed to be usable. "She must have been terrified. If only the passing car had stopped."

"But they didn't… Why wouldn't they have stopped?"

She shook her head. "Could be any reason. Not everyone wants to help a stranger on the side of the road."

I thought for a moment. A terrifying realization crept over me. "No. You don't stop if you think the problem is already being dealt with."

"Casey, what are you saying?"

I shook my head, hating the idea, but it was clearer than any other. "You don't stop to help when there's a patrol car already securing the scene."

TWENTY-SEVEN

It was dusk in the Outer Banks, families setting out for fun on the boardwalk, the evening chasing the sun across the sky, and rose-colored light filling my apartment. The day had been relentlessly long. Jericho's news conference weighed heavy on me, his texts short, a few going unanswered. I grabbed for some spring water, my hand brushing the side of a wine bottle, a craving for the taste making my mouth water, but knowing better.

In one of his rare texts that day, Jericho had confirmed he was stopping by my apartment, sticking to our plans to continue packing and to put more of my things into storage before I moved into his house for good. We'd made good progress already, the walls bare, a heap of half-filled boxes lining one side of the main room, and much of my furniture already gone. The floors were bare too, save for a nightstand with a lamp and a lone air mattress covered with a sheet and blanket.

Stepping around to inspect the place, the sound in the room different with it empty, I froze at the sight. Without realizing it, I'd recreated my old apartment in Philadelphia, from before I'd come to the Outer Banks—sparse, drab even, my life simple back then so that I could concentrate on one thing only: finding my missing daughter. I flashed a cautious eye toward the largest wall, half expecting to see clues and pictures and notes tacked up from floor to ceiling, along with thick yarn looped from thumbtack to thumbtack, the colors indicating the strength of a lead. I shuddered. I had found my daughter, something I'd never really thought possible. Despite the setbacks of the current case, the knowledge that a killer was still out there, and that worse might be coming for Jericho, I never wanted to return to the life I'd had before, and I would never have to.

"Sure looks bare," Jericho said, entering, his arm around me a greeting I'd become accustomed to. I leaned back, letting him hold me, the sadness from his press conference battling with the words I tried to find.

"Why didn't you wait?" I asked, spinning around in his arms, facing him, feeling surprisingly angry. "I could have done something."

"Done what?" he asked with a shake of his head, a look of defeat on his face. Though I had nothing to back up what I was saying, I began to counter, ready to argue. He put his finger to my lips. "I love that you wanted to do something. But it was already over."

I fell silent, understanding that what was in the press conference might have just been the tip of the iceberg. And like the *Titanic*, it was what was beneath the surface that had sunk Jericho's campaign.

He took to the air mattress with a thump, his hand guiding me to sit next to him, air hissing, slowly leaking from a tiny hole I'd never been able to find. We lay there in the near quiet of my empty apartment, the ceiling aglow in a wash of pink and orange, shadows from my patio's outdoor plants stretching forever in the ending daylight, and the sound of breaking waves carrying on an ocean breeze.

Jericho had closed his eyes and was breathing deeply, and I sensed he didn't want to talk. But it was in my nature to need to know the answers. Rolling onto my side, my arm draped across his chest, holding him, I asked nervously, "The district attorney?" He nodded, a grim look on his face. My heart began to sink like the sun below the horizon. "What do they have?"

"I wish I knew," he answered, voice gravelly and low, his hand pressing flat against his forehead. "It can't be what the girl on your team wrote. I think we've done some good damage control there."

"What about the money? It's a solid motive," I said. "I mean, I know about the trust fund going to Ryan. And my team knows about it too. But the reporters? They don't know."

"They do now," he answered, a slight sigh of relief showing as he shifted onto an elbow, our eyes locking. I cocked my head, unsure of what he meant. "The new PR guy likes his favors, keeps a constant tally of those owed and those he owes. He made the rounds and passed along the word that Ryan is the sole holder of the trust. Enough of the press knows there's no money, that there's never been any money."

"It's off the table?" I said. Jericho nodded. "That's good. But what else could the DA have? I mean, the rope analyzed isn't the same as that found on the victims. That'll help to clear any suspicions—"

"What rope?" he asked, blinking rapidly, his gaze drifting over my shoulder toward the packing boxes.

I clasped my eyes tightly shut, wishing I'd told him about the rope, and about wanting to use it to exclude him. "It was supposed to help."

"How?" he asked, rolling onto his back, his fists digging into his eyes. "You sent rope from my house to the forensics lab? Right?" I couldn't speak, afraid of how he was going to react. "You did!"

I pressed my hand on his chest and felt his heart drumming against my palm. "Jericho, let's stay calm. I sent the rope in to exclude any possibilities."

He rolled his eyes until I saw the whites of them and gave me a look that made me feel utterly stupid. "That type of rope is everywhere on the island. And as a Marine Patrol officer, I'll definitely have some here and on every boat I have access to."

"I know that now," I said, trying to explain. "But the ropes on the victims, they were from the same bundle, the ends cut, serrated, and identifiable. The killer has the rest of it."

"Why didn't you tell me about it?" he asked, ignoring my explanations. He sat up, deep disappointment on his face. "Casey, first there's the paper, which almost single-handedly destroyed my campaign…" He swiped his eyes, looking more fatigued than I'd ever seen him. I reached for his arm, beginning to feel afraid for him. He threw up his hands, voice cracking. "I honestly don't know if you just meant well or if you actually suspect that I *could* have killed those women."

"Of course I wouldn't believe that," I told him, choking up at the thought of it.

"Wouldn't isn't couldn't," he said flatly, gripping my hand in his, eyes narrowed. "So which is it?"

I had no answer, the words sticking. What if he was right? What if I didn't know? The questions raced in my mind, circling like water around a drain. I took a deep breath and carefully raised two fingers. "Jericho, at the time, the ropes were a huge piece of evidence. The two victims had been close to your wife. And then we had Joseph Choplin making those claims about you, along with my team reading Tracy's paper and presenting a damn good case. When the rope showed up in your house—"

"You grabbed it as evidence," he said interrupting. His lips thinned as he let go of my hand.

"*Not* as evidence," I said forcefully, trying to convince myself, hating that there was the possibility of doubt. "I wanted the rope checked to verify that it couldn't be the same and eliminate any possibility of suspicion."

He gave me a look that told me he didn't believe me, and for the first time since we'd met, we were uncomfortable together. Strangers. "Casey, you still haven't answered: is it *wouldn't* or *couldn't*."

My head throbbed with the painful truth. "At the time, in that moment, I didn't know what to think, okay?" I answered in a near shout, the words scaring me, frightening me to death with the weight they carried and what they might do to us.

Jericho jumped up, his face in his hands, his suit wrinkled. "This is bad," he mumbled into his fingers. He paced the room, his silence deafening. When he stopped, he swiped his hands against his clothes and straightened his jacket. His eyes darted around the room as though he was searching for something lost, but without knowing what it was. He found his car keys in his pockets and said, "I think I should go."

"Please, Jericho," I pleaded, my voice cracking. "Please, come and sit with me so we can talk." He continued to shake his head as he edged toward the door. "I love you."

"Uh-uh," he answered, daring a painful look in my direction. He clutched his chest, his eyes glistening with tears. He was on the verge of crying, and seeing him like that sent a shiver through my body. I stood to go to him, but he stopped and took in a raspy breath. "It breaks my heart to think you could ever consider such an idea."

"I only wanted—"

"I've got to go," he said, without giving me a chance to explain any further. The front door opened, the sunset setting the sky on fire and putting Jericho's frame in silhouette. He turned once as if to say something, but his look was brief and he stayed silent. And then he was gone.

I rolled onto my side and held my middle, protecting our baby. I stayed like that until the evening shadows came alive, a full moon giving them life as they moved in time to the beat of the ocean waves. As my apartment grew dark, I cursed the stupidity of my oversight and cried myself to sleep.

*

It was three in the morning when I got the call. Emanuel was on the other end of the line, his voice a weak rasp, the sound of the ocean in the background.

"Where are you?" I asked, certain I'd misheard him.

"I'm at the beach. I'm at the location where Jessie Flynn's body was found," he answered, his tone turning dire. "Casey, come quick."

I jumped up, losing my footing in the deflating air mattress, cursing as I snatched at a pair of jeans. "What is it?" I begged, terrified of what he was going to tell me. "Is it Jericho?"

More breaking waves. "He's here; some officers we've worked with are with him. But he's been drinking."

"Drinking?" I asked, throwing on the first shirt I could find and grabbing my gun and badge in a run to the car. I'd never once seen Jericho drink, recalling him telling me how he'd drunk a lifetime's worth after Jessie died, and that he'd never have the need to touch the stuff again. "But he's okay?"

"He said he killed his wife."

TWENTY-EIGHT

I knew Jericho hadn't killed his wife. I knew he wasn't capable. So why would he say such a thing? And why now? The beach was pitch black, the breaking waves a stone's throw from where I walked but invisible in the night. A scatter of blue lights bounced ahead of me, along with beaming flashlights where the patrol officers and Emanuel were waiting with Jericho. I had to stop before approaching. I had to collect my thoughts. I was terrified of seeing him like this, and even more terrified of what else he was saying.

"How is he?" I asked as Emanuel greeted me, taking my hand to help me walk along the heavier sands. My heart broke as I saw Jericho slumped against a dune, head crooked to one side, a bottle of whiskey cradled in his arms like a baby. His hair was mussed, his suit jacket and slacks soiled, shirt hanging over his belt, the front of it stained with vomit. His breath came in short gasps, his chest hitching up, a snore sounding, before subsiding again. "Thank God he's breathing."

Emanuel motioned to one of the officers, "Gary here gave me a call; the two of us go way back and he wanted to help."

I took Gary's hand, shaking it gratefully, trying not to show any tension or concern regarding what Jericho had confessed to them. Middle-aged men, they'd been on patrol long enough to have heard just about every drunken, belligerent confession there was to know. He handed me his flashlight, saying, "He's a good man. Helped me more than I can ever repay."

"I really appreciate you calling us," I told him, taking to my knees next to Jericho, the stench of whiskey powerful. "We'll get him home."

Jericho opened his eyelids to the sound of the patrol car leaving, his eyes swimming sideways. He was a sorry sight and it left me feeling uneasy and sick to my stomach. "Babe?" I asked, voice cracking.

His eyes found me. "I killed my wife," he slurred.

Emanuel shuffled his feet against a ridge of sand. He was noticeably uncomfortable, and I glanced over to him, shaking my head. "I don't think he knows what he's saying."

"I do!" Jericho pawed at my shoulder, his fingers snagging my shirt. He tried to right himself, the bottle tipping forward, his strength jerking me downward so that I fell into him with a thud.

"Jericho!" Emanuel yelled, coming to my side to help.

"It's okay," I told him. Jericho sought the bottle he'd lost, releasing me without even realizing I'd fallen. Emanuel clutched Jericho's arm to lift him, but I intervened, making an excuse, insisting, "I'm fine. It was an accident."

"Accident," he mumbled sloppily, trying to pry the bottle open.

"Man, you had enough of that," Emanuel said angrily. He yanked the bottle from Jericho's fingers and threw it into the darkness, the neck whistling as the bottle turned end over end. Jericho sat mesmerized, staring at his empty hands as though trying to figure out the magic trick that had made his whiskey disappear. "Let's get you on your feet."

"Casey, I killed her," Jericho said, pawing at me again, lips drooping and wet, his focus returning, eyes bloodshot and bulging but straight.

"Wait," I said to Emanuel, raising my hand. Emanuel let go of Jericho's arm, and the three of us sat together, our faces lit by flashlights like children telling a ghost story. "Jericho, what do you mean?"

He pointed toward the ocean, the first glimpses of a sunrise forming, showing us the horizon. "She was there. Right, Emanuel?"

"I remember," Emanuel replied.

"Why did you say you killed her?" I asked, pressing the question.

Jericho balled his hands, his strength feeble, his fists loose as he rubbed tears from his eyes. "I worked with them all that time. I should've known. It's all my fault."

"Kotes and Barnes?" Emanuel asked. Jericho rocked his head back and forth. "We all worked with them, and none of us knew."

"But I was closest. I could have stopped it."

"You and everyone else," Emanuel argued.

"Let's get you home," I said, urging him to stand. A pair of joggers appeared with the rising daylight. "You need to sleep this off."

Jericho stood, his legs folding like a broken chair. Emanuel caught him and slung Jericho's arm around his neck. "I got you," he said, Jericho belting a nonsensical laugh.

We made it to my car, belting Jericho into the passenger seat, where he found a cup of coffee I'd picked up on the way. "Need mouthwash," he said as I closed the door.

"Thank you," I said to Emanuel, my hands shaking with cold and shock.

"I can follow," he offered.

I shook my head. "I called ahead; Ryan's home and can help me."

"The mouthwash," Emanuel said, eyeing Jericho through the car window. "It's for later, in case it gets bad."

"What do you mean?"

"When his wife died, he was a drinker. A drunk."

"He mentioned it," I said, though I was beginning to understand that Jericho's drinking had been more of a problem then he'd ever let on.

"He used to drink mouthwash to get him through the day," Emanuel said, looking as though he was breaking Jericho's trust.

"I'm not sure I follow."

"He should be good tonight, but you'll know he's still drinking if you see mouthwash."

I watched Jericho fumble with the radio. It was like watching a stranger.

Sleep came and went in a blink, with Jericho's hoarse snores making me toss and turn for the remainder of the night. Emanuel's warning of what might happen if Jericho decided to continue drinking added to the worry and the growing unease and tension. I'd never seen Jericho like this and didn't know this man next to me. I decided I didn't want to know him either. I shut my eyelids as a pang of guilt tugged on my soul, a reminder of how we'd got here. While I hadn't put the bottle to Jericho's lips and tipped the whiskey into his mouth, I couldn't help but believe that the rope and my not telling him about it had set the events of the evening into motion.

As the sun climbed over the horizon, I found that place between sleep and being awake, my head heavy and gaze unfocused. With the morning light, a silent blue light flashed into the room, the familiar flicker of a patrol car approaching the house. I blinked the morning into my eyes, waking myself, seeing more of the blue lights. I heard the squeal of brakes, followed by car doors opening and thumping shut.

"Jericho!" I said, nudging his ribs with the point of my elbow.

"Wh—"

I dug deeper, stirring him, as a rumble came from beyond the open window, the mutterings of men and women, with Cheryl's voice talking over all of them.

"Jericho!" I hissed, rocking him awake.

"What is it?" he asked, the smell on his breath pungent, the whiskey in his system seeping from his pores.

"Get up!" I said, launching from the bed and grabbing him a fresh pair of slacks and a shirt.

"What's happening?"

"Cheryl happened," I said, dressing as fast as I could. Cheryl had gotten her way. She'd made her case to the district attorney and was at Jericho's house bright and early to take him in for questioning. "Jericho! Listen to me," I said, my voice shaky. "You're being taken to the station and you're going to be questioned."

He sat up, face in his hands. He seemed oblivious to the night before, which had me wondering who else he might have spoken to, who else he'd offered his drunken confessions to. The butt of a patrol stick hammered on the front door, startling me. Jericho lowered his hands. "Who's that at the door?"

"Please, babe!" I urged him, trying not to cry as I lifted his hands and slipped them into his shirt, rolling deodorant beneath his arms. His eyes came alive with the blue lights, his pupils growing large as my words seeped deep enough into his sodden brain for him to realize what was at stake.

"Reporters?" he asked.

I peeked through the window's shades, seeing the top of Cheryl's head first, and then a line of parked vans, men and women jockeying for position, cameras poised, satellite dishes being raised. "Shit," I muttered, feeling our world coming apart, my body growing weak as I thought about the humiliation Jericho was about to face. I went to the bed, kneeling, hands shaking horribly as I helped him into the slacks.

Once he was dressed, he went over to the window, rubbing his eyes. When he saw the news vans, preparing to broadcast live, his skin went pale, blood draining from his face as his arms dropped and his expression blanked.

“Babe?” I asked, afraid of the sudden change in him.

He turned slowly to face me. “I’m in no hurry.”

TWENTY-NINE

It was another beautiful morning, with wispy clouds like a silk veil colored tangerine and purple. Any other day I would have taken a walk on the beach or around the bay, my feet in the water, a breeze blowing through my hair, staying outside until clear blue skies marked the start of daylight. But this morning, Cheryl's was the first face we'd seen, and it marked the beginning of the end for a lot of things.

She stood at Jericho's door and politely explained to him how it would be in his best interests to join her at the station, where they could discuss the murders of Ann Choplin and Judy Granger. He stopped short at the edge of the house's front stoop and gave her a sharp look, but said nothing. Before we left the house, he had called a criminal lawyer he'd worked with before. And on the advice of the attorney, he knew to say nothing until he had representation.

Jericho's every step, every breath, every bleary-eyed glance up and down the street was broadcast live on Outer Banks television stations. I could do nothing to help him directly, and instead chased a text message from Nichelle. She'd texted a few times about working through the night and cracking the code. I had no idea what she meant by this and had missed the messages entirely.

I drove into a parking space, slamming on the brakes, the tires skidding enough to make a chirp. I checked my phone again, seeing another text from Nichelle. There was nothing from Jericho's attorney, leaving me to stare at the screen, a black mirror reflecting my dim mood.

As expected, more reporters were in place at the station, crowded along the steps. I shoved past them, instinctively guarding my middle with my bag while avoiding questions about Jericho. There were more reporters inside too, taking up the benches normally reserved for the public, the smell of sweat and tobacco and coffee telling me they'd been there for hours. For a moment, I thought about texting Cheryl, warning her about the mass of reporters, suggesting she and Jericho enter the station through the rear. I hesitated and looked at the camera lenses pointed in my direction, jutting through a row of heads and shoulders like long snouts ready to suck in every pixel. This was exactly what Cheryl wanted.

"No comment!" I shouted as two reporters blocked my way. I swung my badge in front of me as Alice, the desk officer, helped clear a path through the gate and into the safety of the station proper. I stopped short on the other side, spinning on the tips of my toes, the gate clacking shut. There were twice the number of reporters here than at Jericho's house. There was blood in the water, and they'd become sharks in search of the source, their appetites voracious, a scandal in the waiting for them to write about. "There is no comment now, tomorrow, or any time after. Understand!"

But they didn't understand—or didn't care—and swarmed the gate, thick fingers holding microphones and cameras, flashes piercing my eyes and forcing me to turn away. Jericho was right, no campaign could survive this, but it was the case Cheryl was building that left me scared. How many horror stories had I read of wrongful convictions, men and women spending decades in prison for crimes they hadn't committed?

Nichelle was jumping around like a jackrabbit, her hair bouncing out of sync with her feet, her brown eyes enormous and red-lined, with puffy bags. Like she'd said in her text, she'd worked through the night. In her hands she held a ream of paper, the edges curled and frayed. These were the letters to Paige Kotes. And the letters she'd sent.

"I'm assuming those are for me?" I asked, approaching slowly.

"Wait until you see this," she said, hand raised to the sky, fingers splayed as though praying in a church.

Tracy joined me as I settled in my cubicle, handing me a cup, the coffee black and steaming. "I saw you coming in and got one for you," she said, her eyes shifting toward the front gate, the noise building with Alice yelling over the reporters and threatening to kick them out.

"Thank you, but you didn't have to do that," I said. "I could've gotten my own coffee."

"You sure about that?" Tracy said, glancing at Nichelle, who was pawing at my arm, eager to show me what she'd found. "I doubt she'd have given you a chance to do much of anything."

"Maybe you're right," I joked, the humor lifting my spirits. A dimple on Tracy's cheek showed as she dared to smile. It was good to see. "This isn't your fault," I reminded her. "Remember what I told you. The power wasn't in your paper."

"I remember," she answered. "I can't help the way I feel, though."

"I know," I said, my heart with Jericho and how much I'd hurt him. "I suppose that's what makes this job so damn hard at times."

We entered Nichelle's cubicle, which looked like a cyclone had hit it. Her desk was littered with energy drinks, an open box of NoDoz next to them, the plastic wrapping showing she'd had more than a few. Her cat calendar and pictures had been completely covered by poster-sized paper, every inch of it marked with letters and numbers, with arrows pointing to more letters and numbers. On her whiteboard, strings of letters filled the top half, but they read like gibberish, complete nonsense. The bottom half contained proper sentences, a match in length to those above.

"What are we looking at?" Tracy asked.

I smirked, seeing the answer immediately, the taste of coffee waking my senses, making me alert. I pointed to the letter substitution chart. "That's a cipher alphabet."

Nichelle's eyes got bigger than they already were, the sight comical. "You're familiar with the basics of cryptography?" she asked. I was about to answer when she picked up a book about codes and encryptions and continued, "Codes have been used for hundreds of years. Very basic mappings. Very simple. Almost too simple. Tricky part is coming up with the substitution bank. A bank of letters—"

"Can we get you a glass of water?" Tracy asked, interrupting.

Nichelle took a deep breath and fanned her face. "Why?" she asked, shaking her head.

"Maybe we'll skip this one," I said, taking the open energy drink from her desk. I gave it to Tracy, adding with emphasis, "A very tall glass of water."

"Fine," Nichelle said, conceding.

"Sit," I told her, my tone demanding. She did as I asked, her color bright, skin glistening. I grabbed my chair as Tracy made her way back. She grabbed hers as well and we each took a few pages from the pile of letters. "Now, tell us what we're looking at."

"Okay," Nichelle began with another deep breath. "Paige Kotes' mail. Most of it was fan mail. I didn't even know people got off on that stuff."

"On serial killers?" Tracy said. "More common than most are aware."

"Yeah? Well it's gross," Nichelle answered.

"And you found something?" I asked, desperately trying to steer the discussion, knowing the two of them had a penchant for conversational tangents when given the chance.

She stood abruptly, pants swishing as she went to the whiteboard, pointing to the top. "Fifteen letters in the last six months with writing like this, letters all mixed up."

"You figured out the cipher," I said, glancing at the letters and numbers with arrows. "It's a good thing they didn't use symbols."

"Like the Zodiac Killer," Tracy said, familiar with the case. "This one is fairly rudimentary."

Nichelle frowned. I realized how what Tracy said must have sounded, and added, "This is very good work."

"Thank you," she answered, her exhaustion possibly lending to some sensitivity. "I guess it is a simple one."

"I think it was meant to be," I said. "That way, it could be committed to memory and pass in and out of the prison mail system without a second look."

"That's a good point," Nichelle said. "They don't read the mail. They just search for contraband. And this gives enough cover to hide anything the guards might glean while scanning the pages."

"What do the letters say?" Tracy asked, leafing through the pages she was holding.

"Pamela Levine is in there," Nichelle began.

"Choplin?" I asked. Nichelle gave a slow nod. "How about Judy Granger?"

"All the victims are mentioned, as well as Lisa Wells."

"This confirms Paige Kotes is working with someone. Do we have an address?"

"Address, name, and record," she answered, bright teeth showing as she tried to hold back her smile.

"Who?" Emanuel asked, joining the meeting, his eyes darting between us. "Nichelle, what happened?"

"Never mind that," I answered. "We have a very strong person of interest."

"His name is Robert Odin, a local. He's a fisherman," Nichelle said, reading from a printout.

"He used his real name in the envelope's return address?" Emanuel asked, his tone doubtful.

"Please!" Nichelle punched her hip with a fist and cocked her head to the side. "Do you really think a serial killer would do that?"

"I'm just asking," Emanuel said, hands raised.

"There's a post-office box, a commercial one. But they're not anonymous. A few phone calls and the manager of the establishment gave up the name without a second thought."

"This is excellent work," I told her again. "Any priors?"

"Just the one, and he did some time for it too. Stole a fish and tried to sell it."

"A fish?" Tracy asked, as incredulous as I felt.

"Apparently you can do time for stealing bluefin tuna," she said.

"Sure can. Given the time of year, that's a ten-thousand-dollar fish," Emanuel said. "We broke up a ring a few years back."

"Robert Odin does some time. He gets out of prison. Still works as a fisherman, and on the side he's interacting with Paige Kotes through encoded letters," I said, summarizing. "How did they pick their victims?"

Nichelle hit the space bar on her keyboard, bringing up the newspaper clipping with Jericho and Ashtole and Joseph Choplin playing football in the background. The victims, along with Jericho's wife, were the four cheerleaders. "In the caption, we can see the victim's names, along with Jericho Flynn's name. From the first letters, there are occurrences of the names."

I braced the back of my chair, hating that Jericho had to be involved, wishing this case was less personal. "How?" I asked, my voice shaky.

Nichelle picked up one of the letters and pinned it on her board, the gibberish impossible to make sense of without the cipher alphabet. She pinned the translation next to it. "After some initial back-and-forth letters, Odin asked Kotes if he could do anything for her." She gave a firm nod. "He asked specifically what he could do to be worthy of her respect."

"That sounds convincing enough," Emanuel said.

I skimmed the translated letter until I came across Jericho's name, and read aloud. "'List the women in my love's past. I already took Jericho's wife. Take them all, take the other women as your own to win my favor.'"

"That almost sounds like a puzzle," Tracy said.

"Not a puzzle," I replied. "It's her commandment. He used social media to find anyone Paige would deem significant."

"Which included Jessie Flynn's best friends," Tracy said.

"But why Pamela Levine?" I asked.

Nichelle held up a finger. "I wondered the same thing." She tacked up another letter. "Lisa Wells was the next victim, but Paige directed him toward Pamela Levine, wanting to select someone from Jericho's past they'd both had contact with, a history in unrelenting pain." She breathed heavily. "It's all in here."

"Paige Kotes was in physical therapy too," Tracy said. She glanced at me briefly before continuing, "Multiple surgeries to fix her face and leg after she attacked Jericho. She must have had contact with Pamela then."

"The gossiping," I suggested, turning to Nichelle. "You mentioned how much Pamela Levine liked to gossip."

"I don't think it was just the gossiping. There were a lot of pictures online of Pamela Levine with patients, including Jericho." Nichelle brought up pictures from the places where Pamela had worked.

In one of them, there was Jericho in the background, his arm still mending, Pamela working with him.

"The killer searched social media," I said. "That's how he got the newspaper clipping of the victims. It makes sense, since Paige wouldn't have had access to anything online."

"Who else?" Emanuel asked, concern in his voice. "If Robert Odin is working from connections he's finding online, and getting approval from Paige Kotes, then who else might they be considering?"

"I wasn't sure how to figure that out, so I searched social media the way Robert Odin might have done. I started with Jessie Flynn's posts since she was the first from the newspaper photo to have died. From there, I counted the occurrences of people she was close to."

"You switched to Jericho, though, didn't you? Following Paige's letter about Pamela Levine?" I asked, suddenly understanding. "Who was pictured with him the most? Who had the most hits?"

"My analysis is incomplete," she began, her face going gray, her high energy stifled by what she'd found.

"I'm fine, you can say it," I assured her.

She looked away. "Detective Casey White," she answered. "It's you."

THIRTY

As expected, the sun was blazing by mid morning and had burned off the colorful ribbons that had followed me to the station, leaving behind blinding sunlight and an unruly heat wavering off the surface of car tops and the pavement. Even for the Outer Banks, the heat was above normal, the wind from the ocean weak, which showed in a slowdown of vacationers, the piers and beaches empty as they stayed indoors where air conditioners ran non-stop.

But the fishing piers knew nothing of the heat. They knew nothing of the cold either, their commerce based entirely on the seasons of each species fished and brought to market. As Emanuel explained it, the Outer Banks was one of the largest and wealthiest fishing locations on the east coast. Especially when it came to bluefin tuna, which was exported for top-dollar prices to Japan, a fact of which our person of interest was keenly aware.

What I saw and smelled when we reached the docks was fish. All kinds of fish—small and large, slender and long, short and fat, with men and women hoisting them on thick ropes and carrying them in netted bags the size of my car. They worked knowing nothing of the hot day that had shut down much of the Outer Banks. They only knew they had a catch in hand and buyers with money to exchange. The fishing center was hustling and bustling with activity, and finding Robert Odin would be a challenge.

"How far up the coast does this go?" I asked Emanuel, having never been to one of the marinas. I shaded my eyes to see that the docks continued for a great distance. I couldn't see the last merchant, the last moored boats. The pier was made up of concrete edged with enormous timbers, the wood assaulted by years of high tides and sea spray, soaked wet and glistening black. Every five yards there were wood pilings driven down to bedrock and holding the timber in place, making for a wall where there'd once been a beach. A sleepy brown pelican sitting squat on one of the pilings opened a lazy eye to regard me a moment, and then returned to its slumber.

"Not sure, but it's a long way," he answered, beads of sweat on his brow and scalp. He swiped his face, breathing heavily, and guzzled water from a bottle. "We don't exactly fit in, so let's just walk along and keep an eye out for the guy."

"Certainly don't match, do we?" I was wearing business casual, slacks and a blouse, my gun holstered, my badge hanging around my neck. My phone with Robert Odin's picture was in my pocket. We'd caught the eyes of workers from the first vessels. Garbed in rubber slickers from chest to toe, their hands were beefy, and toughened by the work on the seas.

I recognized the crab boat in front of us. It was owned by a man Jericho affectionately called Old Man Peterson. At one time Jericho had thought to buy into the crab business, but then decided to stay on with the Marine Patrol. I searched for the old man, his first mate tipping his hat in greeting.

"Peterson around?" I asked.

"He'll be back in a few minutes," the man answered, a stack of crab pots in hand. "Can I help you with something?"

"I'll catch up with him on my way back," I said. Emanuel was tugging on my arm. "What is it?"

"I think that might be our guy," he said, motioning fifty yards ahead to a larger vessel. Odin was working a stout forklift, burlap straps threaded around the forks, hoisting massive fish from its deck.

"That's him," I confirmed, as a deck worker crossed us sweeping fish guts into the sea, another worker shoveling mounds of ice from the back of a pickup truck. "Let's take it slow, casual, like we're here for anyone else but him."

My plan lasted a second, maybe two. Emanuel became distracted when he stepped in something and stopped to scrape it from the bottom of his shoe, drawing attention. Odin spotted us and jumped from the forklift's cab. "I'll go around," Emanuel said, taking to the left to head him off, leaving me to chase the man direct.

"Robert Odin!" I yelled. A flop of black hair lifted and fell as he ran. In his denim coveralls, tattered and frayed and soiled by his day's work, he was difficult to spot on the crowded pier. "Clear the way!"

Odin ran across the path of another forklift and under an enormous fish dangling in the air, dark blue skin and oyster-colored belly gleaming in the sunlight. He peered over his shoulder as he ran, brow furrowed. I was gaining now, my shoes slapping against the wet pavement.

"Watch it!" a voice bellowed as a motorized cart with tubs of ice rolled in front of me. I took to the air, vaulting the load, sweat stinging my skin, my lungs filled with the hot smell of fish.

"That way," Emanuel yelled, flanking Odin's position, keeping right toward the end of the pier. Odin was trying to blend with a group of fishermen, Old Man Peterson amongst them, but he was taller than most and the top of his head appeared. Peterson caught my eye and instinctively snatched hold of Odin, grabbing his coveralls, a gut reaction I'd thank him for later. Odin let out a high-pitched yelp, his skinny frame struggling to escape, boots skidding against the slippery dock, his body flopping in Peterson's tough grip, which was fixed and unmoving, the old man's strength like a machine.

"That's it," I shouted, and began to close the distance. "Hold on—"

The strike came from out of nowhere. The left side of my body was crushed as I was launched sideways and off my feet. Peterson and Odin disappeared. Air left my lungs in a sickening whoosh. My head rocked, my body bounced off the pavement and I tumbled head over heels over the edge of the pier and into the water.

I stayed conscious, a scream ringing in my ears as I sank below the surface, blinking rapidly, trying to get my bearings in the murky water. Slanted sunlight eked through an opening; I'd fallen between the pier and a moored boat, the ocean's wake shoving it against the dock, rocking it slowly, trapping me beneath its hull with the sound of wood banging against wood, other boats bumping and grinding. Had I been struck a moment later, I would've fallen onto the deck, which would have broken bones instead of merely drenching and embarrassing me. I tried to rise, but stopped, the boat's motion stealing my chance to resurface. Light reappeared a second time and I dared to put my hand up, but the hull was on the move again.

My lungs cramped, the need for air coming quick, my feet hitting the soft bottom, which sucked at the soles of my shoes as I pushed against the mud. My shoulder and head ached as I tried to find another opening, the sting of saltwater against my forearm telling me I must have gotten cut and was bleeding. The combination of an open wound and fish scraps in the water struck me. Nerves turned me cold as I feared the worst, for me and my baby. I started clawing at the water, climbing it like a ladder in a race to get a breath of fresh air.

Daylight snapped shut and disappeared like someone had flipped a light switch. I couldn't hold my breath anymore and swam away from the boat toward the pilings. The wood was covered in barnacles, their hard shells rooted into the algae-covered timber, jutting sharply for me to clutch onto. I surfaced just as my lungs were about to burst.

"Casey!" Emanuel appeared at my side, splashing and gasping, having jumped in to help. "Are you okay?"

"Fine," I managed, spitting to clear my mouth.

Peterson was lying on his belly, his long arms draped over the pier's timber for me to grab, browned by years of sunlight, his silver-gray curls sprouting from beneath his dingy fisherman's cap. The tide was low, leaving him out of reach, his fingers dangling. "Can you stretch?"

"I can," Emanuel said, one of his hands crooked beneath my arm, the other clutching the pier.

"Odin?" I asked, choking and coughing, hopes high that we still had him.

"Gone," Emanuel answered, droplets in his hair glinting sunlight. The news of Odin's escape added insult to injury. "We'll issue an APB. Let's get you out of the water."

"Grab onto this," Peterson hollered, lowering a rope similar to the one I'd sent to the forensics lab. Sadness zapped my strength, Jericho's voice in my head telling me the rope was everywhere in the Outer Banks. "Hang on, and we'll lift you out."

I did as he instructed, Emanuel guiding me, as a group around Peterson watched him raise me effortlessly from the ocean. I fell onto my side, the pavement beneath me warm, sharp embarrassment filling me. Emanuel came up next, three men helping him onto the pier. "Thank you," I managed to say as Peterson knelt to check my arm, the cut superficial, needing only to be cleaned and wrapped.

The old fisherman's hands were gnarled and tough, but his touch was soft as a feather and his face was concerned. "Have to have eyes all around you in these parts," he said. Behind him the crowd thinned, a forklift with a pallet of crates appearing, the driver holding his cap and looking terrified. "You're lucky he only dinged you a bit. Could've been much worse."

"I suppose," I said, just as a stab drove into my belly, a cramp twisting like a towel being wrung dry, its hold lasting half a minute or more, which was half a minute too long. Panic stole my breath: it was the baby. I grabbed Peterson's hands. "Please, help me up."

"You'll be okay," he said, hearing the fear in my voice, his clear blue eyes kind and surrounded by age, a forced smile trying to reassure and comfort me. "You're not the first to get knocked over."

Emanuel joined him, seeing at once that I wasn't right, a look of stark concern on his face. "What is it, Casey?"

Another cramp came, its power stretching and pulling inside me, the pain of it sharp and clear and filling me with a sudden uncontrollable dread. "Emanuel," I said, voice wavering. I took his hand, the two men helping me stand as my legs wobbled. "I need a doctor."

THIRTY-ONE

Emanuel drove while I shivered in the passenger seat of my car and called in an all-points bulletin on Robert Odin. The radio dispatcher took down the details.

"How you doing, Casey?" Emanuel asked, his fingers tight around the steering wheel, knuckles straining. He wore a frown and there was sweat on his brow. He knew something was terribly wrong, but had no idea what it was. I tucked my phone away and cradled my front, a tear in my eye and a sob on my lips. I clenched my jaw as a fresh cramp emerged. It rose to a peak, making me wince, and then faded. From the corner of my eye, I saw Emanuel glance at me and spot where I'd placed my hands. A look of understanding came to him. "How far along are you?"

"Far enough to worry," I said, biting my lip.

"It could be normal," he said, trying to sound reassuring.

"I know," I said. "I remember."

"Almost there," he said.

I'd had normal cramping when I was pregnant with Hannah, the doctors explaining it was expected. But there'd been another baby. A child before Hannah. We'd lost our boy as I approached the third trimester, and I'll never forget the feeling inside, his life ending as we said goodbye too soon. I couldn't go through that again.

Thankfully the doctor's office was nearly empty. Emanuel wanted to stay, but I insisted he return to the station so the investigation into

Robert Odin wouldn't miss a beat. With some reluctance, he agreed and left me alone. Alone was what I wanted. It was what I needed.

The waiting room had rows of chairs, empty except for mine, which I no doubt made damp given the state of my clothes. An enormous aquarium made gurgling sounds, the colorful fish swimming back and forth, passing the time like hands on a clock. I shut my eyes and closed my arms around myself in a hug. As my clothes began to dry, I tried to think of anything other than losing my baby.

"Casey," I heard Jericho say, and opened my eyes to find him standing over me. He knelt down, his hands on mine, his face unshaven and his eyes weary, the past days taking their toll, his night off the wagon making everything worse.

"How—" I began, my hands shaking as I reached for him.

"Emanuel texted me. He told me there was an emergency," he answered, taking my hands. "The baby?"

"I don't know anything yet," I answered, cupping his fingers tightly and bringing them to my heart. "Thank you for coming." I found his eyes and held his focus a long minute. "I am so sorry about the rope. I meant well, I did."

"This is what's important," he said as I guided him to the seat next to me. "Your clothes are soaking," he added, his hand on my belly. "What happened?"

I winced as the next cramp began, and kept my eyes shut tight as it climbed to a peak. Only this one wasn't as bad and didn't reach the painful heights of the earlier ones. Instead, it felt more like the type I'd had early on when I was pregnant with Hannah. Jericho watched as I breathed through it, his eyes round, the whites bloodshot, days of stubble on his face.

"I'm better," I said, brushing my fingers along his jaw, liking the salt-and-pepper beach-bum look with his ever-present Outer Banks tan. "You look better than last night," I exclaimed, trying to make light of the situation.

"Better get used to it," he warned with a smile.

"Full-time beaching?" I joked.

"Close. When I finished the interview with Cheryl, I made a few calls. I can be back in uniform with the Marine Patrol as early as tomorrow." I was speechless, tears springing to my eyes. He'd really wanted to be mayor, but he was already looking to move forward, to move past this. I kissed him hard on the lips, a sob coming as I held onto him. I could feel his breath on my neck as he continued, "And I was told I can stay on as long as there's no more trouble from the DA."

"What happened in the interview?" I asked.

"A lot of show for the reporters," he said, his focus falling to the floor, where he brushed my shoe with his. "They wanted to review that report, and brought up the rope, but there was nothing concrete, nothing they could hold me on."

"If they can't hold you," I said, squeezing his hand through a fading cramp, "surely that mean your campaign doesn't have to be over?"

"Breathe," he said with a look of resignation. "It's over. The reporters are eating it up. They love a scandal. And voters do not."

It crushed me to believe I'd been indirectly involved in ending his dream. He would never be mayor now.

My name called, we stood, Jericho taking my arm as though I'd busted a knee. I smiled at his gentlemanly manner and laced my fingers with his. "Well, I might have a twist in the story to throw the reporters for supper. We have a suspect. Robert Odin."

"The fisherman?" Jericho asked, an unsettling frown forming.

"You know him?"

He ran his hands through his hair. "The guy's a petty thief. Arrested a few times. He got sent up for a bluefin tuna sting a few years back."

"Well, he's also been writing to Paige Kotes, and the evidence makes him our number-one suspect."

Jericho stiffened at the mention of Paige, his body language showing concern, his expression turning cold. "Can't imagine what those two would have to talk about."

"Let me worry about that," I said.

In the examination room, Jericho sat close to me. "So were you swimming with the fishes down at the pier?"

"Something like that," I said as the doctor entered, flipping through pages on her clipboard.

"You're wet," she said, stating the obvious with sarcasm in her voice. She rolled a stool to the examination table, raising the seat before sitting, her brown hair thinning and disheveled, her skin without a single blemish. "Now, what's happened to you today?"

The examination was over before my clothes had time to dry. Dr. Pandit checked everything possible and brought in equipment for us to hear our baby's heartbeat, the subtle swooshing thumps reassuring us. Jericho's smile was brimming. I could have listened to that sound forever. The relief was enormous, and the weight of concern lifted as Jericho held my hand to help me down from the exam table.

An expanding uterus, the doctor explained, telling us it was quite normal. But knowing my history, she also warned me to limit my physical activity, and to rest. I agreed, but felt the diagnosis was a staple that doctors used when they lacked any direct causes to address. The important thing was that our baby was okay and my fall into the ocean when chasing Robert Odin hadn't caused any damage.

"Odin's not your guy," Jericho said, holding the car door for me, the brief moment of relief over.

"Why are you so certain?" I asked, welcoming the heat from the seats.

He closed the door gently. "He isn't the type," he answered, getting into the driver's seat and starting the car. "I've known him for as long as I've been around the Marine Patrol. He's a goof-up, not a murderer."

My phone buzzed: a text from Emanuel telling me Odin was in custody at the station. I held up my phone for Jericho to see. "Well, it looks like I'll have the opportunity to find out for myself."

THIRTY-TWO

Robert Odin had long, stringy hair, a carry-over from his younger days, refusing to succumb to his receding hairline and a bald patch expanding atop the back of his head. But the crisp lines webbing his eyes and riddled on his forehead spoke for him, showing he was nearing forty. He had spent much of his adulthood in and out of trouble, rehabs, and jails. His right leg bounced without rhythm, the heel of his boot clopping against the interview room floor while Emanuel, Nichelle, and Tracy sat across from him, waiting for me to begin.

I'd cleaned up after my unexpected dip in the ocean amidst bloodied fish scraps and barnacle-ridden pilings, but as I stood at the doorway to the interview room, sipping coffee to warm my cold bones, I could still smell the fishing pier, the odor pungent, almost relentless. It was coming from Odin's coveralls, the denim fabric dingy, his boots soiled with the workings from the dock, the cleaning of fish and hauling of crabs and their pots. His record showed he'd done just about every job there was to offer in the fishing industry, and that he'd also tried stealing from more than a few folks he'd worked for. I glanced at my team. Emanuel's face was fixed in a grimace, Nichelle had covered her mouth, and Tracy's nose scrunched as she tried blinking the stink away. The interview room would probably never smell the same again.

"How's the fishing?" I asked Odin, taking a seat and plunking a folder onto the table, the pictures of the victims and the Paige Kotes letters inside and at the ready.

"How's the swimming?" he answered, opening his mouth wide in a sarcastic laugh, his teeth yellow and crooked, some of them chipped.

"Probably better than the market for stolen bluefin tuna," I retorted, setting boundaries, telling him I was a cop and he was still an ex-con.

"Is that what this is about?" he asked, spittle dripping to the tip of his chin. He swiped at it and continued, "I swear, every time there's any shit going on around that place, I'm the first to get pulled in and questioned. That's harassment."

"Well, in my experience, it's the guilty ones who run," I replied. "Is that why you tried to escape? You're involved in some shit going on around that place?"

Odin snapped his mouth shut. He was guilty of something, but what?

"Once a convict, always a convict," Emanuel commented.

Odin lowered his head, scraggly locks falling onto the table. He tucked them behind his ears, his leg bouncing again. "I've been clean," he said. "Really! I ain't lying." He peered up at us. "I got a daughter I'm trying to support."

I searched his eyes, searched for the evil I'd seen in murderers who'd sat across from me. I found none of it. From the folder, I pulled a copy of a letter he'd sent to Kotes, sliding it in front of him. "What can you tell us about this?"

He held the page, eyes moving from left to right and then top down, a frown showing as he tried to decipher the mixture of letters and numbers. "How did you get this?"

"You recognize it?" Emanuel asked.

He shrugged. "Can't really say. I've seen one like it before, but dunno what—"

"From Paige Kotes?" I asked, interrupting him. At the mention of her name, Odin placed the letter down and tucked his hands beneath the table.

"I just sent her a few letters, fan mail is all," he said, his voice solemn. We weren't here to talk about stolen fish, he knew that now.

"Fan mail?" Emanuel asked. "So you admit to communicating with Paige Kotes?"

"Uh-huh." Odin tipped his chin toward the letter. "She never answered any. But then I got one of *them*."

"Why?" I asked out of pure curiosity. "Why send her mail?"

The corner of Odin's mouth curled into a smile. "'Cause she's famous. And I don't mind the scar none, I told her so in my letters. I think she's beautiful."

I turned to Nichelle. "We'll want to review the terms of Robert Odin's probation as set by the judge and courts." Odin's eyes became huge, his attention concentrated on me as he realized what he'd just admitted to. I continued, "We'll need to determine if he's broken any conditions by communicating with Paige Kotes."

"Aww, come on!" he pleaded. "I'm six months out from being done with my probation."

I had no idea what the terms of his probation might be, but I wanted to quicken the questioning, have him open up so we could get to the point of the interview. I pushed another letter in front of him, this one marked by the prison's mail room as outgoing, sent to Robert Odin by Paige, the encoded words including the names of the victims, Ann Choplin and Judy Granger. "Then you won't mind telling us what this says."

He picked up the page, his lips moving, skin gleaming with grease and sweat, the smell of his days on the fishing pier intensifying and making it even harder to tolerate. Tears welled in his eyes. "I can't go back inside," he blubbered. He braced the letter, his focus firm as though taking a test, elbows perched, eyes straining, bugging out from his skull. "I… I have no idea what it says. I couldn't read the one I got neither."

"There was only one?" Nichelle asked, puzzled.

"Like I said, she never replied to any of my fan mail," he answered, shoving his palm against his forehead, resting his head. "But then I got one of these."

"What did you think it was?" Tracy asked, the look on her face showing that she shared my concern. Odin shrugged and shook his head. "The first letter we showed you, why did you send that?"

Odin's eyebrows lifted and he pointed to himself in disbelief. "You think I wrote that?"

"You wrote it and sent it to Paige Kotes," I said, stating it as fact but beginning to believe what Jericho had said. This man wasn't capable of composing a letter with encoded words and sentences, let alone orchestrating a murder spree. "Tell us about the letters you sent."

"They ain't nothing like these," he answered. "Couple of poems; telling her how much I liked the television shows about her. That sort of thing."

Silently I pulled a picture of Ann Choplin from the folder and placed it in front of him. It was a still taken of her face following her autopsy. "So. How do you know this woman?"

Odin shoved at the picture, his face losing color, the gravity of the situation becoming clear as he understood he was here in connection to a murder. He shook his head vigorously, answering in a flustered stammer. "I… I got nothing to do with no dead people."

"And this woman?" I asked, placing a picture of Judy Granger on the table.

"Aww, shit!" he yelled, reeling, his hands guarding his face like a child viewing their first horror movie. "I never seen her. Never seen either of 'em"

"These people?" I asked, putting the newspaper cutting on the table next. Odin lowered his hands, his face blank. "I ain't never seen her, or her, or him. Not even that one!" He pointed to the football field where Ashtole, Joseph Choplin and Jericho stood.

Beneath Odin's tobacco-stained finger there was a fourth person, standing at the goalpost watching the festivities. I'd overlooked it until now, but seeing his hand spread over the image somehow framed the extra person. Had we overlooked the possibility of another victim?

As Odin continued discounting all that we'd proposed, I texted Nichelle telling her to investigate the additional person in the picture. I also sent a copy of the photo to Jericho, asking him if he knew the individual.

"You don't recognize these women?" Emanuel asked again, trying to find any hint of Odin lying. He placed the autopsy photos next to the cutting. While the women had aged since their days as cheerleaders, I could still make out the resemblance.

Odin reeled back again, the sight of death too much. And by the look of him, I believed he was telling the truth. I let out a sigh, feeling defeated and disappointed. In my head, I'd built him up to be this mastermind serial killer who was working with Paige Kotes, continuing to do for her what she couldn't do while incarcerated. But that wasn't who we had in the interview room. I glanced at him again, his head lowered, cowering and sniffling. He wasn't a murderer.

So how did the encoded letters get addressed to him? Regardless of Jericho's warnings, I'd have to visit Paige Kotes to find out.

THIRTY-THREE

It was nearly dark by the time I reached the prison. As I drove, the view from my rolled-down car windows had changed from seashore to rural country, the ever-present salty aroma replaced by farm smells. My heart thumped hard in anticipation. I'd called ahead, notifying the prison of my visit, telling them it was of the utmost urgency. Robert Odin wasn't our guy. He wasn't the killer. The only thing I believed he'd ever killed were brain cells doing whatever it was that he liked to do with the money he made trafficking stolen bluefin tunas.

The bleak colors of North Carolina Correctional Institution for Women looked even bleaker with the sun having set. The overhead lights buzzed with electric energy, putting the walls and floors and people in a shade of green as night bugs bounced off the tin and glass enclosures. The damp prison smell hit me the moment the first iron door swung closed, the metallic clamoring followed by a deep echo of inmates hollering in response. I took a breath through my mouth, adjusting to the musty odor and the faint tang of cleaning fluids, the floor having been mopped earlier perhaps. There was more to the prison. I hadn't been able to put my finger on it in previous trips, but the night's dampness helped to bring it out. It was an undertone of decay, of petulant illness and rot, life withering away, the kind of stench we instinctively avoided. I wanted to run away, but continued on, desperate to get to the bottom of this case.

I followed a guard to the interview room, a different guard to last time, the later hour biting into another shift. He glanced at me as we walked the corridor, his eyes fixed longer than I was comfortable with. I guessed he'd recognized me from one of the television shows about Hannah's kidnapping, and hoped he wouldn't ask any questions. Our footsteps bounced off the cinder walls, his leather belt creaking as he hung one hand from his thumb and motioned with his other to the interview room's entrance. Paige was sitting with her arms on the table, wrists shackled, chains sliding over the metal table and clanged between her legs, where they connected to her ankle restraints.

"I'll be standing right outside if you need anything," the guard said softly, a faint smile appearing, and my discomfort dissipated as I looked into his friendly blue-green eyes.

"Would you mind removing those cuffs?" I asked him. Paige held her arms in the air, a fake smile crossing her lips. Her hair was a tangle of curls, appearing uncombed in the days since I'd last visited. There were heavy dark pouches beneath her eyes too, leading me to think she hadn't been sleeping. And by the gauntness in her cheeks, I guessed she hadn't been eating either.

"Yes, dear!" she said to the guard in a snappy tone. "Please do remove these bracelets."

"Settle," the guard warned as she playfully waved her hands in front of him in a game of catch-me-if-you-can. Perturbed, he stepped back. "I'll leave them on if you don't mind yourself!"

"Fine," she said holding still, conceding, allowing the guard to remove the cuffs. She looked me square in the face, expressionless. "Did you bring me some fun?"

"Possibly," I answered, handing her a candy bar.

She was looking for more details from the case, some autopsy photos maybe, but when she saw the candy, her eyes blazed and she snatched it from my fingers, the silver and brown wrapper no match for her eagerness and appetite. Bringing a treat to a prison interview was one of the oldest tricks. It wasn't just the psychological aspect, the giving of a reward for cooperation being the obvious tactic. It was also physiological. After the first bites, the body converted the sugar into pure energy, while the chocolate triggered pleasure zones in the brain. I didn't know all the science behind it, but I had seen enough to know it worked wonders. I needed Paige to be pliable like putty and tell me about the letters.

"It looks like you could use a meal… a shower too," I said.

"It's this place," she said, side-eyeing the door, the guard standing in the corridor. "I got into a fight, haven't been able to leave my cell much."

"More than one?" I asked, seeing old bruises around her cheek and neck. They were fading, but still visible. I wanted to establish some ground before diving into the letters, and asked, "What happened?"

"News reports," she said while chewing. She peeled away the candy bar's wrapper, the guard turning his head at the sound of the tearing paper and foil, then held it up, saying, "I'm sorry, where're my manners?"

"It's yours, thank you," I answered.

"Maybe your *baby* wants a bite," she said, sounding reasonable, even a little compassionate. Revolted by her, keeping myself in check, but wanting to strengthen our rapport, I broke off a piece of the bar and popped it into my mouth, the chocolate melting instantly. "There you go." She let out a light laugh, then folded the wrapper around the rest of the bar and tucked it into her coveralls.

"Saving it for later?"

"Yeah," she said, gazing out of the narrow prison window, the night in full bloom with stars and moon appearing in the corner. "I miss it."

"Chocolate?" I asked, fishing the folder from my bag, my hands clammy, my insides fluttery with nerves.

"Life," she answered quietly. My gut reaction was to make a snarky remark, but I didn't want to spend any more time with her, or at the prison, than I had to.

"Paige," I said, raising my voice to get her attention. She turned her head slowly and let out a sigh. I opened the folder to show her copies of her encoded letters. A look of deep hurt registered on her face, a frown appearing. Immediately she picked at the ragged scar, which turned white as the rest of her complexion went red. She was furious. Those letters were never intended to be found. "We know you've been working with someone," I said. "And I'm sure you're aware that makes you an accomplice to murder—"

"Accomplice!" she yelled, the guard turning his head again. She scooted over the table, her chest pressed flat against the metal, her face inches from mine, chocolate wafting from her breath. "Look around you, *dearie*. I am never getting out of this place!" She slunk back into her seat.

"I know that. That's why I'm appealing to you." I held out one of the letters. "Who have you been communicating with?"

"Guard!" she yelled, ignoring me, voice cracking. For the first time since we'd met, her demeanor was chinked, her armor cracked. The sight of the letter hurt her, which meant we were never supposed to have seen it. She eyed the pages, visibly shaken. Whatever bond she had with the killer was far stronger than I'd accounted for. "Guard!"

The man entered the room swiftly, giving a concerned glance toward me before attending to his prisoner. Paige held up her hands, peering once more at the letters before snapping her wrists together for the guard to lace the handcuffs and chains. "Take me back to my cell. We're done here."

As quickly as she'd unwrapped and eaten the chocolate, Paige Kotes was taken away, arms and legs fettered with iron, her chains rattling and scraping against the concrete. A second guard came to my side to escort me back to the exit.

As we traversed the maze of corridors and reached the holding locker, where I handed in my temporary ID and gathered my gun, I pondered. Paige would never set foot outside this prison as a free woman again. Logically, she had nothing to gain in helping us reveal who the murderer was.

But despite that, something in me knew that she would have helped if she could. Her ego needed the attention. It wasn't that she didn't want to help; she couldn't. Paige Kotes had no idea who her murderous apprentice was.

THIRTY-FOUR

I shook the prison's damp air from my skin and hair while moths bounced hurriedly around a street lamp, a white halo shining from the glass dome and brightening the roofs of cars in the parking lot. I was glad to be outside. The meeting with Paige was a breakthrough, albeit small. The fact that she'd shut down at the sight of the letters and had no idea who it was she'd been writing to was new information, an indication that the killer was smart enough to outwit her. It also meant we were looking for someone even more dangerous than she was, a lethal killer who might already be many steps ahead of all of us. I'd gotten to know her well enough to believe that if she did know, she would have wanted to twist up the knowledge into a word puzzle and then offer it to me as a clue, making a game of it for us to play.

Her silence was a hard blow and gave me nothing to take back to the station and the team. More than that, I only had the letters with the victim's names to offer Cheryl and her investigation. Would it be enough to clear Jericho? Or would she twist the letters into a story where Jericho was Paige's secret pen pal? My gut told me it would be the latter.

All but a few cars remained in the parking lot, the evening in full swing as bells rang and whistles blew on the other side of the prison walls. I glanced at my watch, thinking it must be chow time for the inmates, my stomach growling with the thought of food. It was getting late. The day's sunlight was long gone, the moon half lit and slipping in and out of cloud cover. The summer heat kept the nights warm, the parking lot pavement still hot, the air thick. In the west there was lightning, but it was the silent kind, sheets of it flashing as though the sky was blinking.

It would be almost midnight by the time I reached the Outer Banks. Traffic sounded from the only access in and out of the town bordering the prison, and bright beady eyes lumbered, the headlights of cars and trucks driving along the two-lane road. A truck braked to slow down, and I heard a rattling as it drove away.

Paige not knowing the identity of her pen pal had become a puzzle to solve. I spun around to face the prison, the bottom of my shoe grinding against the pavement. My thoughts drifted to the process. The mail room. The solution was in the letters. We'd learned about how incoming mail was opened, inspected and scanned before being delivered to the prisoners. This would have to work for outgoing mail as well. Paige would write her encoded responses, the prison mail room would open the letters, inspect them and send them to Robert Odin's PO box address.

Which meant the workers in the prison mail room were the only ones who could have intercepted the correspondence, substituting Robert's letters with their own, hiding their identity.

I checked my phone: a single bar showed a weak signal, so I walked around my car to seek another bar. When it appeared, I texted Nichelle about the prison employees; how I wanted to review each of them, the guards as well as the office staff and anyone else with access to the mail room. When I hit send, I saw there were three missed calls from Jericho. The sight of them scared me. Like any parent, I thought first of Hannah, my throat tightening as I feared the worst. Nothing could jar my emotions as sharply as fear for my child. It was the kind of fear that came from a different place. A primal place. And it was all-consuming. But maybe the calls were about the campaign. Maybe it was good news.

"Hey, you called?" I asked, Jericho picking up on the first ring. "Is everything okay?"

"Where are you?" he asked with urgency, his voice crackling with static, the reception in the rural location terrible.

"I'm at the prison," I said reluctantly, my phone's speaker hissing. "I interviewed Paige about a lead we—"

"Come home!" he said abruptly, voice rising and turning tinny, the cellular service over-compressing the audio.

"What's happened?" I shouted, instinctively raising my voice so he could hear me.

"We're fine here," he answered. Relief settled in me with a sigh. "It's the… newspaper pic… the… guy… asked about… the… field by the goalposts."

"What about it?" I asked, trying to decipher his words, feeling silly circling in a street lamp's light like a night bug as I tried to lock in a better signal. "Do you have a name?"

"His name is Du… y Jones," Jericho answered. "… works at… prison. Come ho…"

"Babe, you're breaking up bad," I yelled, the service dropping, my phone beeping and showing no bars.

"Ma'am?" I heard beyond the bleeding edge of the lamplight, the figure merging with the dark evening.

"Who's there?" I asked warily.

"Sorry," the voice said. The prison guard who'd escorted Paige stepped into the light and approached at a saunter, his gait easy in comparison with the at-attention demeanor I'd seen inside the prison. "I didn't mean to startle you. Are you having car trouble?"

I lifted my phone. "My car is fine. It's this that's having the trouble."

He gazed into the sky, putting a hand on his hip. "Yeah, the nearest cell tower is a quarter-mile up the road." His dark hair had the faintest of gray streaks around his ears. He came closer, his step cautious. "Did you get what you wanted today?"

His question took me by surprise. "I'm sorry?"

He dipped his chin, blue-green eyes shifting back and forth without focus. "From the prisoner?"

I understood why he was asking. It was common for prison guards to ask case-related questions. At one time he had probably wanted to be a cop, but might not have been able to make it happen for one reason or another. "Sorry, but that's part of an ongoing investigation."

He lifted his chin, eyes locked with mine. "She's pretty popular," he said.

"She is," I agreed, assuming he meant with the press and other police officers wanting interviews with her over the years. In the distance, a train whistle blew, and bells clamored, sounding an alarm to give notice of a road crossing. I used it as a cue to go to my car, tucking my phone in my pocket, anxious to get on the road. "I really must be going."

The guard sidestepped with a swift motion, mirroring my feet to match my steps. The hairs on the back of my neck stood poker-straight, a sense of looming danger taking my breath. The fear was primal. He dared another step, close enough for me to see the whiskers on his chin and smell the prison on his clothes. "Did… did you ask about my letters?"

Works at prison, Jericho had said, his words a warning. My hand was on my gun in a second. But it was a second too late, the guard's lunch pail already in full swing, the metal box crashing against the side of my face and tipping me over like a top-heavy sack. I tumbled onto my side, my head bouncing off the pavement, a flash of light dismantling my sight and turning the evening black.

*

As I opened my eyes, panting heavily through my nose, I found I was on my back. A terrible pain rifled into my legs, a feeling like my feet were being amputated, a clamp on each ankle, squeezing hard enough to break bone. I tried screaming, but my lips were sealed with a thick swatch of sticky tape. My hands were tied, my wrists clasped together tightly enough to cut the blood flow into my fingers. Above me, the lighted halos of the street lamps were oblong, stretched… and moving.

Only it wasn't the lights on the move. It was me. I was being dragged, my arms behind me, the backs of my hands rubbing against the hot pavement. I kicked my legs, the pain in my feet and ankles fierce, the guard tightening his grip as he looked over his shoulder, a sickening grin appearing. When I kicked again, my heel nailed his thigh, bringing him to his knee for a moment, a hollow laugh spilling from his mouth.

"I don't want to play yet," he said, one booted foot on my thighs, pressing down with all his weight, the pressure immense. I let out a muffled scream, choking against the tape, certain he was going to break my legs if he didn't let up. "You gotta play nice until it's time."

Another train whistle sounded, then a car horn on the two-lane road, stealing his attention a moment. I reared upward, striking his groin with my clenched fists, my fingers purple and numb. He answered with a powerful swing, uniform rustling, and I felt a solid strike between my eyes. The force of it was blinding and threw me backward. I landed with a breathless thump, my skull spitting, my senses dulled, making everything vague. My nose gushed, blood streaming down the sides of my face and into my throat, which made me gag and spit.

I was groggy, my head swimming, eyelids fluttering as I slipped in and out of alertness. The guard spun me on the ground, turning me over again and again, his strength surprising me as he bound my ankles and knees like a spider wrapping its prey. In the dizzying blur, I saw the rope he was using. Green and white.

A moan slipped from my lips. It felt like I was losing who I was, losing the years of training to handle situations like this. The sound stopped him, his fingers wound tightly inside the loops of the fishing knot he was tying, and his face appeared above mine to see if I was going to fight back again, his arm cocked, his fist balled. I couldn't fight, though. His face dissolved as my arms and legs became rubber. I hated what I'd been reduced to. I'd become the killer's next victim.

THIRTY-FIVE

Paige Kotes sat on her bunk. The prison was quiet. The usual back and forth cries and yelling was absent, replaced by late-night murmurs and evening chatter mixed with singing drifting in echoes from the common area. Most of the inmates were huddled around the televisions to watch *American Idol*, a favorite of theirs.

But Paige couldn't relax. Not now. Not while Detective White had her letters. She bowed her head, sucking on a morsel of chocolate, the disappointment weighing heavier than anything she'd ever felt before. This might even be worse than Jericho's rejections. After all, the letters were sacred, they were a bond, her soul to his, the makings of a union to advance their work. How could he have been so sloppy?

Footsteps. Single, a lone guard making rounds. He'd probably come to see her undress, or to make small talk. Some of them were lonely, and she often thought they'd taken this job for the company, the unspoken benefits, the favors granted for an extra fifteen minutes in the yard. It was the sickening side of incarceration: trading yourself, using your body like currency.

"Kotes," the guard said, appearing suddenly. She recognized this one, and relaxed some. He'd never asked for a thing. But she'd caught his eye more than once as he stood at the far entrance, perched like a statue, unmoving, but all the while watching her cell. He held up a handful of forms in one hand and shackles in the other. "Get your shoes on."

"What's this about?" she asked. She peered toward the small window, the outside as black as ink. "Someone visiting? At this hour?"

He flashed a smile, raising his brow. "I'm taking you out of here."

A couple of inmates appeared behind the guard, curious about the activity. Paige gave them a courtesy nod, a gesture to tell them she was okay. The pair often invited her over to their cell. She'd always turned them down, but had stayed friendly, keeping close, needing someone who'd have her back for occasions such as this.

"What she do?" one of them asked, her voice high-pitched and cracking.

"Yeah! Nobody gonna go anywhere this time of night," the other said.

"Mind yours," the guard snapped at them. Leather creaked as he turned enough to scowl and warn, "Move on, or you'll lose privileges."

"Come on, Rose," one said to the other, hooking arms and giving Paige a wave.

When they were gone, Paige asked, "What do you mean, taking me out? Where are we going?"

The guard's face turned stony, expressionless, his patience wearing thin. He entered her cell and shoved the chains forward, gripping the paperwork. "It's a transfer, Kotes."

"A transfer?" she asked, bemused by the idea. She realized then what had happened, and anger roiled inside. "It's that detective, isn't it?" she spat. "She thinks if I'm closer to her—"

"Can't say for sure," he answered, interrupting. Reluctantly Paige slipped her shoes onto her bare feet and held her wrists out, all the while cursing beneath her breath. "I'll try to make this quick for you."

"Yeah, whatever," she answered, uninterested. "The sooner we get this over with, the better."

*

Paige said nothing during their walk through the prison. As they passed along empty corridors, a series of gates unlocked and then relocked behind them. Her feet shuffled, the chains rattled, and her anger for Detective White stewed to a boil. She dreamed of freedom, dreamed of cornering the detective for interrupting her stay, dreamed of making her pay. How dare she think she could do this? At last they reached the outer barrier, an exit door a few yards from her, a counter and glass bubble, thick Plexiglas with unarmed men and women inside it.

Paige's guard skid her paperwork beneath the Plexiglas. "What's this?" the desk clerk asked, taking hold and reading the opening pages. "A transfer? Now?"

"There's some urgency with this one," the guard answered, his fingers twined with her cuffed hands, his skin touching hers. "We're taking her east."

"It's an odd time of day," the clerk said.

"No press," Paige's guard was quick to answer. "Request came to avoid reporters and television crews."

"Right." The clerk nodded, pushing a curl of auburn hair from her face. "I suppose that's what happens when you're famous." She armed herself with a massive stamp and ink pad, the rubber bouncing off the pages with a loud thump. "ID wristband, Kotes?"

Paige held her arms in the air, the heavy chains making it an effort. The clerk beamed the reader through the window, scanning the barcode, the red LED flash finding her identification with a screechy beep and clearing her from the prison's system. "Can we get a move on?" Paige asked. "Sooner this is over, the better."

"You're clear," the clerk answered. She turned to her computer. "Who is performing the transfer with you?"

"Michaels," the guard answered. "She's bringing the wagon around."

"Good enough." The clerk stifled a yawn, the sight of it making Paige do the same. "Safe trip."

The guard turned and led the way to the doors, his pace increasing, Paige struggling to keep up, the chains bouncing along the tiled floor. When the doors opened and she stepped outside, she stopped, holding firm, the guard stopping with her, and gazed around, eyes wide. The night had stolen the sun but had given her the moon and stars. It was warm and humid but the air was still fresh, and didn't carry that morbid undertone she could smell in every sickening breath inside the prison.

"Maybe this won't be so bad."

Impatiently, the guard jerked her arms forward, and they crossed the landing dock, passing through landscaped shrubs and bushes until they reached the parking lot. "Stay with me. We're almost there."

"Almost where?" she asked, confused, searching for the other guard, the one he'd called Michaels.

He stopped, the two of them standing between street lights buzzing with electricity, the evening's darkness merging with his clothes. His eyes shone with reflections of the overhead lamps, a smile on his face. "This is safe enough."

"Safe enough for what?" she asked, tone demanding.

"Lift," he ordered, pointing to her hands. Reluctantly she did as she was told, his hold firm as he removed the handcuffs and shackles and metal fell to the asphalt. "Does that feel better?"

Paige rubbed her wrists. Excitement built within her, the taste of freedom on her tongue and the feel of it in her arms and legs. "Immensely," she answered, as understanding hit her. Now she only needed confirmation. Taking a chance, she approached the guard and held his face in her hands, his cheeks scratchy to her touch. "You're *him*."

He bowed his head and placed his hand over his heart. "That I am."

"And I'm free," she said, letting out a breath of joy, her insides welling with giddiness. She wanted to scream at the top of her lungs, but held back. She searched his face, appreciating the ruse, the fact that her apprentice had been so close to her all this time. "What do I call you?"

"If you like, you can call me Jericho?" he said with a question. She looked at him cautiously, and he quickly added, "Dusty. My name is Dusty."

"Well, Dusty, it's good to make your acquaintance in person," she said, spinning around in front of him.

"I was so happy when you responded to my letters," he said, playing along, holding her hand as she twirled. "I thought you might have ignored them, maybe thought it was some kind of a trap."

Paige stopped. "Is this a trap?" She let out a comical laugh at the thought, knowing it was real, that the man behind the letters was standing in front of her. "You know, it was a huge risk, trusting you the way I did. But you kept sending those letters." She moved closer to him, chest touching his, saying with a shrug, "I had nothing to lose, I wasn't going anywhere, so I answered them."

"You did. You answered them," he said. His face reminded her of Jericho's, the dimple in his chin and the same green and blue colors in his eyes.

Before she could ask him another question, he slammed his mouth on hers, his lips parted, teeth cutting. Paige reeled back, shoving him, the taste of blood on her tongue. "Easy. Plenty of time for that later."

"I've been waiting so long," he said. From his pocket, he produced a small red jewelry box trimmed with gold leaf. "I have a gift for you."

Intrigued, she took it from him. "For me?"

"They were all for you," he answered. "I did it for you, just like you told me."

"You did well," she said, examining his face, appreciating his level of commitment. She'd had the same devotion before. This man would do anything for her. "Let's open this together."

They eased the lid of the jewelry box open, revealing locks of hair and trinkets, something from each of the women he'd killed. "I did like you said," he said, searching her face for approval. "I did it so nobody would see what I took."

"That's the right way," she said, giving him the approval he was searching for. She turned toward the prison, noticing activity at the front gate, and told him, "Let's get a move on."

"They can't see this far," he said, his tone the same as he used inside the prison, full of confidence.

"What did I say?" she demanded.

"Yes. We'll move," he answered, bowing his head, softness returning to his voice. "I have something else for you."

"Another gift?" She smiled, appreciating his child-like efforts to win her affections. "Let's make it quick."

"Over here," he answered, approaching a car and opening the trunk. Paige joined him, careful to stay submerged in the dark. Inside the trunk, there was a woman's body, her head covered in burlap, patches of dried blood on the cloth, some of it glistening and still wet. Her arms and ankles and wrists were tightly bound, the knot exactly as Paige had instructed in her letters. And the rope was the same, a bundle of it still wrapped in torn plastic acting as a pillow of sorts beneath the woman's head.

"So this is Lisa Wells?" Paige asked. Although they hadn't discussed killing her, the woman was next on the list.

The guard reached into his pocket and drew out a piece of paper: his copy of the newspaper picture. It was creased where he'd folded and refolded it a hundred times. Ann Choplin's face was crossed out with a red X, as was Judy Granger's. Jessie Flynn's was also marked, the initials PK covering her eyes and nose and mouth. Lisa Wells' face remained clean, unmarked, leaving Paige to wonder who was in the trunk. The body shifted, giving her a start; the woman was still alive, abducted but not killed. "I brought her for you."

"You did, didn't you," Paige said, excited by the idea of her first killing outside of prison. But her puppet had gone off script, branching out, doing his own thing. The idea was unsettling. He was coming into his own, and she'd have to unleash him soon or he'd turn on her.

He held the newspaper picture closer. "Did you know that was me?"

"Who?" Paige asked.

He pointed to the figure near the goalpost. "I was every bit as good as Flynn and Ashtole. And better than that Choplin kid."

"I'm sure you were," she answered. Seeing her lack of interest, the guard carefully placed the newspaper clipping back into his pocket. Sensing that it troubled him, knowing he was in a dangerous state, she said, "You did this on your own." She touched his face again, and a smile appeared. "This is all you, and I'm very proud of you."

"I brought her to you," he said. A vicious look came to his eyes as he added, "I was going to finish. I wanted to finish. But I stopped myself." He yanked the burlap from the woman's head. Detective Casey White appeared, eyes swollen as she squinted against the sudden light.

Paige's breath was taken. Her chest tightened in shock. There was duct tape over the detective's mouth, drying splotches of blood at the corners and fresh blood dripping from her crooked nose. But what Paige saw that gave her pause was the look in the woman's eyes. It was terror, a rabid fear that death was imminent. She'd seen that look before, seen it in all her victims.

"The detective. His woman. She's yours."

"She is," Paige answered, clasping her hands together joyfully, amenable to his pleasing her but trying to mask how she really felt. "The ocean!" she exclaimed. At the sound of those words, Detective White shook and moaned, tears streaking her face, the sight of her pitiful. "Get the car started and I'll close up here."

"Yes. The ocean," he said, nodding vigorously, an expression on his face like that of a young child pleasing their parent.

When the guard had gone to the front of the vehicle, Paige leaned into the trunk, her hand on Casey's chest, her face inches from the bruising and the sweat and the tears. "Listen to me carefully. Do exactly what I say and follow my lead. I'll get us out of this." Casey's swollen eyes opened wide, a terrified dance of confusion and fear in them. "But first, understand that I have to do this." With that, Paige swung wide, the back of her hand striking the detective's face, hard enough to be heard by the guard. Casey reared up, a scream stuck behind the duct tape. The guard returned and peered into the trunk, eyes blazing with joyous satisfaction, and Paige joined him in a giddy child-like laughter.

When he turned away again, Paige winked once at Detective Casey White, and slammed the trunk.

THIRTY-SIX

Darkness. Utter and total darkness. My wrists and ankles and knees were bound tightly by the marina rope, the nylon shredding my skin, turning it raw, the sores stinging as sweat dripped from every pore. The trunk of the car was a hot box, the air thick with the smell of fear. I wasn't the first to make this trip. I suspected Pamela Levine had been in here before me, her body placed exactly where I was now, my skin touching death. Was I going to die? How long would they let me live? How long did the other victims live?

The car's tires thumped rhythmically, a steady thrum as we drove along one of the highways with expansion joints, the separations an exact distance. I head breaking waves, distant and almost unrecognizable, but it gave me some idea of what was next—a boat ride, trekking out to waters deep enough for them to watch me drown.

"You knew them all?" I heard Paige ask, her voice barely registering through the thick material between the seats and the trunk. I shuffled closer to the car's back seats, pressing my ear against that place where the seats separated and folded. "Jericho and Jessie and their friends?"

"Thick as thieves, they were," the guard answered. "We grew up together, but once they became popular, they forgot me."

"Well they won't forget you now, will they," Paige said.

"Nobody will forget me," he exclaimed, his voice deep. "Especially Flynn."

"Were there others?" Paige asked.

"What? What do you mean, others?" he asked, raising his voice. When Paige didn't answer, he added, "I kept to the newspaper clipping like you said. I didn't deviate, not once, not ever."

"Ann Choplin was first?" Paige asked. I wondered if she knew I could hear them, and whether the questions were intended to keep him talking. It gave me hope that she'd stay true to her strange promise to help me escape. But in the back of my mind, I knew not to trust her.

"Choplin? Yeah, she was first. I got her on the jogging trail. She remembered me."

"Remembered you?" Paige asked.

"Well," he started shyly, "not at first. But then she finally recognized me. She'd dropped her water bottle and that was when I dosed it."

"Drugged?"

"It was the best way," he answered. "Granger too. For Levine, I'd set up a trap, and that worked too."

"And then you took them to the ocean?"

"All of them, just like Jericho's wife. I gave them a saltwater grave like you gave Jessie Flynn."

"Very fitting," she said, sounding delighted. "And everyone thinks Jericho did it. It's ruined him."

"Just wait until we finish with this one," he said, the coldness returning to his voice. "We can do her like the others, but without the drugs."

My muscles clenched. They wanted to drown me, throw me alive into a saltwater grave. Fear seized me. I was terrified of being dropped into the ocean with my arms and legs tied together, terrified of drowning. And there was my baby, and Hannah, and Jericho, who I'd made such a mess for. I couldn't leave them now.

I rolled onto my back just as the car swerved, causing me to lean against the turn, my left arm pinned beneath me. There was nothing on the roof of the trunk, the dismal gray light showing only shadows making up odd shapes. But of course there was nothing. The guard had made the trunk secure. The child-safety release was missing, the glow-in-the dark T-shaped handle removed, leaving behind a stub. Forcing my legs straight, straining, muscle fibers tearing, I shuffled toward the rear light's enclosure, believing I might be able to knock it out from the inside. The place where the plastic housing with the wiring harness should be was gone. Brushing my forehead against the surface, I felt a piece of wood, the rear lights armored, protected, another escape idea thwarted.

The car swerved again, and I shifted to release the pressure on my arm, where the blood had stopped flowing. It had turned deathly cold, with pins and needles riddling my skin. Stretching my other arm, my fingers flexed to touch my pants, checking for my phone. My pocket was empty; he must have snatched the phone after attacking me. I could do nothing from inside the trunk. Nothing except listen.

They continued talking as we made a left turn, the breaking waves louder: we were approaching the dock. He told her more about his days in high school, about his work as a prison guard and how he'd got access to the mail room. He bragged how he'd been an admirer since her arrest, his sole goal in life to mirror her success, to please her. The conversation shifted, Paige asking specifics about his letters, her voice rising to a scold, a shout, angry that I'd discovered them. He didn't argue, but apologized, telling her he'd make up for the mistake, make it all better. Delivering me was his way to atone.

The car bumped over a ridge, causing me to bounce. The tires were now on gravel, stones spitting and pelting the underside of the vehicle, the noise covering the rest of their conversation. We braked, tires skidding to a stop, pitching me forward like a rag doll. Car doors swung open and slammed shut, and I followed the sound of their footsteps to the trunk.

The lid opened, and I saw their faces black and stony against a street lamp behind them. I squinted against the brightness and felt fingers clawing, gripping my clothes and arms, dragging me from the trunk and dropping me onto the ground.

I flopped like a fish, rolling and turning, coating my sweaty skin with gravelly dust. We were at a marina, a dock with a gas station like the ones I'd had Emanuel research. I wondered if this one was on the list. Not that it mattered now.

"Where you going?" the guard said, a whooshing sound heralding a strike to my belly, the tip of his foot stabbing my middle like a dull blade. Every bit of air escaped through my nose as vomit stirred in my gut, threatening to choke me behind the duct tape on my mouth. Concern for my baby raged in my head. Paige came to stand between me and the guard and slapped his face, his shoulders slumping at her reprimand.

"Not like that!" I heard her yell as pin lights zigged and zagged in front of me, the suffocating blow excruciating, turning every breath painful. "So much to learn."

"Teach me," he said, trying to appeal to her ego. "Show me."

I curled into a tight ball and shut my eyes, my instincts turning primal, taking over, all training as a cop forfeited to my abysmal state. My baby's life was in danger. My own life was in danger. I began to black out again, any hope of escape, of being saved, dangling precariously from the words of a serial killer.

THIRTY-SEVEN

When I came to, eyes drifting and head throbbing, I was on a boat, lying on the lower deck near the rear, surrounded by a wraparound couch. The guard stood with Paige at the boat's wheel. We were cutting through the vaulting waves at high speed, sea spray raining on me, the watery chill making me alert. My face hurt and felt heavy like a bowling ball, lungs aching as I breathed through my mouth, my nose broken, the insides clogged and impossibly painful. Pouches swelled beneath my eyes in a way I could see and feel with every heartbeat.

But it wasn't the damage to my face that frightened me. It was thoughts of my baby. The guard had struck my middle with the tip of his boot, knocking the air out of me, an endless cramp circling my middle. I was terrified he'd done more than crack a rib. Paige must have smelled the newly intense fear on me; she turned as terror rose into my throat and put her finger to her lips again, telling me to stay quiet.

I searched around the boat. It was a bowrider cabin cruiser, high-end and a popular style in the Outer Banks. It wasn't new, but it wasn't old either, and it had been kept pristine, plush and spotless, the instrument panel's electronics modern. Even in the dark and with the moon covered by clouds, the polished metal gleamed, and the canvas seating was unstained and bright. The guard had made certain not to leave behind a single piece of evidence after he'd brought his victims out into the ocean and thrown them overboard.

Was that my fate too? I lifted my head as far as I could manage, looking at the display panel by the wheel. The console showed our route, and I could just make out the lines of previous runs out to sea. I knew each path would be dated and time-stamped. The GPS unit was a high-definition one that would allow steering at night. The guard was following a previously plotted path, blindly racing to the same destination coordinates as before.

"What are you looking at?" Paige asked sharply, raising her voice over the roaring motors, giving me a subtle wink. The sea breeze lifted her hair, whipping it around her head as she pawed at the scar on her face, her expression changing as the bow struck the choppy surface. I said nothing and lowered my head, the hard ride pummeling my insides. I was unsure about trusting her. Every warning I'd been given about Paige Kotes came alive in me, invading my thoughts. But it was Jericho's words I heard loudest. He had begged me to stay away from her.

"Well?"

The guard caught Paige's tone and looked in my direction, his focus shifting from my ankles to my knees, checking the rope and the knots he'd made. "You better check her wrists," he said, unable to see my hands pinned behind my back.

"Aye, aye, Captain!" Paige said, giving a sarcastic salute. "Checking ties, sir!"

She knelt in front of me, her eyes never leaving mine, her grin fixed as though permanent like her scars. "Please?" I begged when she was close enough to hear me. She brushed her body against mine, holding me as the boat lurched.

"Bumpy ride," she quipped, holding us in place. She gave the guard a look, saying softly, "He's not worthy."

"You okay?" the guard asked.

"We're fine!" Paige yelled. She held up her palm and revealed a blade beneath her sleeve. It was a prison shiv. Her brow rose and she smiled again. "I never leave home without it."

"We're almost there," the guard shouted.

Before I could say anything else, Paige went to work cutting the rope. The boat swung hard to the left, our weight shifting, and her hand slipped, the edge of the blade riding the inside of my arm and slicing it open. "It's okay," she reassured me, sounding apologetic.

The pain faded fast but my fingers went instantly cold as blood covered my wrists. She was silent and my heart dipped. The boat came to a stop, the motors sputtering, seawater rushing against the transom in a cloud of burnt fuel. Paige brought her face close to mine. "You have to finish this."

"What's wrong?" the guard asked, raising his voice.

"Oh sweetie," she said, keeping his attention on her and standing between us. "Paranoia looks terrible on you."

My heart beat harder than ever, walloping uncontrollably against my chest, pressing against my temples. The fingers of my right hand were numb, almost lifeless, Paige's accidental cut clearly deeper than she'd let on, but my left hand was fine. I found her prison shiv embedded in the rope's knot and continued to saw with the makeshift blade, vibrations driving into my wounded arm, my mind scattered with thoughts of my baby, of Jericho, of Hannah, and of how it was that Paige could have made a weapon in prison. The license plates, I realized, attempting to focus my mind as Paige kept the guard busy.

"It's time," I heard him say, his words fierce, turning my veins to ice. Paige put up an argument, buying time. Their voices intensified. "I said it's time!"

"I know, baby," Paige said, humoring him. "Let me do her the way I want to do her."

"You mean you want to kill her like you did Jericho's wife?"

"Will you help me?" she asked, running her hand over his shoulder.

"Yes! Yes, anything for you," he said, playing into her hands, his face bashful.

I braced to fight, one hand coming free. Life began to return to my other hand. I'd need it to fight. I tightened my fingers around the shiv, ready to drive it into the guard's neck at the first opportunity, his death being the only choice if I was going to live.

The two of them approached me. I sensed it wasn't time to move yet and kept my arms behind my back as though I was still tied up. In the dark, he didn't see my spilled blood on the deck. Paige gave instructions, telling him to hoist me up by the arms while she lifted me by my knees. She flashed me a brief look, and I waited for her cue. And then I was in the air like before, their footing awkward as the ocean swells lifted and dropped the boat.

"Get her near the edge," Paige instructed. "When I say the word, you drop her head-first into the water while I keep hold of her legs."

"She won't last a minute."

"Well, let's hope she lasts a little longer than that," she laughed.

They'd hold me just beneath the water's surface the way Paige had done to Jericho's wife. It was a horrible way to die. I clutched the shiv and ran my thumb over it, finding the sharper edge. A gull swooped overhead, telling me we weren't too far from land, the moon and stars hovering behind thin clouds, the eastern sky already warming with a touch of orange and red.

When we reached the side of the boat, the guard lowered me, the small of my back digging into a cleat as I was held upside down. He manhandled me like a sack, his arms thick, his grip tight. I peered up; his eyes were fixed on Paige. When I followed his focus, I saw her left arm beneath my knees, her right hand untying the ropes around my ankles. "Leave it!" he demanded.

"Trust me," she said, raising a finger to her lips as she'd done with me. A perplexed look appeared on his face. Paige locked eyes with me, my blood turning cold at the sight. For a split second, I thought she'd broken her word, that she'd been lying about helping me, that she'd been enjoying giving me one last hope. But instead she said, "Detective, now would be a good time."

Without hesitation, I gripped the cleat with every ounce of strength I had. With my feet unbound, I had the leverage I needed, and swung my arm like a baseball bat, as fast and as hard as I could. The point of the shiv entered the guard's shoulder, missing his neck but driving deep into his skin, catching him blindly and unawares. He let go of me instantly, a sour look of disappointment on his grimacing face.

"Wait! What?" he yelled.

I kept hold of the shiv, the boat tipping while I jerked him forward, his falling off-balance toward the water. The shiv came free, his muscled arms pinwheeling wildly. He grabbed hold of Paige's prison coveralls to save himself. She let out a scream as the two of them fell overboard, his foot striking the boat's instrument panel, the throttle bumping, the boat jumping into gear. I got to my feet as a swell swallowed the guard whole, Paige screaming, her hands clawing the side of the boat.

"Hold on!" I yelled, taking hold of her arm. Her body was plastered against the boat, the water's chop threatening to consume her, pummeling us both. The guard's hand appeared from the ocean, clutching at Paige, the sheer size of him a threat.

"Kill him!" she screamed, terror on her face, his weight threatening to drag her under. "Casey! You have to kill him!"

The boat turned to starboard, our weight pitted to one side and causing a steep lean. The speed was slow, but the boat was steering on its own while I hung onto Paige with my good hand, the guard dragging close behind. In the low light, I saw a dark green buoy marker; the bow grazed it, the shallow impact taking us into a boating channel, at the mercy of any oncoming ship traffic. A distant horn wailed with a warning call, a spotlight shining briefly in the darkness as the boat continued to circle.

I raised the shiv, readied my nerves, poising it above to take the guard's life so that I could save Paige's. Paige grabbed hold of a cleat, her fingers bending to the point of breaking, the guard stealing most of her strength as he struggled to keep hold. The rough waters were becoming too much, and his face dipped below the surface, his mouth horribly open, sucking in seawater. Paige seized the moment and used her elbow, hammering it against his head and face in a vicious volley, shouting as he gagged and gulped and fought for his life. When the struggle had weakened him, she kicked him loose.

I followed his descent, running toward the rear of the boat, watching his head bobbing in and out of the water, his voice crying out to Paige, asking why. He yelled for her once more before being sucked beneath the boat, where I felt him bounce against the hull and then tangle briefly with the twin motors, the blades running through him with enough force to end his life.

The moment of relief was short-lived as I ran to rescue the woman who'd just saved my life.

"I've got you," I shouted, straining to pull her aboard. The horn blared again, the oncoming ship approaching.

Paige hoisted herself up, one arm flailing until she secured it over the side, the other hand still holding onto the cleat. Then she stopped.

"What's the matter?" I asked, peering down at her.

"Did you ever hear the story of the scorpion and the frog?"

"What?" I gasped, my strength failing, blood pumping from my forearm, turning my hand into a red sleeve. "What story?"

As the ocean swells crashed around us and the oncoming ship lit up the inky blackness, Paige's expression turned frightening. "A scorpion asked a frog if he would carry her across a swollen creek. The frog objected, telling her she'd surely sting him. The scorpion replied that she'd do no such thing since if she did, they would both drown."

"Shut up and climb!" I screamed at her, uninterested in her story and desperate to get out of the shipping channel.

"Let me finish!" she shouted, her eyes blazing. "So the frog let the scorpion climb onto his back and he carried her to the other side of the swollen creek. But before they got there, the scorpion stung the frog. As the poison took hold of his body, the frog asked, 'Why would you do that? Now we'll both drown.' With a look of regret, the scorpion replied, 'Because it's in my nature.'"

Merciless terror came to me then as I understood what she intended to do. She'd said the guard wasn't worthy. What she meant was that he wasn't worthy to kill me. I glanced at my arm, the bloody sleeve turning black in the moonlight. "You cut me on purpose?"

Paige lunged upward as though propelled by a mermaid's tail. Suddenly her hands were around my neck, jerking me down, slamming us both against the side of the boat, her lips close to my ear. "I tried to do good. I wanted to do good. But like the scorpion, murder is in my nature."

My muscles strained, fighting her as she squeezed and stifled my breath. The oncoming ship blasted its horn once more, the beaming flash of its lights turning Paige's skin a pearly white as the bowrider veered around into another circle. Her laughter was maniacal as stars appeared in my eyes, sharp, colorful rays dancing an interlude with black fog.

Death was coming. I raised my hand in desperation and struck out, driving the shiv into Paige's head, giving her a bloody teardrop to match her scar. Her emerald-green eyes were filled with rage and shock, her grip loosening at once. The surprise gave me a chance to strike again, her arms battling me defensively, absorbing my onslaught, opening new wounds as I struck her repeatedly. I was screaming, crying, driven by terror and a gruesome darkness I didn't know I possessed. Then her fist struck me square in the face, turning the world dull in an instant and sending me backward to fall flat onto the deck.

The bowrider rose and fell with a massive swell, the oncoming ship towering over us. Paige's hands appeared over the side, her arms next, followed by her face and shoulders. She cocked her head, wiping the blood from her cheek, coming for me to finish what she'd started.

The ship struck. The sound was enormous, the metal giant barreling into the bowrider, sending us end over end in a single motion. The front of the boat splintered, the bow exploding into confetti and chunks of fiberglass, throwing debris into the air along with our bodies, tossing us into the sea like ragdolls.

I slammed into the freezing water, the force driving me below the surface, into the dark. I heard the ship's enormous propellers thumping mechanically, the water pulsing, the feel of it telling me I was still alive. When I surfaced, my head was swamped by a sea of foam as the ship passed, taking much of the bowrider with it, sucked beneath the hull with metal screeching on metal. Shivering desperately, I waited to hear alarms from the ship and see sailors in the wheelhouse and on the decks. A spotlight flicked on, and then a second and a third, the beaming lights circling and swaying, darting from one side to the other in search of survivors.

"Over here!" I screamed, my voice hoarse from Paige's crushing hands. "Please!"

Paige was in the water with me, but I'd lost her when we were struck. I tugged on the last of the marine rope; the guard had tied my knees together using the same knot he'd used on his other victims, but I'd learned it well enough to untie it in the dark. Another splash, debris floating next to me. I snagged a long piece of the bowrider's siding, the foamy insides jutting from beneath the torn fiberglass. With my arm draped over the remains, I waved again, but the ship was moving away, leaving me behind. *Too big to stop*, I told myself. But they knew they'd struck something, they had the coordinates, and they'd surely radio it in and send help.

The ship continued west, its port and bow lights becoming indistinguishable from the stars edging the horizon. In the east, a glimpse of sunlight was bending around the skyline, the first crisp signs of the new day. I wouldn't be in the water long. If the calls were made, the Marine Patrol would find me, taking into account the time and the currents to calculate my position.

Salt touched my lips and tongue. Blood flowed from my aching forearm, weakening me. Had I lost too much already? Was my heart strong enough for two? Could the sharks smell it in the water? I struggled to tear the bottom of my shirt free and tied a makeshift tourniquet, stopping the flow for now. I was terrified of sharks, and now that stupid movie theme was on repeat in my head. Jericho often teased me about it, assuring me there'd been no shark attacks in these parts for as long as he could remember. A desperate hysterical laugh escaped my mouth amidst a cry, the adrenaline taking its toll. I fell silent then, the darkness and the quiet unnervingly eerie. It wasn't just the sharks that left me worried. I didn't know if I was alone. I wondered if Paige was near, if she was hunting me, if she was staying true to her nature like the scorpion. With stabbing fear, I believed she was.

THIRTY-EIGHT

Paige never surfaced. The sharks never came either. I stayed conscious long enough to see the sunrise, its magnificence unencumbered by clouds, the sky free of blemishes, the horizon's colors like a painter's fresh palette. I believed it would be the last sunrise I'd ever set eyes on.

I was colder than I'd ever thought possible: a bone-deep cold that numbed me. And I'd become pale. Not just pale, but I lacked all color, the blood loss heavier than I'd first thought. Even the color beneath my fingernails had faded, disappearing like the moon had, its round shape turning the color of denim against the dusky sky until I couldn't find it anymore. The wound on my arm never closed enough to stop the bleeding, the tourniquet I'd made soaked with seawater and proving ineffectual.

I had also become incredibly weak and sleepy and had no idea how far I'd drifted. There were no helicopters looking for me. There were no boats circling in search of me. And there was no land to be seen anywhere around me. A seagull or sandpiper, any bird would have been a hopeful sight. But there was nothing.

The ocean swells and the current had swept the remains of the bowrider far from the shipping channel we'd slipped into. While the shattered section of boat I'd hung onto wouldn't sink, it wasn't big enough to carry me anywhere, leaving me to bob up and down in the water while straining to hang onto it. But I wasn't going to be able to keep hold for much longer.

As I drifted and the sun rose, the ocean waters became clear. Looking down, I could make out my shoes, my pants and shirt loose, swaying in the current, the depths beneath me a deep blue that went on forever. With the beauty and the tranquility there came a sinister truth, a heartbreaking reality. There was blood below my waist, near my pants, a wispy trail of it I hoped desperately had come from the wound on my arm. But it hadn't. I tried not to cry as my mind raced in tortured slow motion, filling me with a cold understanding of what was happening inside my body. The blood was the truth, and it was coming to light like the day to tell me we were both dying.

I never saw the search helicopter or heard the boats. The next thing I saw was Jericho's face, wearing an expression of utter terror. He was dressed in his Marine Patrol uniform, and it dreamily crossed my mind that it was like he'd never run for mayor, like he'd always been with the Marine Patrol. For a moment I wished all of it had been a dream, the kind that ended with me plummeting to earth and waking with a jerking start just before my heart gave out. Only this wasn't a dream and I feared I wasn't going to be able to wake up.

"The guard," I said in a rasp, voice too dry to speak.

"Drink," Jericho said, holding me in his arms while the helicopter blades thumped the air, the whoosh-clop-whoosh-clop sounding a lot like our baby's heartbeat. "I know all about him."

"Prison guard—"

"His name is Dusty Jones," Jericho said, his blue-green eyes wet, his lips trembling. He peered over his shoulder. "Move faster!"

"I'm so cold," I said, coughing on the water and shivering.

"We're not far," he told me, pulling me closer and brushing his fingers though my hair.

At my feet, in the rear of the rescue boat, I saw a body bag, a manilla tag on the zipper, the paper and its writing sleeved in plastic. "Who is that?"

"We found Dusty's body," he said.

"Paige—" I tried to say, as my heartbeat skipped and slowed with a strange sensation.

He shook his head. "There was no sign of her."

"She did this," I said, motioning to my arm. The gauze wrapping was saturated, and Jericho tightened a new tourniquet around it. Excruciating pain fired into my shoulder, telling me I was still alive.

"Faster!" he yelled. "Radio the hospital, there's been massive blood loss."

"Our baby," I said with an endless ache. I laid my hand on his chest, feeling his heart beating under my palm, and braced him as though I could possibly soften the pain. "I'm bleeding."

He put his lips to my cheek, his body shaking with a sob. "I know," he whispered.

Like the moon, Jericho's face began to fade, my body turning numb as I slipped away, unable to stay with him. I felt dead from head to toe, the patrol boat motors and Jericho's voice bouncing distantly, the rescue helicopter overhead, my sense of the boat rocketing over the ocean becoming a dream.

Hospital smells filled my nostrils and lights raced back and forth across my eyes. I felt safe, Jericho weaving his fingers with mine, a blanket warming me, a pinprick shooting hot fluids into my veins. I was too weak to open my eyes but heard the talk of an emergency blood transfusion. I was slipping in and out of consciousness, but I managed to ask about my baby. There was no answer. From the commotion, the heart monitor and the heavy clap of shoes against the floor, it was clear I was in trouble.

"Casey," a doctor shouted near my ear. "Casey, can you tell us your blood type."

"I'm O negative," I mumbled.

The doctors and nurses went quiet then, Jericho shifting uneasily. "What? What's wrong?" he asked. Through my confusion, he sounded very far away.

"We don't have any," I heard a nurse answer.

"I don't follow. What do you mean, you don't have any?" I imagined his face draining. His voice was cold and angry. "I'm AB positive. Can you use it?"

"You can donate blood," a nurse said politely. "But even if it was a match, we couldn't transfuse it directly."

I felt someone brush my arm gently. "Everyone can receive O negative. That's why we use it as part of our major hemorrhage protocol. We would normally be stocked, but I'm afraid we had a major trauma earlier and used every unit."

Through the confusion and fear, a thought crystallized. "My daughter," I said, Hannah's blood type was the same as mine. The room grew dim and my eyelids heavy. "My—" I was too woozy to speak. Part of me longed to pass out again.

"Hold on, Casey," Jericho begged, his voice thick with tears. I hated that he worried so.

"It's okay," I managed to say. "Nothing hurts anymore."

It was the Rh factor. While I had a blood type of O, I was also Rh negative, which meant I could give blood to everyone but could only accept it from another O negative person. They'd find someone. I was sure of it. There was Hannah, and even my ex-husband, who was also the same type, a joke we used to share about being bags of reserve blood for one another if it was ever needed. The emergency room dimmed, the voices went in and out of my hearing, a hand touching mine became no more. I tried holding on, tried to listen to what they were saying, but I couldn't.

"Paige!" I tried to scream, my throat burning as a whisper spilled on a gush of air. A man was next to me, his face blank, clutching my arm firmly. I tried raising my hands, but they were enormously heavy. I righted myself with a start, the needles beneath my skin holding me back and rifling pain up and down my arms. I screamed again. "Dusty! Paige!"

"Casey," the man said as a woman wearing paisley scrubs rushed to my side. "Do you know where you are?"

"She's delirious," the woman said, the two of them holding me down. I couldn't fight, and a shrill cry escaped my lungs. It was Paige and Dusty, their fingers shiny like sharp blades, preparing me, getting me ready so they could finish what they'd started.

"Casey?" Jericho's face came into focus, and the fog in my head lifted.

"Jericho?" I whispered. "Jericho, it was the guard, his name was Dusty. And Paige—"

"Yes, I know," he said, his cheeks wet, his touch soft as he tenderly held my hand. "Do you remember talking to me?" I shook my head as the nurse tended to a bag of medicine. "The boat?"

"The boat," I said, trying to raise my voice but failing. I drew a rattly breath. "They took me. I think they took me like they took the other women… and they tried to kill—"

"I know," Jericho said again, massaging my wrists gently, skin burned raw by the ropes.

"Dusty targeted those women," I said, the case and his motives clearer in my head. His motives, and Paige's. "He did it with Paige's help, with her direction."

"We know," he said. "Everyone knows now."

"Paige wanted it to look like you killed them," I said, piecing together memories from their conversations, voices muffled by the trunk. "And the guard, he'd been communicating with her, exchanging letters, doing as she told him."

"Your team searched her cell," Jericho said, his voice weepy and tired. "They discovered the newspaper picture, and pictures of us, along with her journal. It's all there."

"He's dead," I said, a vague image circling my mind, a helicopter overhead, the floor of the patrol boat with a body bag. "He did this."

"I remember him now, from high school," Jericho said with sad understanding. "If only he'd never met Paige—"

There was guilt in his voice. "This wasn't you," I said, interrupting.

"But maybe if we'd been nicer, if we'd let him in our group, he would have been different."

I thought about his words, my head spinning, my mind slipping again. "There wasn't any changing him. If he hadn't found Paige, he would have found someone else." I winced and let out a groan when the nurse pinched my arm, replacing a needle I'd accidentally pried free. "Jericho, he was a murderer. He didn't become one. He already was one."

"I'm sorry," Jericho said, his words becoming distant as my eyelids grew heavy again. "Nurse!"

THIRTY-NINE

It was daybreak when I woke again, a bag of blood on the pole next to my bed and a needle buried in my arm. I felt like I'd been split into a thousand pieces and then haphazardly sewn back together. Paige and Dusty were gone. The talk with Jericho was fresh on my mind. The nightmare was over.

The outside was bright with sunlight as a nurse opened the curtains. Her face was familiar; I'd come across her before. But this time I was the patient. She was older, dark skin, thinning gray hair with a tinge of blue. She came to the side of the bed, checking the tubes, the skin on her hands shiny, her nail polish bright like gold. I was beside myself with worry and took hold of her fingers.

She looked at me with a start. "Look who just woke up."

"My baby?" I asked. I winced as I tried to swallow.

"You'll be sore for a while," she said.

I went to squeeze her fingers but couldn't. I asked again, needing confirmation. "What happened to my baby?"

She raised my bed, her eyes never quite meeting mine, and put a straw in my mouth. "Fluids and rest."

"Casey?" Jericho asked from the doorway, coming to the bed and taking my hand. "We thought we might lose you there for a while."

Hannah appeared at the door too, and I was shocked to see Ronald, her father, next to her. He put on a smile, waving.

Jericho's eyes were red-rimmed, his cheeks sunken and riddled with stubble. What felt like hours, must have been much longer.

He'd changed out of his Marine Patrol uniform. I spat out my straw and looked at him. I didn't have to ask again. He shook his head sharply, his palm on the side of my face, telling me what I already knew. I needed to cry, and I was certain it would come, but not yet.

"You've been here a few days," he said, wiping his eyes. "You've had a lot of visitors."

I managed a smile, and reached out my hand to Hannah. She took it gently. Ronald followed her, standing by the bed. "It's good to see you awake," he said.

"They found blood?" I asked, the nurse's voice in my head. "Were you guys my personal blood bags?"

"I couldn't give directly, but I donated a pint to the blood transfusion service," Ronald said.

"They shipped blood in from another hospital," Hannah said. "I donated too," she continued, patting my hand, a look of disappointment and pain coming to her face. "And then… I got an email from them, which included a temporary blood donor card."

"Can this wait?" Jericho asked sharply.

"What happened?" I asked, finding strength. They exchanged looks, sharing uncomfortable news and keeping it from me. "Tell me."

"It's my blood type," Hannah said, shoving her bangs from her face. "It's B positive."

"B positive?" I shook my head. With that blood type, it would be impossible for her to be my daughter.

I felt every bruise on my face pulse. I pushed on my hands, trying to sit up, tears bridging my swollen eyes and setting up a sting in my broken nose. "Uh-uh. That's not possible."

"Casey," Jericho said, taking my hand, helping me. "We can talk about this later."

"It's not possible!" I said, raising my voice.

Hannah burst into tears, her hands shaking. "I have to go," she said, turning sharply, her fingers slipping from mine, before running from the room.

"I'm sorry," Ronald said, rubbing his arm. "I wish things had been different."

"They're wrong!" I insisted, anger rising, my voice grating against the rawness in my throat. "Wrong!"

Ronald held out a folded piece of paper. I knew what it was and refused to take it. He swallowed dryly and placed it on my bed. "I got the DNA test result yesterday. It confirms what the blood test showed."

"Leave!" I demanded, snatching the paper, crumpling it in my fist. I glared at Ronald and then Jericho, my anger swarming and misguided. I was apt to strike at anyone close to me. "Please! I need to be alone."

"Casey—" Jericho began, trying to take my hand.

"Now!" I shouted, a cry wavering. "Please. I need a few minutes alone."

The men left, Jericho's steps faltering at the doorway before he exited the room. The gray-blue-haired nurse returned with a tray of food. I took the coffee she offered, cupping it in my hands, the tears that wanted to come staved off by brewing rage. My hands trembled with the coffee's bitter taste, my insides becoming bitter too, which was the beginning of the end for most cops.

I couldn't speak or hear or see anything. It was as if a black hole had formed around my hospital bed and sucked me into it. The world had disappeared, leaving me alone to dwell on what was gone. I'd lost the case, the killer finding me instead of the other way around. Jericho stood to lose everything, his political career gone, his house mortgaged twice over. I bit my lip, clenching with the pain. I'd lost Jericho's baby, my baby, and now I'd lost Hannah too.

FORTY

Her name was Shannon Grace. She had been Hannah's age when she was kidnapped from her home. She had the same light brown, summer-red hair color as me and my daughter. And she also had the dimples and bright baby-blue eyes of Hannah's father. The two girls could have been cousins, sisters even.

Shannon's mother was inside their house when her daughter was taken. Her father was doing yard work in the rear, stacking a cord of wood for their stove. They lived on the mainland, in North Carolina, fifty miles west of the kidnapper's home. According to the police report, Shannon was playing alone, jumping in and out of piled leaves her father had raked for her, the first autumn winds putting a sway into the trees and scattering their browned leaves for the change in the season.

The parents reported that they'd heard a car door open and close but hadn't given it any thought. When they went to check, Shannon was gone. And like me, Doug and Lisa Grace never gave up searching.

Tracy entered my hospital room, carrying Shannon's case file, the edges worn from the years of review and even more years of sitting in a drawer, fingers brushing over it time and time again. There was a new addition for us to place in the folder so we could close the old case—a sheet of fingerprints Tracy had collected with Nichelle's help, the results a positive match to Shannon Grace.

"I guess that settles it," I said, taking the sheet from her, my arm nearly as white as the hospital bed's linen. Tracy had noticed, her face grave with concern when she saw me. "I'm still anemic, and it's going to be a while."

"Are you feeling any better?" she asked, offering an encouraging smile, a dimple warming me.

"All things considered? Some, I guess," I said, deciding not to sugar-coat my response.

"I'm sorry," Tracy said, her gaze falling to the floor.

"Don't be," I warned, patting the bed, encouraging her to sit. Tracy took to the end, the mattress sagging. She looked glum, clearly still feeling responsible for Jericho's predicament. "Tracy, you were doing good detective work and came up with a credible theory. Just because we come up with a lead doesn't guarantee it's the right lead."

Her blue eyes were wet, her cheeks flushed. "I'm just sorry," she repeated. She put her hand on my leg. "And I'm really sorry for everything that's happened to you."

"We're not going to win every case," I said, the words another of the hard truths we had to learn if we wanted to survive in this job.

"Am I interrupting?" Jericho asked from the doorway.

I waved him in. "Tracy, could you give us a minute?"

"Mr. Flynn," Tracy said, standing, tears on her cheeks. "Mr. Flynn, I had no idea that paper—" She crumpled, putting her face in her hands, unable to finish.

I held my breath, feeling for her, unsure how Jericho was going to react. The ramifications of her paper had changed his life, changed his future, and the consequences might still be coming if he couldn't pay down on his home's double mortgage.

Jericho paused, his expression showing conflict. I was sure he wanted to scream and shout, but that wasn't his style. Instead, he braced Tracy's arms. "Tracy, that woman over there," he began. Tracy uncovered her face and looked to me and then back to Jericho. "She's the best teacher you'll ever have. Promise me that from now on you'll work closely with her."

"Uh-huh, I will," Tracy answered, a sob rattling her breath. "Thank you." She was gone in a flash, her sneakers chirping against the hospital floor as she turned to leave.

Later that day, I faced the girl I'd thought was my daughter. She entered my hospital room cautiously, mindful of my health, uncertain if I was asleep. I wasn't, of course. I didn't think I'd ever want to sleep again. When she saw I was awake, I urged her to my bedside, Jericho on my other side. The news I was about to deliver was like another small dagger in my heart, a confirmation that my daughter was still out there somewhere, still missing from my life. But for the young woman I'd believed to be Hannah, the truth about her identity would be amazing news. And it was right that I should be the one to tell her.

"Hannah, do you remember getting fingerprinted when you were arrested?" I asked her, softening my words, wishing I didn't have to bring up a painful time from her past, before I'd found her.

"I never meant for that fire to get out of control," she answered, shaking her head.

"I know you didn't," I replied. "This is about the juvenile detention center."

"What about it?" she asked, face emptied by the shame of that time.

I smiled at her, a painful smile that tore my heart. "About a year after my daughter's disappearance, another girl went missing."

"Me?" she asked, her voice breaking. "Was it me?"

I nodded, staving off the cry that had stolen my words.

"What… what's my name?" she asked, swiping at her tears.

My chest cramped as I held out my hands for her to take, squeezing her fingers as I told her, "Your name is Shannon Grace."

"Shannon Grace," she mouthed.

"And your parents…" I started to say, but couldn't finish.

Jericho put his hand on my shoulder, continuing. "Your parents are very eager to see you."

"They are?" she asked, eyes darting back and forth nervously.

He nodded. "They still live in the same house, an hour's drive from here,"

"I don't think I'm ready," she said, a tear racing down her cheek.

I gently wiped it away. "You're ready," I told her.

"What if…" she hesitated, "what if I just stayed with you guys? Like we planned?"

I cupped my mouth, my heart breaking into a million pieces.

"You'll always be welcome with us," Jericho answered for me. "But you should go and meet them."

"They'd love that," I said, trying to encourage her.

"Okay. I guess I could try." Her face cleared, and she nodded. "I could see them."

I fought the weakness, pushing myself to take hold of her in a hug, the embrace quick. I could feel her curiosity pulling her away from me already, my time to say goodbye cut short.

Jericho checked his phone and read a text message. "They're downstairs in the lobby, waiting for you."

Shannon's face went white as she pawed at her hair, and then the neck tattoo. I took her hands again. "You are whoever you want to be," I told her fiercely. "They are enormously lucky to have you." Her eyes settled on mine a moment. "Just like I was," I added.

She hugged me hard then, her body shuddering a cry. "I love you," she said, before letting me go.

"Go on," I said, keeping a smile pasted on my face. "They've been waiting a long time."

"I'll take her," Jericho said. He had been the one to contact the Grace family and coordinate the reunion.

I held a grim smile, trying to show I was happy for the girl I'd thought was my daughter, but inside I was crumbling. I waited till they'd left the room, then held a pillow over my face and screamed until I almost blacked out.

FORTY-ONE

I'd become a vampire, or maybe it was a zombie. I wasn't much into horror films or creepy television shows, but I'd seen my share to recognize the look. I was anemic, and would remain so until my body's blood count caught up, producing enough of the stuff to return the color to my face and the bounce to my hair. It was the strength in my legs and arms I needed, the weakness debilitating. I'd also stopped going outside during the day, taking the recovery slow, spending all my time in my apartment, a steady flow of visitors bringing me enough food to last a year.

After everything that had happened, I'd wanted time alone in my own place. The move in with Jericho would have to wait. No matter how much he wanted to know, I couldn't give him an exact reason why I needed to stay in my apartment. Hugely disappointed and hurt, he'd argued that I was putting my life on hold. I assured him that I wasn't. But as I mulled it over, I decided he might be right. After all, life had been interrupted and *had* put everything on hold. It had also triggered an old itch and awakened an incessant need to investigate my daughter's kidnapping. I loved Jericho with everything that I was, but maybe deep inside, I knew I couldn't reopen the search for my daughter while I was living with him.

I'd taken to sleeping during the day and staying awake at night to avoid the constant onslaught of reporters, the television shows and radio broadcasts and online articles filled with stories about Hannah and Shannon. The Graces held a press conference immediately following their reunion with their daughter, the story going national in an instant. I could hardly bring myself to watch it, but made myself do so with Jericho's help, the two of us happy for the Graces but with a punishing sadness weighing on us. Seeing a kidnapped child reunited with their parents was one of the reasons I was still a cop. It was just so different when you'd once believed the child was yours.

During my recovery, Nichelle was in my apartment several nights a week. I'd supplied the funds for her to build me a high-end computer system that even she had become jealous of, and we turned my empty dining room into a home office, which included four enormous screens to help with my research.

In my absence from the station, Cheryl was given the role of lead detective. Emanuel and Nichelle were reassigned to work with her, though they were told it was only temporary. I shook my head when I heard that, knowing all about how permanent the state of temporary actually was. I'd been temporary too, and now I was on medical leave and had lost my team to the woman who'd questioned Jericho about the murder of his wife.

They were a good team, loyal too, sharing the progress of a new murder case with me, Cheryl's inexperience in the lead role showing like the stumblings of a newborn fawn. I encouraged the team to help her, telling them that nobody was perfect their first time. I was also envious, but I could never have kept up, not in my current state.

Tracy was the one team member not to make the cut. Cheryl never invited her on the team. She was still working as a crime-scene tech, but her internship as an investigator was on hold until I was back in the swing of things. She still had school to finish before landing a permanent position. For now, she'd become my partner, offering to help with my search for what had really happened to my daughter all those years ago.

*

Today I felt strong enough to take the first step, leaving my apartment just after sunset, the barrage of reporters camping outside parting for me, their questions about Hannah and Shannon Grace going unanswered. Nichelle had warned how hot the topic still was, the online true-crime blogs and podcasts blowing up with the story. Theories involved everything from Mafia retaliation out of Philadelphia to alien abduction.

I said nothing as the reporters followed Tracy and me to my car. And I said nothing when they followed us to the prison where Tommy Fitzgerald was being held. His wife Sheila hadn't spoken a word since the day of their arrest for kidnapping Hannah, leading me to work with Tommy alone. I'd stowed my gun at the station, leaving it there until I was back to full activity, but I'd been allowed to keep my badge, making this an official inquiry. The district attorney was interested in my findings as well; now that there were two kidnapped girls, there would be further charges to file. Was it possible that there were more than two? Selfishly, I only wanted to know what had happened to my daughter.

Tracy followed me into the prison, the hall narrow, the chairs and tables reminding me of a police station. This place was colder than the women's prison where I'd visited Paige. Not just in the sense of temperature; the colors and the feel and the noise were dark and melancholy like a dungeon. There was an ever-present sense of being amongst the walking dead. Inmates as pale as me, wearing drab blue overalls, paraded past us. One of the younger prisoners side-eyed Tracy and made a cooing noise, the sound raising the hairs on the back of my neck, making me shift protectively in front of her as the guard in charge rapped a club against the bars. I could see Tracy breathing heavily, jumpy at the constant clamor.

We made our way to the interview room, a scatter of dust floating in the overhead lights, the air stiff with a thick smell of damp stone, like concrete after a rainstorm. A metal table stood in the center of the room, surrounded by seats fixed to the floor. It was similar to Paige's interview room, only this room lacked any windows. In fact, I didn't think I'd seen a single window since we'd entered the prison.

A pair of guards brought Tommy Fitzgerald into the room, his shape rounder, doughier since I'd seen him last, his diet unscathed by the time spent behind bars. "You've got twenty minutes before the prison closes for the evening," one of them told me.

Tracy and I took our seats, a pad and pencil in front of her, my hands in my lap.

"Mr. Fitzgerald," I said,

"Detective," Fitzgerald replied in a steady voice, his wavy gray hair slicked back, tucked behind his ears. He briefly presented his hand to shake, but then retreated with an awkward look on his face. "I know why you're here. I saw the news. I read in the newspaper too about that Paige woman—"

"How many?" I asked sharply, my skin turning hot, a flush on my neck and face. The feeling was impossible considering the anemia, but this man and his wife had taken my child, and the sight of him made my blood boil. "How many children did you and your wife kidnap?"

He shook his round head, his eyes glassy, his puffy cheeks jiggling, his gaze shooting to Tracy and then back to me. "I want you to know, I haven't asked for an attorney."

"Oh, I'm not your attorney," Tracy replied.

"How many?" I repeated, resisting the urge to clutch his thick neck and squeeze the answers out of him. There was a wary look on his face, as though he was rethinking his position. I'd come on too strong, and reworded. "I'm only interested in my daughter's whereabouts, but the district attorney is going to speak to you about Shannon Grace."

"Just the two," he said in a breathy voice, seeming to shrink in front of our eyes as he prepared to tell us the truth.

"Two girls," I confirmed, aware of Tracy scribbling beside me.

Fitzgerald sat up quickly. "But my wife had nothing to do with the second kidnapping." He lowered his head. "She only took your daughter."

"Please," I said, weakness flooding my body, threatening to end the interview before it started. "Please tell me what happened to my daughter."

"She got sick," Fitzgerald answered, emotion in his voice hinting at the darkest of notions and stealing my voice. "I don't know why I didn't say anything before, but I wish I had."

I braced the table, trying to regain my composure. Tracy spoke for me. "What happened to her?"

Fitzgerald cocked his head, staring at Tracy again, and then back at me. "She's working with me," I assured him, realizing that he thought Tracy was a reporter.

He leaned his arms on the table, folding his hands. "When your daughter got sick, I was afraid to take her to hospital," he said. "It was an infection, a bad one. I think it might have been her appendix."

Leaning in, closing the space between us, I asked, "So what did you do with her?"

"We couldn't take her to an emergency room. I was afraid they'd find out she wasn't ours."

"What happened to her?" I demanded.

"I left her," he answered, tears springing from his eyes.

"*Where* did you leave her?" I asked, fearing the worst.

"A hospital's parking lot, I think." His eyes wandered frantically. "It might have been a firehouse. I don't know."

"What do you mean, you don't know?" My voice rose in frustration.

"I'm sorry," Fitzgerald sobbed. "But I couldn't go inside."

"And then you kidnapped another child?" Tracy asked.

"My wife got really sick again. Like the first time when our Patricia Anne was killed," he said, his gaze falling. "Sheila searched everywhere for our girl, telling me she was going to the police to report a kidnapping. I couldn't let her—"

The shuffle of stomping feet came, an alarm sounding and lights flashing, a pair of guards entering the room, our twenty minutes cut short. "Sorry, ma'am, we'll need to end this."

"I still have more time," I yelled in a near shout. "At least five more minutes."

"But it'll take you ten minutes to return to the entrance," he answered, uncaring, his shift ending soon.

"Where?" I asked Fitzgerald, finding the strength to reach across the table and clutch his hands in mine.

"It was a hospital or a firehouse," he said. "I don't remember."

"Ma'am!" the guard said, raising his voice and approaching the table.

"Which one!" I asked, shaking Fitzgerald's hands.

"I don't remember," he repeated, his face turning waxy, spittle on his lips. "I drove until the gas tank was near empty and put her down gently, wrapped in a blanket."

"That was my baby you abandoned!"

"Now, ma'am," the guard demanded, and I let go.

"I remember rain, a spring rain, the smell of pollen and flowers," Fitzgerald mumbled as he was taken from the room.

Fifteen years ago, my daughter was kidnapped from the front yard of my home. Thirteen years ago, she was left to die in a parking lot. I didn't know which hospital or firehouse; I didn't even know whether she had survived, or if someone had taken her and driven away with her. But as long as there was a chance she was still alive, I would keep looking, and I would find her.

EPILOGUE

Over the course of several days, twenty men and women of the Marine Patrol and the Coast Guard scoured a four-hundred-mile stretch of ocean. While pieces of the bowrider were recovered, no body was ever found. Paige Kotes was presumed dead.

With the press feeding on the mystery of Paige's disappearance, and new docudramas and book deals emerging, the public's fascination with her story was an unstoppable train. It wasn't long before theories of her survival surfaced, even earning a spot on the evening news. According to one theory, when our boat was struck, the current and the ship's massive wake carried her away from the wreckage, after which she was picked up by the sailors on deck and taken to the ship's infirmary to recover.

In an interview with the police while I was in the hospital, I'd mentioned the ship's crew, and how they'd searched the ocean surface with their spotlights. But I'd never seen a rope thrown or the ship slow. The matter was closed, and Paige's death certificate issued. Yet I still wake from every restless sleep bothered by her disappearance. During the investigation, Nichelle produced the names and destinations of the ships that were in the vicinity when the bowrider was struck. One reassuring thought came from this information. The ship that had helped save me from Paige was destined for Asia. If Paige Kotes was still alive, she was far away from me, and far away from Jericho too.

The investigation into her prison escape was short-lived, requiring little more than a day or two to interview the guards on shift that fateful evening. The trick behind the magic of her escape was in the documentation presented by Dusty Jones. It was a near-perfect forgery. He'd used previous transfer papers and methodically removed the inmate name and number, replacing them with Paige's. To any guard working in the prison, the papers appeared legitimate.

With Cheryl heading up the investigation, Nichelle and Emanuel became my eyes and ears, relaying what they learned. They told me what was discovered when Jones's apartment was searched. The team had cleared every shelf, lifted every loose floorboard, and eventually found a workbench with draftsman tools, eraser types graded by coarseness, able to lift a layer of paper pulp, that sort of thing. Emanuel showed me pictures of a small hollow discovered in a closet wall, where they found a shoe box containing keepsakes preserved in plastic baggies, a serial killer's souvenirs. Each of the items was identified by the families of the victims. Paige was telling the truth when she said a serial killer was coming into his own.

And who was Dusty Jones? He was the high-school kid who never fit in. He'd palled around with Jericho and the in-crowd, including Ann Stewart and Joseph Choplin, Judy Granger, Lisa Wells and Jessie Cooper. However, as Lisa told me over the phone, Jericho and Joseph Choplin confirming, he was always on the fringe, and most of them had lost track of him after high school. From my research, I'd learned that he'd been following Jericho, mirroring his career, failing to become a policeman three times, failing to join the Marine Patrol twice. He settled on becoming a prison guard and a part-time security guard working the local mall on weekends.

More than just a guard, he was also a Paige Kotes super-fan, his small apartment covered wall-to-wall with memorabilia, newspaper clippings, books, and poster-sized photographs. When Nichelle searched his computer, she discovered hundreds of hours of security footage from the prison. Dusty had secretly siphoned closed-circuit television recordings from a security camera near Paige Kotes' cell, using a thumb drive to copy and transport it. With the evidence mounting, the investigation into the murders of Ann Choplin and Judy Granger was closed.

Although Jericho was back with the Marine Patrol, that didn't make up for all that had happened. Directly or not, I'd played a part in his political career ending. Even though the actual killer was now known, the reporters' stories about Jericho and the scandal that never was had already sold papers and mouse clicks, and that was all that mattered. Months from now, when life returned to some level of normalcy, there might be a short story, an apology of sorts, a few paragraphs perhaps, buried ten pages deep in the local paper or at the bottom of a web page. Nobody would see it. Nobody would read it. Nobody would care. Accidental or not, it broke my heart to think I had had a part in it—or worse, missed an opportunity to stop it.

The summer was almost over, a light sprinkle wetting the late hour in the day, the last of the tourists soaking up the evening with a walk on the boards edging the sea. Although I'd kept my own place, Jericho giving me space, we'd made an effort to see each other every chance we had. Today was Wednesday, which included a long walk on the boardwalk, followed by pizza and fries. With my arm looped in Jericho's, we joined the parade of tourists along the ocean front as my wet flip-flops squelched with the rainwater.

My phone buzzed with an alert from Nichelle, a news flash coming across the wire about Hannah's kidnapper, Tommy Fitzgerald. The man had been involved in another altercation. Only this time, he didn't survive. The very last person on this earth I knew to have had contact with my missing daughter was dead. The news stated that Fitzgerald had been on the wrong side of a prison fight, but that seemed highly coincidental, or at least my mind told me it seemed that way, my endlessly seeking new clues everywhere. Had his murder been provoked? Could there be a connection to Hannah?

"I've gotta go home," I said, ignoring Jericho's quizzical look as I exited the boardwalk and took to the beach, my apartment only blocks away. Since Fitzgerald's interview, my world had settled into a daily routine of waking, working, eating and sleeping. I'd found myself back where I'd been for so many years, a single purpose in life—finding my daughter.

Jericho followed me into my apartment, stopping short at the sight of the news alerts flashing across the monitors, his focus shifting to the wall with the pinned pictures and the leads strung in colorful yarn. "I guess this answers any questions about what you've been up to during your recovery."

"Uh-huh," I said, barely hearing him as I stepped around the air mattress and slid a stack of cardboard boxes away from the wall. I pecked his stubbly cheek with a kiss. "Sorry, I have to work. I'll catch you later."

"Casey," he said, his voice breaking. I sensed sadness from him. Or was it disappointment? I wasn't sure I cared. Not in the moment, anyway.

"Just a minute," I told him, gathering yarn and thumbtacks, along with pictures of four hospitals I'd found within twenty miles west of where Tommy Fitzgerald's home was. Ideas popped into my mind like weeds, my trying to find new connections—after the prison attack, was Fitzgerald taken to one of the hospitals? Maybe someone at the hospital was involved with Hannah's second disappearance? I picked up Hannah's picture next, holding it against the wall, deciding on another place to start.

Jericho shifted, placing a hand on his hip, the other on his chin. From the corner of my eye, I could see him thinking. I organized the different-colored yarns, the best leads being marked with red. I felt Jericho next to me, his presence a distraction. I needed time.

"Babe?" he said.

"Listen, I'm going to be busy for a while—"

"Casey," he said again. I shot a glance at his face, finding sadness and pity, a look I'd come to loathe after Hannah's kidnapping. "What are you doing?"

I couldn't face his questions or his mounting discontent. I knew where my place was now, where I needed to be. And I wouldn't be judged. "Jericho, I'm searching for my daughter."

Without another word, he began to leave. As the apartment door's hinges creaked, I stepped back into who I once was as though the last year had never happened. I found the bitterness that had driven me all those years before coming to the Outer Banks. I found it deep inside me like finding an old song on the radio and tuning to its familiar melody. Outside, a car roared to life, the tires chirping as Jericho sped away from my apartment, leaving me alone. I didn't dwell on his departure; I needed the time, needed to work.

I studied where I was with Hannah's case, reviewing the notes on my phone, piecing together what Tommy Fitzgerald had told me. Nearly two years to the day after her kidnapping, my child was abandoned outside a hospital or a firehouse, the summer rains pelting her fevered skin, her cries going unanswered. There were no records of what had become of her after that. No reports or television news stories about a child abandoned in the rain. Nothing.

I scanned the apartment's last empty wall, decided on where the center of it was and pinned Hannah's picture there. From a foldable TV tray, now covered with thumbtacks, index cards and spools of colored yarn, I draped a line of red yarn from her picture to one of the hospital photos, then did the same three more times. When I stepped away from the wall to see what I'd completed, a part of me wanted to collapse onto the mattress, curl up into a ball and cry myself to the brink of insanity. Instead, I did as I'd told Tracy to do, which was to look forward and work the next part of the case, no matter how impossible it might seem.

With the help of Nichelle's computer system, I had become a regular on the true-crime sites and a frequent contributor to the podcasts about Hannah's kidnapping. Online, I had a new team working with me who had miraculously found archived surveillance footage from the days surrounding Tommy Fitzgerald's trek west of the Outer Banks with a sick child.

There'd even been the most amazing discovery this evening, eclipsing the news of Fitzgerald's death. Leaning in, the monitor's bright pixels shining on my face and hands, I clicked through the links until the video footage opened, its originating source still being investigated, the playback a black-and-white feed, the video grainy and without sound. On the screen, lying on the pavement at the doors of a hospital, a bundle, an unconscious child. A woman in scrubs entered the frame and kneeled next to the child, checking for a pulse and then lifting the blanketed bundle. But she didn't enter the hospital. Instead, she glanced around her and then quickly exited the way she'd come, taking the child with her.

There was one frame that showed some of the woman's face, the black-and-white pixels a blur, but clear enough to identify her as Caucasian, dark-haired, of average build and a height I'd yet to determine and thought Nichelle could help me with. I printed the still image and pinned it to my wall. It was a great clue, the timing right, the story matching with Tommy Fitzgerald's. It was a powerful lead and it lifted my hopes. I also knew it would consume me for the foreseeable future, leaving little time for anything else. From the pinned picture, I threaded red yarn, the lead the hottest I'd had so far, and wound the other end around the thumbtack holding Hannah's photo.

As I tightened the lead, adding an extra loop to secure the yarn, it wasn't lost on me that I'd returned to being the mother spider tending to her web. I think I was okay with it too. On my wall, I'd established the initial links for this case, my course for the investigation set. With a deep breath, I shed the person I'd been in the Outer Banks and became the person I once knew—the woman who'd stop at nothing to find her daughter.

A LETTER FROM B.R. SPANGLER

Dear Reader,

I want to say a huge thank you for choosing to read *Saltwater Graves*. If you enjoyed it, and want to keep up to date with all my latest releases, just sign up at the following link. Your email address will never be shared and you can unsubscribe at any time.

www.bookouture.com/br-spangler

I hope you loved *Saltwater Graves*; if you did, I would be very grateful if you could write a review. I'd love to hear what you think, and it makes such a difference helping new readers to discover one of my books for the first time.

I love hearing from my readers—you can get in touch on my Facebook page, through Twitter, Goodreads or my website.

Thanks,
B.R. Spangler

ACKNOWLEDGMENTS

There are a few people who have really been so helpful in supporting my writing journey and also helped me with Casey White's stories, reading every idea and draft, helping me guide the stories to become what they are. Thank you to Ann Spangler, Chris Cornely Razzi and Monica Spangler.

From the team at Bookouture, thank you to the very talented Ellen Gleeson for her help in editing every draft, and my immense appreciation and gratitude to all who work so hard at Bookouture to make every book a success.

Printed in Great Britain
by Amazon